ESCAPE FROM

THE

CENTER

OF THE

EARTH

GREIG BECK

SEVERED PRESS

HOBART TASMANIA

ESCAPE FROM THE CENTER OF THE EARTH

"Descend, bold traveler, into the crater of the Jokul of Sneffels, which the shadow of Scartaris touches before the calends of July, and you will attain the center of the Earth. Which I have done, Arne Saknussemm" — Jules Verne, Journey to the Center of the Earth.

SCIENTISTS DETECT SIGNS OF A HIDDEN STRUCTURE INSIDE EARTH'S CORE

March 5, 2021: Researchers have found evidence that Earth's inner core appears to have another even more inner core within it.

"Traditionally, we've been taught the Earth has four main layers: the crust, the mantle, the outer core, and the inner core," explained Australian National University geophysicist Joanne Stephenson. "Our knowledge of what lies beneath Earth's crust has been inferred mostly from what volcanoes have divulged and seismic waves have whispered."

But now, Stephenson and colleagues had found more evidence Earth's inner core may have two distinct layers.

"It's very exciting," she added. "And might mean we have to re-write the textbooks!"

PROLOGUE

They laughed at him. *All* of them. But he had been right.

Arkady Saknussov held his arms wide, face turned heavenward, and basked in the hot, red glow from the boiling ceiling miles above.

Stretched out before him, a near-endless sea sparkled with its reflected crimson, amber, and fiery highlights. Things swam languidly in its warm primordial depths, some hidden just below the surface, and some lifting long, chitin-armored snouts above the waterline to bellow in bass-deep calls of mating or warning.

What a wondrous world, he thought and closed tired eyes, sat down, and drew in a deep breath, inhaling the scents of a brine ocean, drying seaweeds on a shimmering black shoreline, and a hint of primordial sulfur. A far cry from the frozen Russia he had left behind—how long ago—weeks, months, years? It didn't matter anymore.

Saknussov suddenly opened eyes rimmed with a touch of madness and jerked to his feet to stand rod-straight.

"In the year 1485, I claim this land in the name of Ivan III, first Tsar and true ruler of all Russia."

He slapped hands over his mouth, eyes rolling, and he jerked back down, sniggering. *Shut up, fool, they'll hear you.* After another moment, satisfied he was still alone, he exhaled in a long sigh.

This place had taken its toll on his body and mind, but at least he still lived, unlike his team that were all now gone. Some had fallen from heights, some drowning, some simply vanishing in the labyrinths, and some dying the most horrible deaths from strange infections or by the tooth and claw of the terrible things that inhabit this inner world.

Death would come for him as well soon, and he looked down at himself. He was nearly destroyed—his clothing was just tattered rags, his stick-like arms and legs were covered in abrasions and open sores, and the broken bones in two of his fingers had erupted through the skin.

Saknussov decided to just watch the sea for a while. He already knew he'd never make it back to the surface, never be able to talk to anyone about his wondrous discoveries. And worse, he'd never be able to warn anyone.

He looked up at the hellish red sky. "Don't follow me." He

lowered his gaze. "For God's light does not reach down here."

But he knew they would come. One day. Because curiosity was an irresistible drug…and in the end, just as deadly.

EPISODE 11

"I thanked God for having led me through the labyrinth of darkness to the only point at which the voices of my companions could reach me." — Jules Verne, Journey to the Center of the Earth

CHAPTER 01

Kol'skaya (Kola) Superdeep Borehole – Pechengsky District, Oblast Province, Russia

Oskar Svegeny was bored, like he was every time he and Grigory Valadin had pulled a long shift at the borehole. Though the hole itself had been closed for nearly thirty years, they still needed to monitor and maintain the site, as the many miles-deep hole had never been filled.

Oskar quickly read from the monitors and checked off the never-changing details. And he guessed *never-changing* was good.

The Kola Borehole was a scientific "what-if," the result of a drilling project that was to bore as deep as possible into the Earth's crust, with the project goal being a target depth of just on forty-eight thousand feet—nine miles.

Drilling began 24 May 1970 and by 1989, they had reached a depth of forty thousand two hundred and three feet, which at the time was the deepest man-made point on Earth. It was a satisfying display of Russian ingenuity and engineering.

But then, just a few months later in that year, drilling abruptly stopped. Reasons given were that they encountered higher than expected temperatures that damaged their drills. Also suggested was that there was a change in the rock characteristics with a strange decrease in density and greater porosity, which caused the deep geological matrix to behave like plastic.

But Oskar knew that wasn't all—there were other reasons, whispered ones, that stayed out of official reports. The engineers refused to work on the site at night, as from the depths there were noises that unsettled the crews—low mumbling, grunting, yelling, and agonized screams—the voices of the damned it was said.

Then there was "the attack." A crew working at the lowest level said they were set upon by things that literally forced their way out of cracks in the walls—human-like but not human. They dragged several of the crew away before they could be helped. They searched, but they were never found.

The Kola Borehole was sealed that year and never reopened.

People never talked about it again, and it quickly vanished from scientific interest.

Now, just a few monitoring staff remained. Good money to sit, bored, and babysit a hole drilled, as the rumors went, all the way down to Hell.

It was Grigory's turn on the monitor, and as he listened, his eyes screwed shut and mouth turned down in distaste. "*Ach.*" He shook his head. "They should blow this abominable place up."

"*Huh,* what?" Oskar continued to read his magazine. "Why?"

He took the headset from his ears. "Like they say, the voices of the damned." He tossed the headset onto the desk in front of Oskar. "Listen."

Oskar's mouth turned down. "I've heard it. A thousand times. It's supposed to be just the geological strata shifting. So what?"

"Just… *listen,*" Grigory pressed.

Oskar sighed, put his book down, and lifted the headset. He held it to his right-side ear.

He bobbed his head from side to side. "The usual: popping, clicks, weird grating noises from the depths. Maybe it's whales." He scoffed. "Nothing new." He went to pull the headset away.

"Wait," Grigory urged.

Oskar lowered the headset. "No, I have better things…"

Grigory flicked a switch and put the sounds up on the overhead speaker.

After another few seconds, there came something that could have been a woman sobbing. Oskar frowned. And then looked up slowly.

"*Help me.*"

The Russian swallowed the dry lump in his throat. "Is in English," he whispered. "This is a joke, yes?"

Oskar shrugged. "How? There are no other listening devices linked to this site, and we are a long way from any potential external surface or atmospheric interference."

Grigory closed his eyes and concentrated.

"*Help me. My name is Ally, Ally Bennet.*"

"Horse shit. It's a prank." Grigory lunged for the speaker and switched it off.

"Sure it is." Oskar shared an uneasy smile. "So, we do what we always do: record, record, record." He placed the headset on the desktop. "And stop listening to ghosts from nine miles down."

***

5

Days later, Oskar uploaded the recording to a haunted hotline site in Moscow as a bit of a joke and because he knew it would interest them.

An hour later, it was picked up in the normal data scoops carried out by one of the American spy agencies and now other ears listened to the strange recording of a woman calling for help from nine miles below the Earth's surface.

CHAPTER 02

Western Pacific Ocean, The Mariana Trench – 36,201 feet down

"You won't believe this, but I think there's a cave down here."

Barry Gibbons slowed the deep-submergence vehicle, or DSV, down to little more than drifting speed. The eight tiny propellers around the craft worked in bursts just to keep him near motionless in the inky black water.

"Big one. Real big." He leaned forward, staring out of the reinforced bubble screen. "This is going to sound insane, but there looks like there's some sort of structure in there."

"Say again, DSV Omaha, did you say a *structure*? Like, a man-made structure?" Topside, Frank Abbott, head of his surface crew, sounded like he brought the mic closer to his mouth.

"That's right, Frank. But I didn't say man-made, did I?" Gibbons chuckled.

"Barry, make sure you're—"

"Recording. Got it, and..." Gibbons started the video recording feed, "...transmitting."

***

Frank Abbott, up in the ship's monitoring and control room, saw the small screen flick to life and the images start to be revealed. He strained to make out the huge cave at the bottom of the Mariana Trench—the water pressure there was a crushing eight tons per square inch, or about a thousand times the pressure at sea level. It was also bone-numbingly cold, and as lightless as Hades, so, when something was black in the already stygian blackness, it was damn hard to see.

They were working in an unexplored area of the trench, and given the massive rip in the ocean floor was 1,500 miles long with an average width around 43 miles, there was a lot of real estate down there that no one had ever even gotten close to, let alone seen.

Abbott narrowed his eyes; the images relayed weren't as clear as he would have liked, and so far, the feeds were limited to the circles of light from the DSV's multiple, powerful lamps. Beyond them was a seeming infinity of nothingness.

He knew that usually at those depths, there was a form of deep-sea mud made up of degraded rock and detritus that rains down from above. He expected there to be some large, heavily armor-plated copepods, some blobby cephalopods, and an occasional rare and boneless-looking fish. But not now.

Abbott sat forward, his mouth hanging open. A few of the other support crew had turned from their own control panels to watch over his shoulder.

He began to smile. "This is impossible."

There were columns, towering edifices, and steps—had to be—and using the DSV's arms for comparison, they were all on an unbelievable scale. And everything seemed as old as time itself.

Some of the columns were broken or crumbling, encrusted with grey-green mosses and strange growths hanging between the ancient stone edifices like monstrous cobwebs.

"Is that some sort of sunken city?" Benson asked from over Abbott's shoulder.

"Maybe if they were giants," Abbott replied. "See the DSV's claw out front?"

"Yeah." The sound engineer rolled his chair closer.

Abbott clicked on the mic. "Barry, hover and rotate slowly."

"Roger that." Barry Gibbons in the DSV slowed and spun the craft in the ink-black water.

The powerful lights illuminated more of the carved stone around the edges of the hole in the ocean trench's floor. Much was still out of range of the lights, but what they could see was of titanic proportions.

"You getting this?" Gibbons asked breathlessly and extended the claw.

"Oh yeah," Abbott said over his shoulder. "That utility claw is ten inches across. Now using it as scale, look at the step riser."

Benson and the group surrounding him leaned closer, and Abbott drew the image back a little as the DSV maneuvered along the giant step's side.

"Holy shit. I thought that was a wall." Benson blew air between his pressed lips. "It's only one of the steps. That's crazy."

Sure enough, the set of step risers must have topped out at around twenty feet—each—and they led from a platform surrounded with broken columns, downward toward the edge of the hole, and then kept on going.

"I'm going to take a closer look," Gibbons said almost reverently.

"Over."

Abbott nodded and then remembered to speak. "Yeah, okay, Barry, roger that. Watch your clearance. Over."

"You bet, Frank, over," Gibbons replied.

The DSV pivoted in the water and then headed toward an opening that was more like a cavernous wound in the bottom of the ocean.

Up in the command center, the DSV's signal fragmented for a moment.

Abbott frowned. "Barry, you okay?"

"Yeah, yeah, but check this out," Gibbons answered.

The image cleared to show something hanging mid-water.

"They look like rocks, but they're just hanging there. Floating." Gibbons hovered over the hole and reached out with the DSV's utility claw. He nudged the object, making a solid sound as if he struck stone. But the thing floated away like a kid's balloon.

"Maybe like some sort of pumice." Abbott looked at Benson and the pair shrugged.

"I'm marking it down as just another anomaly among all the other anomalies." Gibbons chuckled. "Wanna know something else weird? The water over this hole is warm, seventy-six degrees warm. That's tropical."

"Must be some sort of volcanic vent in there," Abbott replied. He checked the depth reading of the craft. "Barry, you're now at 36,201 feet—the Mariana basement."

"And there's more to go." Gibbons angled the DSV to look down into the massive void. "Dropping a globe."

In another few seconds, the DSV ejected a small, round illuminated ball that gave off light in all directions. It was weighted and should have plummeted down into the abyssal void. But instead, it too hung in the water just like the stones.

"It's like everything over this hole has negative buoyancy. But there's no current I can detect," he said, and then, "I'm taking her in."

"Roger that." Abbott couldn't tear his eyes away. Or even blink.

Gibbons started the DSV's motors and began to enter the void. Almost immediately, the screen started to crackle with static.

"*Whoa*," Barry Gibbons said.

"Speak to me, Barry. What's happening?"

"I'm in. But strange. Picking up speed. Even though there's no current," he replied.

On the screen, there was no sensation of rushing water or

turbulence, but the depth readout from the DSV started to accelerate.

"What the hell is going on?" Abbott's brows snapped together. "Jesus, Barry, pull up, you're accelerating."

"*I... can't... (crackling static) ... stop...*" Barry Gibbons sounded like he was straining, and Abbott could picture him pulling back on the controls.

Then the screen totally whited out.

"What just happened?" Abbott shrilled. "What's the read?"

"He's still there but going down. Fast," Benson said.

"Pull back, Barry. Do you hear me? *Pull back, for God's sake.*" Abbott half stood in his chair as he leaned over the console.

"Thirty-five thousand—forty thousand—forty-eight..." Benson shook his head. "*Eighty thousand, and still accelerating.*"

"That's impossible. It can't be that deep!" Abbott yelled.

"Gone." Benson sat back, his face beaded with perspiration. He turned. "It's gone."

"Implosion." Abbott sat back slowly into his chair.

"I don't know," Benson said. 'The signal faded out and wasn't cut off. More like he..."

"Like he just went out of reach. Because he kept descending," Abbott whispered. He turned. "But to where?"

CHAPTER 03

Boston, Massachusetts – Ellery Street

Matt Kearns whistled softly as he stopped at his front gate to open the mailbox. There were several letters, most of them those annoying ones with the little plastic windows in front that let you know how much you owe someone for something.

He tucked those under his arm and reached for the final piece of mail, a small box all the way from a place called Huntsville, Alabama.

He turned it over, and then shook it. There was something small inside that was heavy, *unusually* heavy, and he closed his mailbox while looking again at the handwriting on the front—neat, professional, and in ballpoint.

Matt couldn't remember if he had ordered something online lately but was intrigued by the small package.

Entering his front door, he tossed the letters on the entrance table and headed first to the kitchen to grab a beer from the refrigerator. He glanced at the phone to see if there were any messages—none—and then headed to the front room where all the light was streaming in the windows.

He flopped onto the couch, had one sip of the beer—a big one—and then he went to work opening the box's wrapping of brown paper and way too much tape.

It took him several extra seconds, as there were more layers than he expected, but he eventually got to the ordinary-looking box, and lifting the lid, he found cotton wool. He pulled the top layer away and his eyebrow rose.

"*Whoa*," he whispered. "Hello there, beautiful."

Matt lifted the not quite silver-dollar-sized coin free and held it up. He could immediately tell it was gold by the weight. And it was old, very old. Even gold can oxidize and "pit" with age, but it can take thousands of years.

He put the heavy coin on the table, pushed his long hair back, and leaned over it, studying it minutely. The side he looked at contained a human head, but with three faces. *A king or kings, perhaps*, he wondered.

11

There was writing around the outer edge, which he squinted at but couldn't make out. He turned the coin over.

"*Mother of mercy.*"

The beast depicted was hideous and compelling at the same time. It was also familiar, and it nagged at his memory. The hulking thing had tendrils or tentacles hanging from a monstrous face with mesmeric gaze, and huge arms that ended in grasping claws.

"I've seen you before somewhere." Matt rubbed his chin for a moment before he jumped up and headed toward his desk. He dragged out the top drawer and grabbed his magnifying glass. On the way back, he also took a few ancient leather-bound books from the shelf and then dropped back onto the couch.

Matt flipped open the largest of his books; it was an ancient cryptozoological text about mythical creatures from the past and present. He had an idea what he was looking for and quickly found it. He sat back.

"*Dagon,*" he whispered. "The slumberer beneath."

Matt lunged forward and grabbed up the magnifying glass, focusing on the tiny lettering. He slowly began to grin—he didn't recognize it, and therefore couldn't read it. And that excited him even more.

Matt was one of the—if not *the*—top paleolinguists in the world, and if he didn't recognize the writing, then no one would.

"A new language. Thank you, whoever you are." He picked up the box again and pulled out the remaining cotton wool. Sure enough, there was a small note in the bottom. He read it.

The lost city in the crystal cave.

His mouth dropped open as he read the last sentence.

That exists at the center of the Earth.

CHAPTER 04

University of Alabama, Huntsville – Lecture Room M106 – today

Jane Baxter stood on the podium feeling right at home after two years away from teaching.

Back to my roots, thought the biology teacher, who had attained her doctorate specializing in evolutionary biology following her visit to the vast world at the center of the Earth—her secret, and her cross to bear.

But the legacy of her trip lived on, and she hiked the collar of her shirt a little higher to hide the lesions from the skin cancers that were forming on her neck. They also dotted her back, and as far as the oncologists were concerned, were untreatable, aggressive, and would eventually eat into her, just like they did to the old Russian woman, Katya Babikov.

She felt a twinge in her stomach as she knew that Mike Monroe was in an even worse condition than her—it seemed their curiosity, or stupidity, had a high and terrible price.

Jane pushed the morbid thoughts from her mind and inhaled the comforting smells of old wood, floor cleaner, and whiteboard marker. It was just what she needed to take her mind off the hand she and Mike had now been dealt.

Jane smiled as she heard the students start to fill up the theatre. There was a mix of murmuring, coughs, laughter, shuffling feet, and books being slammed down on desktops. Some were bright-eyed with enthusiasm, some slouched, and some were only here to draw a few extra university credits, or maybe just catch an extra hour of sleep after a heavy night.

It didn't matter, she loved them all and had missed this. Because the job was more than rewarding—it was safe, secure, and in a way, it was the psychological iodine to apply to her mental wounds.

It had been a year since she and Mike had climbed out of the Gadime Cave in Kosovo. Everyone that had traveled with them had been lost, brutally, with the question mark still hanging over Harris and Ally who never surfaced. But they had to be dead. Had to be.

She and Mike were a couple now, and at first they had treated their ulcers with the remains of the red people's salve he had kept—and it worked—but when it ran out, the cancers came back, bigger and hungrier for more of their flesh.

Just before Mike had left, one morning Jane had stood before her full-length mirror examining herself. Clothed, she could forget about the cancer as she and Mike both were still physically strong. But naked, her skin reminded her of a suit that the moths had gotten into and left tiny holes in the fabric.

Mike noticed and had smiled ruefully and said, "*Looks like we're going to be eaten alive after all.*"

A horrible thing to say, she had told him. And immediately regretted it, as he was trying to lighten their predicament with humor. But it was horrible because it was so true. And she hated it.

I'll never give up on us. I'll fix this, he had told her. And then he had begged her to come with him to his cabin to be surrounded by nature, and not concrete, glass, smog, and shouted voices. She didn't fight it because she understood it. But she didn't go with him. *Not yet*, she thought.

Jane rubbed at one of the ulcers on her shoulder, sighed, and gave her lecture notes a crooked smile as she assembled them. Butterflies tickled in the pit of her stomach, and she breathed deeply. *Focus*, she demanded of herself, *you need this*. So, she sucked in a deep breath and scanned the title on her first page: *The evolution of giants*.

Her background in biology and what she'd been through had forced her to become an expert, and this was the way she expelled her demons—via a lecture room exorcism. She'd talk about it like it was a laboratory experiment, pretend that it happened to someone else, and keep putting distance between those horrifying events and the new Jane Baxter she was making today.

She checked her watch, 2:01 pm: *go time*. Jane knocked on the lectern to draw the room to silence and looked up at the rows of youthful faces—lots of them—a full house; there had to be a hundred and fifty people. Interest in her topic was gratifying.

Jane's presentation was about gigantism brought about by evolution, and her presentation focused on the massive marine creatures of today and those from our world's past, and *long* past, and how evolution would always fill a niche with whatever raw materials it could find.

She began. "In the beginning, there was the sea. And only the sea." She hit keys to project a silent movie onto the screen behind her.

"Let me take you back in time... to the warm waters of the Devonian period, some four hundred million years ago."

The screen image first showed harsh sunshine on an endless expanse of water before it dove down to where curtains of light reached into the shallow depths.

"It was warm, mid-eighty degrees, and there were no polar ice caps, so the sea level was much higher than today. The oceans were vaster than at any other time. In effect, our Earth was a water world."

The video rolled on, as if they were gliding through the empty water. Jane looked up briefly and saw the blue glow from the screen reflected on their youthful faces.

"Life on land didn't exist at the beginning of the Devonian. But down below, the creatures of the vast oceans exploded in diversity. And when there are few predators, creatures thrive and grow big. But eventually, the predators respond by also growing huge to be able to prey on them."

The film then showed a trilobite, its multiple spindly legs maneuvering along the sandy sea bottom. And then, a shadow passed over it.

The armored creature hunkered down as it sensed the threat, but it didn't do any good. Huge claws grabbed it from the sea bottom and held it before clamping down and filling the water with a mist of blood and flesh fragments.

The camera pulled back to show a huge, armored arthropod that looked like a mix between a spider, lobster, and scorpion.

"One of our first super predators to exist on our planet—the eurypterid *Jaekelopterus*, or giant sea scorpion."

Jane paused to let the *oohs* and *aahs* die down.

"Nine feet in length and built for speed, it had large, eighteen-inch claws with embedded teeth for gripping their prey, plus the forward-facing stereoscopic vision of a hunter. The Devonian was a time when arthropods ruled the world."

"Then we are lucky it didn't last, *hmm*?" came a voice from the audience.

"Indeed we are." She looked up but the faces were in darkness. She continued. "The Devonian was also a period of massive change in lifeforms."

"Adaptive radiation." That voice again. But it sounded too mature for a student.

"Yes, a term used to describe explosive and varied changes. Life

15

exploded in the seas, then plants colonized the land, and then bony fish evolved throughout the world. Finally, it was followed by the animals, arthropod and tetrapod, leaving the oceans."

She smiled ruefully. "The arthropods had a head start, but the fish grew more efficient lungs and became amphibians. Then they learned to lay dry eggs that didn't need to hatch in the water. Then they grew big. And it was game, set, and match for the arthropods who were pushed back into second place."

"But imagine if they won—the arthropods—what the world would look like. Can you imagine? I would think it would be a very frightening and dangerous world."

She looked up and searched the area the voice had come from. There was a larger-than-normal figure there, but the face was obscured. She'd check again when the lights came up.

"Moving right along." She hit the keyboard to advance the film. "The oceans gave us the first giants."

The screen image showed a few bobbing ammonites, the coiled shells with large eyes and tentacles blooming out of the open end. Then came something looming up out of the blue haze of the sea depths.

"The first of the real giants appeared during the Triassic, the marine reptiles or fish lizards, and quickly dominated the seas."

Something that looked like a giant pointy-headed dolphin appeared on the screen, except its tail moved side to side like a normal fish.

"The ichthyosaur grew to fifty feet in length and could move extremely fast for something so large."

There were whistles of awe from the crowd, and Jane looked up. "I know, a big animal, but then in 2016 on a southwestern English beach, a large storm exposed the remains of *Shonisaurus sikanniensis*, a species of ichthyosaur that was eighty-five feet long—almost as big as a blue whale."

She turned briefly to the screen as the huge fish glided out of the deep blue to swim past the camera. It seemed to take forever to go by them, and then an eye that must have been as large as a truck tire swiveled to give the camera a glassy stare before it continued into the endless blue water.

The camera zoomed back to lift high above the ocean and then the planet, and they watched as the single massive continent began to break up.

"Late in the Triassic, seafloor spreading led to rifting between the northern and southern portions of Pangaea, separating into two continents, Laurasia and Gondwana, which would be completed in the Jurassic Period. Our familiar world was beginning to take shape even then."

The film then followed the coast lines that were shallow seas reaching miles inland and were the hunting grounds for the fearsome mosasaurs. Then, finally, there came a sound like the deep booming from rolling thunder and the screen whited out for a moment.

"But all things must end." Jane tilted her head and watched as the final scenes of the movie showed a ring of smoke and fire moving across the globe. "Sixty-five million years ago, an asteroid impacted with Earth off the Yucatan Peninsula in the Gulf of Mexico with the power of ten billion atomic bombs. It sent wildfires raging across thousands of miles as a vast sulfurous cloud blotted out the sun and drove the entire planet into a decade-long global winter. The fearsome giants of land *and* sea perished."

She shrugged. "But without the mass extinction that ensued, humans would never have had the chance to evolve."

"Ms. Baxter, do you think other giants will evolve—or have already and we just don't know it yet?" The adult voice had a smile within it. "Perhaps they're somewhere hidden from us."

She winced, and then was annoyed with letting herself still be thrown off balance. But the insinuation seemed a little too knowing and it rattled her.

She composed herself and pasted on a smile. "Like I mentioned before, nature hates the vacuum of an empty niche and soon fills it. But there's no vacuum right now, and evolution takes millions of years. Maybe there will be, but we might not be around to witness it."

She stopped and looked up at the theatre. "Questions?"

There were many, but she managed to keep them all on topic.

From a back row: "Do you think those sea scorpion examples you gave us were the biggest those species ever got to?" a student asked.

Jane thought for a moment and shrugged. "Maybe." She turned. "But unlikely." She leaned on her desk. "Think of it this way—the average human being in the US is around five feet nine inches tall." She smiled. "But George Bell, recognized by Guinness World Records as the tallest man in the United States, is seven feet eight inches. Thirty percent bigger than the average."

She came around her desk. "The point I make here, is there are always outliers. Five-nine is the average. But there are lots of people over six feet even in this classroom. There's also quite a few over six-

six, and then a few like George Bell, over seven feet. They're rare, but they're out there."

The time had flown, and she had enjoyed the class. And she thought the students had as well.

"And that brings us to today's finale—the largest creature that ever lived in our oceans and ever will." She called up the last image of the huge beast. "The blue whale, coming in at one hundred and twenty-five feet, and more than thirty feet longer than even the massive ichthyosaur. It is also the heaviest creature that ever lived. So, for those of you out there looking down in the mouth at the loss of the mighty marine reptiles, just remember, we still live in an age of giants."

Jane took final questions, then closed the lecture and watched as the students began to file out as noisily as they filed in.

"One more question, Professor Baxter."

It was the adult voice in her lecture.

"The enormous blue whale was the largest sea creature that ever lived…" He raised his eyebrows, "…on the surface of the planet. But maybe somewhere else, there are bigger things living, yes?"

"I don't know what you mean." She stared, but the guy stared right back.

"What about the legendary beasts? Giants like the Kraken, or Leviathan…" His smile remained. "Or perhaps, Dagon?"

Jane quickly turned the room's lighting up.

The still-seated man was too old to be a student and far too well dressed. He had the tan of someone used to the outdoors, but he seemed too polished to be someone who worked there and had more the burnished skin of someone who lay on the deck of fast boats.

"As far as we know, and we *do* know," Jane replied. "There is or was nothing larger. The fossil record doesn't lie."

"You just finished telling your students that sometimes 'outliers' remain hidden." He smiled and it retained its warmth.

"Well, after centuries of fossil hunting, on land and sea, we're confident we have a good idea in what has existed." She shrugged. "The blue whale is still king."

"On the surface," he repeated. "Have you ever heard of a Russian by the name of Arkady Saknussov?" he asked. "He had a theory about hollow earth."

Jane lifted her gaze to the man and stared for several seconds. *Keep cool*, she demanded of herself. She slowly shook her head. "I'm a scientist, and only dealing in reality today. But I may do a future lecture on mythological beasts. It's an interesting topic, even if it is a little more crypto for my field."

"I admire you, Ms. Baxter." He kept his poker face.

Jane's brows came together. "Have we met?"

The man got to his feet and began to walk toward her at the lectern. "My apologies for ambushing you, but I've been looking forward to meeting you."

He smiled with a perfect set of teeth. "Janus Anderson." He stuck out a hand. "I consult to private and public institutions. And specialize in salvaging and recovery."

Jane took his hand. "Well, you know who I am." She waited.

"Indeed, I do." He motioned toward the screen. "You give a good presentation—informative, fact-based, and enjoyable. And you seem to enjoy it as much as your students."

She sighed. "Mr. Anderson…"

"Janus."

"Mr. Anderson, what can I do for you?" she asked, beginning to gather up her notes.

"I, my company, recover things, Ms. Baxter. Things lost recently, and things lost long ago."

"Let me guess, shipwrecks and the like." Her lips pressed into a line as she continued to pack up.

"Yes, and everything else. There's nothing I can't find, and nowhere I can't get to. I also find lost people." He pulled his phone from his pocket and searched it for a moment before hitting play on something and then holding it up to her.

"Help me."

There came a few scraps of Russian language. And then.

"Help me. My name is Ally. Ally Bennet."

Jane put her hand over her mouth, feeling like she was going to throw up. She glared. "You bastard."

He nodded. "I've been called worse." His smile was crooked. "I know you're dying, and you know you're dying. Aggressive carcinomas, brought about by exposure to various forms of radiation. So is Mike Monroe."

Janus sat in the seat directly in front of her and leaned forward to clasp his hands together.

"Ally Bennet is still down there. And alive." He nodded slowly. "The government wants her back."

"You're insane. Forget it." She looked away.

He sighed. "If it was you trapped down there, would you want us to forget it, or come get you?"

Her head jerked up and she stared. She was confounded by his insights about her and Mike's condition, and what he knew about, *everything*.

"How do you know all this? About me, and Mike, and… Ally?" She hated that her voice came out a little tremulous.

"Like I said, I admire you. And Mike." He held the smile. "What the pair of you two did, where you went, what you lived through, was beyond anything anyone on the planet can comprehend." He shrugged. "And only a handful of people know about it." He snorted softly. "And most of them are Russian."

"Get to the point."

"Ms. Baxter… may I call you Jane?" He lifted his chin.

"No."

"Not yet then." He grinned, but it soon fell away. "You asked me to get to the point. I will, so please excuse my bluntness."

Jane waited.

Janus got to his feet. "We believe Ally Bennet is alive. Trapped beneath the Earth." The man's eyes were dead level. "A listening station at the Kola Superdeep Borehole recorded her voice just two days ago. We want her back, and I have been given unlimited powers to achieve that by our government."

He drew a breath and paced for a moment before he stopped and turned to her. "I know you and Mike are dying from aggressive carcinoma cancers. You're strong now and the cancer hasn't metastasized internally, but…it will." His eyebrows slid in sadness—real or fake, she couldn't tell. "It won't be a pleasant way to go."

Jane felt anger burn within her at this upstart asshole laying out her life and future before her. "Who fucking told you all this?" She stopped as if she was hit up the side of the head. "Mike?"

Janus nodded slowly. "Yes, he's dying and doesn't want to die, and more importantly to him, he doesn't want *you* to die. Not like that." He sighed.

She covered her face and rubbed it. "I can't." She looked up from her hands. "I liked Ally, but I can't do it. I can't do anything, and I can't help her."

"I know that," Janus replied softly. "Mike has given us a lot of information we are able to work with. He gave us detailed descriptions of the lifeforms you encountered, and the devices and techniques you used to prevail."

"We didn't prevail, Mr. Anderson. Everyone died except Mike and me, who will just have the pleasure of dying more slowly, and…"

"And you survived. Remember that." He cut across her. "And so did Ally."

Her mouth snapped shut and her jaws clenched.

Janus went on. "We couldn't reproduce the Russian vibration weapon, and they're not divulging the technicalities. But we were able to reproduce your sonic bug, or at least the pitch, that proved so effective in the caves. Bottom line, we're going. We have to."

"Bullshit," she spat.

He frowned. "What?"

Jane laughed mirthlessly. "I don't believe for a second that you are doing this to try and save Ally Bennet, if she's even still alive."

Janus exhaled and sat down heavily. He held his hands up. "You're right. You got me," he said. "But we really do intend to mount a rescue mission for our missing soldier." He crossed himself. "On my honor."

"And what else?" she asked.

"Several reasons." Janus folded his arms. "Do you know how many people die or get afflicted by skin cancer every year? I'll tell you—about three million. Drug companies estimate a cure or treatment for that form of cancer runs to the billions of dollars." He sat forward. "And if it can in any way be adapted for use against other forms of cancers, then we're talking hundreds of billions. A year. Every year."

"I knew it. It's about the money." She growled. "And there's always some wealthy asshole looking to make even more money."

Janus' eyes locked on hers. "Jane, for your information, I pulled myself up with my own bootstraps. I'm fully aware that for every asshole born with a silver spoon in his mouth, there's a thousand more born with a thorn in their foot." His eyebrows went up. "And by the way, you don't think a cure for cancer is important? Even for you and Mike?"

"Don't you dare try and make it about me," she retorted.

He shook his head. "I'm not."

Jane squeezed her eyes shut as she spoke. "You have no idea of what is down there." Her eyes flicked open, and she turned to him. "Something bigger and more horrible than you can imagine."

Janus' eyes were dead level. "We'll be ready for anything and will be armed to the teeth."

"You're freaking insane. The armaments you'd need, the

manpower, and just getting there through miles of caves, squeeze holes, and thousand-foot drops, it's impossible. Forget it."

"No, very possible. And we don't intend to squeeze through the caves you traversed to get there. We think we have found one of the seaborne gravity wells you mentioned that will take us right to it."

"Mad." She gathered up her notes and computer.

Janus stood. "If we're mad, then so is Mike. He wants to come."

Jane's mouth dropped open for a few seconds and couldn't even think to form words.

"It's true. In fact, we tried to get his brother as well, Jack Monroe." Janus' gaze was level.

"The shark specialist?" Jane just stared, her mind whirling.

"That's right. But apparently he's off chasing a giant shark somewhere in the South Pacific." Janus shrugged. "Jane, look, all Mike wants is for us to obtain more of the salve that cures cancer from the race of people you encountered. He wants it for you, Jane."

She lowered her head. "No." She looked up. "You know he's too sick now. He'll never make the journey."

"We're going via the ocean in specially designed submersibles. Then we take an expedition to the red people. He knows them and where they are." Janus held his hand out, palm up. "We're there and gone in a few days."

She shook her head. "He can't go. He'll die."

"He's as strong as an ox. For now. But we need a guide, and for that he needs to be with us to show us where these people are." Janus nodded. "He loves you. And obviously will risk everything to save you. There's no stopping him, you know that."

She cursed softly. "The fool." She looked at the dapper, young man. "He can't go."

"I think he can, and so does he," Janus replied softly. "And if you really want to look out for him, then go with him."

"I will not climb into those caves again with the monsters in the dark. And I won't let him." Her jaws clenched.

"You won't have to." He smiled flatly.

She frowned. "What? Then what about Ally?"

"There's a separate team to rescue her—Russians. Consider it penance for their attack on us from below the surface." He looked at his watch. "In fact, they'll be dropping into the Kola Borehole right about now."

CHAPTER 05

Kola Borehole – Murmansk Oblast Province, Russia

Oskar Svegeny moved his castle up the chessboard four squares, and then smiled with satisfaction. "Check." He sat back.

Grigory Valadin looked up from his book for a moment, glanced at the board, and then maneuvered his knight over the top of a pawn to take Oskar's castle. He went back to reading his book.

"*Ach.*" Oskar grimaced and then frowned at the pieces. He placed a hand on one of the bishops, but then changed his mind and removed it. He then took the queen up the board to take a rival pawn. He grinned. "Now we will see. Check, again."

Grigory lowered his book, looking from the board to Oskar. "Seriously?"

"Yes." Oskar's brows knitted.

"Okay." Grigory shrugged, and then used his own queen to take Oskar's queen. "Check mate in two moves." He laughed. "You're getting better."

"I let you win. Sometimes." Oskar studied the board with the intensity of a physicist about to split the atom. He still couldn't see how...

"Hey, you hear that?" Grigory tilted his head upward.

Oskar half turned. "Helicopter. Coming now? We're not due for shift rotation for another two weeks."

The two men stood from the board and headed to the steel door. The Kola facility wasn't large now, just a single story remaining. But it was still a heavily fortified construction built over the borehole. There were several rooms around the outside for cooking, ablutions, sleeping, and storage, and at the center, the sealed shaft.

They pulled open the heavy door in time to see the large helicopter landing, its blades whipping up snow dust and forcing them to close their eyes to slits from the gale of wind and icy particles.

"Who are they?" Grigory yelled.

The door was pulled back, men in uniform jumped out, and then they knew.

***

Kapitan Viktor Zhukov leaped from the rear of the chopper and spotted the two men standing at the door of the facility. He ignored them and took a quick look around. He'd heard the stories, but it still amazed him—the entire countryside was frozen or snow-covered, except for about a hundred feet around the Kola Borehole zone. He snorted softly; apparently, heat was still rising from Hell.

He then turned to bark orders to his team and stood back as they grabbed their gear and jumped from the chopper to assemble.

Last out was the only woman in their group, Dr. Valentina Sechin, a medical practitioner and biologist with extensive troglodytic flora and fauna experience—perfect fit for what their mission objective was.

Zhukov watched as his second-in-command, Vladimir Ustinov, organized the team and then waved the chopper off. The ten-strong team then marched toward the facility, and he stopped before the two Kola maintenance crew.

"Good morning, gentlemen." He pointed to one of the men. "You must be Oskar Svegeny." The man nodded and shared a confused look with his colleague. Zhukov faced him. "And that makes you Grigory Valadin."

Grigory looked up at him. "And who, sir …?"

Zhukov pointed. "Inside first."

"Of course. Please enter." Valadin bowed his head as he and Oskar stood aside.

Once inside, Zhukov took in the facilities with a glance; he already knew the layout. "I want that elevator checked and online, I want communications established, and I want a coffee." He looked along his squad's faces. "And if anyone needs to piss or shit, do it now, as we'll be moving fast." He checked his watch. "We drop in one hour."

Vladimir Ustinov barked the repeated orders as he assigned the jobs and the team moved off in different directions.

Zhukov then turned to Oskar and Grigory. "In answer to your question, we have been assigned to a deep Earth rescue mission. In fact, our mission team is called *Glubokaya Zemlya*— Deep Earth."

Oskar clicked his fingers. "Oh, that voice we heard. It wasn't a prank?"

"We've been ordered to find out." Zhukov glared for a second or two. "And if I find it is a prank, someone's head will roll." He turned away to look at the state of the room with its communications equipment, chess board, food wrappers, and empty coffee cups. "Clean this place up. You'll be working for us for the next few days and will be sending messages on to Moscow of our progress."

Oskar glanced at the rubbish and then nodded. "Yes, we were about to." He stepped closer to the big man. "Do you know where this, *ah*, person is?"

"Deep. Our tracking of the soundwaves puts the emanations at around sixty-six thousand feet, and approximately eight miles east."

Grigory whistled. "Twelve and a half miles down. The borehole is only around nine." His brows came together. "But how? How did she get down there?"

"Maybe she fell down a well." Zhukov slapped the man on the shoulder. "Now, we need to do some work. And so do you."

Oskar held up a finger. "Ah, one more thing, sir. The elevator has not been used for twenty years. Or even maintained."

Zhukov glanced at the man. "We have our own engineers. Besides, it only has to work twice more—once down and again back up, yes?"

***

Vladimir 'Vlad' Ustinov urged the men to speed; he had been under Kapitan Zhukov's leadership on many missions and the man had never failed. Vlad always thought if he had a big brother, then Zhukov would be him.

Standing beside him, and looking drowned in her caving suit, was the scientist and doctor, Valentina Sechin. She perspired heavily even though it was around fifty degrees in the room, but this was because there was a warm, humid breeze blowing up from the borehole. He grinned. Or maybe she was just shitting scared.

"Okay?" he asked her.

She just nodded, her lips pressed into a thin line.

Shitting herself it was then, he thought.

The pair watched as two men had opened the large metal tube that was the capping structure for the elevator. The metal shielding that now surrounded it had been added later to keep most of the bore shaft heat contained. But the whispered stories were that it was to shut out the noises from below. Vladimir snorted; the *noises from below* were why they were here.

The elevator itself was a form of typical mining elevator, in that it was a steel, box-like enclosure. But this one was an oversized industrial-strength cage that could fit twenty people. The other difference was, it was made to drop entirely to the bottom of the shaft and even though the elevator moved quite quickly, it still took an hour to fully descend.

Three of their men worked on getting it operational: Mikhail Fradkov, their youngest soldier; Yuri Chaika, a military engineer; and Vyrin Andripov, the muscle dogsbody, who could bench press four hundred pounds.

"Got power," Yuri exclaimed and began to work the controls. The gate slid upward, and the internal lights came on.

"Let's test it. Drop it a few dozen feet and bring it back," Vladimir ordered.

Yuri nodded, but then paused. And began to grin. "Mr. Fradkov, I have a job for you." He turned. "Test pilot."

The young soldier returned the smile. "Always happy to serve Mother Russia."

He stepped inside the large cage and walked its perimeter. He sniffed. "Stinks in here. Like rotting vegetables. Or maybe like the latrines after Vyrin has been in them."

"Very funny," the huge Vyrin replied without humor.

Vladimir folded his arms. "The smell is probably a mix of old gases. Maybe some methane." What was it about methane that nagged at the back of his mind? He couldn't remember, so he let it go.

Mikhail Fradkov jumped up and down a few times, making the cage rattle. "Solid."

"Stop that, fool. The old mechanism hasn't been used in decades," Yuri warned. "Ready?"

Fradkov looked down below the grating where a line of lights was leading down into oblivion. He gripped the cage wall. "Yes."

Yuri brought the heavy gate down. He performed one last check, and then with his hands on the controls, looked up. "Going down." He pressed the descent button.

With a squeal and a shower of rust particles, the elevator descended, slowly to start, and then it picked up speed for several dozen feet. Yuri stopped the cage, and then started it back up. It all ran smoothly and on arrival, he immediately opened the gate.

"Well?" he asked.

Fradkov shrugged. "Was noisy, dropped a shower of iron dust, but works fine."

"Good enough." Yuri stood back from the controls.

Vlad nodded. "Then we are ready."

***

Zhukov and Ustinov checked their supplies and weaponry. They had high-spectrum, computer-enhanced goggles with light and heat amplification, plus a stratigraphic pulse system that could form images through a hundred feet of solid rock. Their weaponry consisted of standard handguns and snub-nose machine guns for maneuverability in tight spaces, plus a range of knives. Zhukov and Ustinov also had several fragmentation grenades each, but these were to be last resort only due to cave-in risk.

All the team had worked with their armaments before, except for one item that had been offered by the Americans—a small black box with a speaker at one end that emitted sound waves. Each team member had one and it delivered a burst of sound that was almost unbearable. Zhukov was told that their potential adversaries in the caves would be repelled by it.

Adversaries? He thought back to their briefings about what they could potentially face in the borehole depths. The information was vague and near unbelievable—beings that lived miles below ground, looked like hairless dogs, and hunted by sound. It was these things that were supposed to be holding the woman captive.

His mission objectives were simple: Kill them or drive them away. Find and secure the American woman or her remains. Return to the surface.

He believed he could achieve these tasks within three days. But if it took longer, that was fine. His team was the best of the best, and hardships and danger were nothing to them.

Zhukov fully expected to succeed and have nothing more than a good story to tell over a warm glass of vodka on a cold night when they got back.

"Last check, load up!" he yelled.

His men and the female doctor readied themselves. Last-minute checks on supplies, equipment, and weaponry were rapidly and professionally examined.

Zhukov nodded to Valentina. "You'll be next to me, Doctor. Your advice and expertise will inform a lot of our decisions below the surface."

Zhukov then went and stood before the Kola Borehole's maintenance crew, Oskar Svegeny and Grigory Valadin. He pulled on a friendly smile, but both men still blanched a little before the large and fearsome-looking soldier.

"Gentlemen, your role is now to work with us and for us. One of you will stay by the communications and controls, twenty-four hours a day, and be prepared to act on our orders immediately. Is that clear?"

Both men nodded vigorously.

"Good." Zhukov patted Grigory on the shoulder, and then turned away. "Then, let us begin." He headed to the elevator door.

"Line up."

The team fell in behind him, and Valentina followed at his shoulder. At the door, he waited for the large gate to be lifted, and he waved his team in.

His trusted second-in-command and friend, Vlad Ustinov, entered first and moved to the far side of the large cage. Then came Fradkov, their youngest soldier. He was joined by Yuri Chaika, their engineer, and the hulking form of Vyrin Andripov. Then came the soldiers; good and brave, every one of them: Anatoliy Serdyukov, Viktor Sobyanin, Igor Ludzkov, and Pytor Shamiev.

The last man seemed to hesitate at the cage rim.

"Problem, Pytor?" Vlad asked.

Pytor quickly shook his head and continued in.

"You're not worried about heights, are you?" Fradkov grinned. "Just because we're standing in a steel cage, over a hole forty-three thousand feet deep?" He chuckled.

Pytor blew air between his lips. "Not a bit." He refused to look down at the grating over the floor that showed a line of lights dropping to a seeming infinity. "Is that all?" He grinned.

"Are you sure?" Fradkov jumped up and when he landed, the cage shuddered.

There was a sound of something cracking, and Vlad leaned toward the young soldier. "You do that again and I'll open the door and throw you into the pit myself. You understand?"

Fradkov nodded. "Yes, sir, sorry, sir."

Zhukov and Valentina finally entered the cage and the door closed with a heavy *clunk* of finality. The captain wasn't afraid of heights, but the weird smell, the warmth, and the incomprehensible depths made his skin crawl.

He circled a finger in the air, and Grigory turned back to the controls. The huge elevator whined to life and then with a grinding of steel it began to move.

"Going down. Next stop, Hell." Vyrin Andripov pulled a silver crucifix on a long chain from his collar and gripped it in his fist.

***

Pytor Shamiev stared straight ahead, seeing nothing. Truthfully, he hated heights, hated doing parachute jumps, and hated cliff climbs. But he was smart and hoped to complete officer's training and climb out of this type of field work within the next few years. *Good riddance to grunt work*, he thought.

His gaze was unfocused as he took himself mentally out of the cage and began to recite some of his favorite poems in his head—poems of love and friendship, and freedom and loyalty, by the likes of Pushkin and Lermontov. He tried his hardest to ignore the rising heat and blank out every clunk, grind, and jerk of the endless rails as they dropped to the bowels of the Earth.

Few of the men spoke, all, like Pytor, seemingly lost in their own thoughts. Beside him, the rock wall traveled upward at a blistering rate, and the lights dotted every few hundred feet were like a strobe light illuminating their faces for a blink to then leave them in near darkness for moments more.

The heat grew, and he remembered Yuri's comment about Hell, and now thought them more than apt.

What Pytor didn't know was that after thirty years of no maintenance, underneath them the formidable cage floor had been eaten through by the mix of caustic gases rising from the depths. The support superstructure had been weakened and the combined weight of the soldiers and their gear was adding a level of strain to the grate not experienced in decades.

After another ten minutes, Pytor estimated they had dropped close to a mile below the earth's surface and had around eight more to go. He stuck a finger in beside his collar to wipe at a tickle of perspiration.

The big man shifted from one foot to the other.

That was all. And that was all it took.

Below him, the floor gave way completely and he dropped, fast.

Pytor had good reflexes and threw out a hand, grabbing the floor edge, but the combined weight of his body and pack dragged him down.

The other big men moved quickly, but the corroded steel floor beneath them groaned and sagged, and Captain Zhukov roared for them to stay still.

The soldiers were professionals and immediately complied with the order—even Pytor remained motionless as he strained with one hand to hang onto a single steel girder.

"Easy now," Zhukov whispered, shrugging off his pack and laying down to inch forward. On his belly, he peered into the hole in the floor and the upturned face of his soldier.

Pytor was bathed in sweat and it stung his eyes, but he couldn't dare blink as he stared firstly at his commanding officer and then at the steel bar he held onto as it began to pop and bend. Downward.

The big man began to drop further below the cage floor. Zhukov reached down but was still a few inches short of Pytor's hand.

Zhukov turned to speak over his shoulder. "Grab my legs. Lower me down."

Both the Russian captain's legs were held, and he was inched forward. It wasn't easy, as the edges of the hole were rusty, ragged, and sharp, and he doubted he'd get his shoulders through.

"No good." It wasn't going to work, but he had another idea. "Get some rope, form a slip knot."

Behind him, there was furious activity. He knew that each man had two hundred feet of elasticized climbing rope, and in seconds, he was handed a length with a sliding noose at one end. Zhukov leaned into the hole again.

"Pytor, I'm going to lower this rope. You must use your dangling hand to grab it and slide it over your wrist. Then I can pull it tight, and we will haul you up. Understand?"

Pytor nodded but grimaced. "It hurts."

"You can do it." Zhukov noticed that just like him, Pytor had not yet donned his caving gloves, and the flesh of his hand was glistening with blood, obviously shredded from the jagged steel. And worse, it would make his hand slippery.

A fist-sized piece of floor steel broke away to bounce off Pytor's cheek and the hanging man quickly turned to look over his shoulder and watch it tumble away further, and further, and then forever—he would never hear it hit the bottom. He turned back, his eyes glistening with fear.

"Stay strong, Pytor," Zhukov urged. "The rope, hurry now, grab it." Zhukov tried to move the rope loop closer to his man's arm, but Pytor was trying to stop himself contorting while he only just managed to hold on with one hand.

Zhukov half turned to his team. "Lower."

His men slid his body out a little further, but it was as far as he could fit into the hole. It was just bad luck or a fluke that Pytor was able to slip all the way through.

The cage bounced and rattled as it continued to drop. It didn't help the trapped man. Zhukov could see Pytor struggling. He needed to keep him focused but calm. "Soldier, listen," he ordered. "You will place your hand through the rope loop. *Now.*"

Pytor nodded and tried to slow his gyrations. As he did, his hand moved a fraction on the blood-slippery girder. Only another six inches of it remained before he fell.

The man shut his eyes for a few seconds, and then slowly reached out. Zhukov tried to match Pytor's movements with the rope. Inches now separated them. Then only one inch.

The elevator passed over a roughened part of the tracks and jerked, just a little, but enough. The corroded steel gave up, snapped, and both it and Pytor fell into space.

Pytor never made a sound as he kept his eyes on Zhukov as his body fell away. Zhukov wondered how long he would fall—thirty minutes, more? And would he be conscious the entire way, gathering speed until he hit bottom?

Pytor finally vanished down into the abyss without making a single sound. Zhukov exhaled miserably. "Pull me up."

He was dragged backward, and he got carefully to his feet. His team were silent and all pressed to the outside of the cage now.

"Pytor is gone. A good man, killed serving his country." He looked along their faces. "We can't stop and can't turn back. We go on. Use your safety lines to hook on to the cage sides."

The team reached into the climbing kits and took out clips and lines and latched them to the cage walls. Zhukov glanced at the young Fradkov. "And I promise you, next person to jump up and down will join Pytor."

***

Vlad counted off milestones as they went, but the rest of the descent was completed mostly in silence as the team remained lost in their own thoughts.

Zhukov stared straight ahead. He knew military mishaps happened, but it was shit that it occurred before they had even touched down. From a resource perspective, he was already down one man.

"Forty thousand," Vlad intoned.

And in the next instant, the cage slowed, and then slowed more, making them all feel the weight of gravity come down on their bones, before bouncing to a stop. The gate opened and Zhukov nodded to Chaika and Andropov, and the two men headed out with guns up. The area wasn't large and in seconds, they gave the all-clear and the rest of the team filed out.

Zhukov turned slowly. They were in little more than an excavated pit, roughly forty feet around and with what looked like a humid mist that came to their knees. It must have been a hundred degrees and the air smelled of methane, oil, and rotten vegetables.

"Where's Pytor?" Vlad asked.

The group all looked one way then the other, but it would have been impossible to miss the man, no matter how obliterated or exploded the body might have been.

Zhukov looked up. "Maybe he got hooked up during the fall."

The others craned upward, but again, there was little space between the elevator sides and the bored hole they had descended.

There was little other possibility—and then they found the breach in the wall.

"Here." Fradkov pointed.

The group joined the young soldier and stood at the rip in the rock face. Zhukov stepped closer and shone a strong beam into the cavity.

"Deep. Natural caves in there."

Vladimir leaned in beside him. "Notice which way the breach has fallen?" He turned.

Zhukov nodded and placed his hands on the edge. "I know, inward. So, the breakthrough came from in there, not from the borehole side." He straightened. "Doesn't matter—this is where we need to go."

Zhukov squinted at the edge of the rip in the wall, and then looked at one of his hands. He held it up to his second-in-command—it was covered in fresh blood. He leaned further in. "I see more blood inside."

"Pytor's? How? Did he bounce?" Vlad exhaled. "I doubt he climbed in there himself."

"I agree." Zhukov wiped his hand on his pants. "As the Americans say: shit just got real." He turned. "Doctor?"

Valentina Sechin joined them, and Zhukov showed her the blood trail. "Your opinion, please?"

Valentina used a flashlight to examine the blood on the edge of the hole and then leading in. "Fresh, so has to be from Pytor. And obviously a dead Pytor."

"Maybe our dog people are real after all." Vlad raised his eyebrows.

She half smiled. "And if they weren't, would they send so many soldiers and so few scientists?"

"SOP, Doctor." Zhukov smiled. "The American woman is estimated to be eight miles due east, and another two miles down." He faced her. "Do you think she could be alive?"

Valentina's mouth turned down. "I think we are more likely on a body retrieval mission."

"I think so too." Zhukov turned to his men. "Listen up, we're going in. Anitoliy, Viktor, take point. Fradkov, you are at rear. Doctor, you are with me." He circled his finger in the air and then one at a time, the men started to squeeze in through the crack in the wall.

CHAPTER 06

Office of Anderson International Salvage, New York City

Matt Kearns left the window with its panoramic view over the city and paced around the enormous office that was larger than his entire apartment. The meeting room he had been left in was sparsely furnished with a few couches and at its center, a single, enormous antique table that looked to be centuries old.

Matt crossed back to it and looked over the spread of Janus Anderson's satellite images of the Pacific Ocean plus varying sea charts. He ran his finger over the bathymetry maps that indicated a fairly uniform 5,000 or so-foot-depth for hundreds of miles in every direction. As expected, there was nothing but a plain of endless ocean floor.

He slid the first of the satellite images closer to the bathy-maps and compared the latitude and longitude grid. They were identical for positioning, and all other aspects except for one thing —the satellite images showed a small island in the middle of nowhere.

Matt looked at the next set of images—*blank*. Whatever the island was, it had vanished, in true mysterious fashion.

He'd read that vanishing islands are natural occurrences and usually they're visible at low tide and then disappear at high tide. The Philippines is home to seven of such islands while the San Juan Islands have many of them.

In the medieval period, explanations for the strange phenomenon of islands that appeared and subsequently vanished were often associated with sea monster stories told by superstitious sailors.

But that only happened in very shallow water, or water that was on the ridge of some sort of volcanic or crustal uplift… not in water that was supposed to be around a mile deep.

There was another occurrence of a now-you-see-it-now-you-don't island, where underwater volcanic eruptions could spew out tons of pumice that was lighter than the surrounding water. They created something called a pumic-raft, some of them miles wide, and were literally floating carpets. But they were thin and only a maximum of a foot above sea level, not like this island that seemed to rise for a hundred feet.

Matt had no idea what it could mean and knew he was out of his depth, so to speak. He had been brought on as a consultant to analyze a lost civilization, lost language, and potential lost world, which he was excited as all hell about. Someone like him who'd studied ancient languages all his life had found the offer irresistible. The coin had been the dangled bait, and he had bit down hard.

He felt he was over the trauma of the extinction plague, as they were now calling it—giant bugs that had burrowed up from below the ground. After a few weeks of psychotherapy, and then a few more months holiday surfing on the Australian east coast, he felt he had been rebuilt both physically and mentally. He was ready to take on something interesting and productive. Plus, the consulting fee Janus Anderson had offered him for a few weeks' work would ensure he could holiday for the entire year if he chose.

He looked again at the large mass on the ocean's surface and smiled; there was an old saying about us knowing more about the surface of the moon than we did about the bottom of the ocean. And he never said never when it came to the inexplicable. Matt knew there was still plenty of that in our ocean. As recent as 1997, an ultra-low-frequency, high-amplitude underwater sound was detected by NOAA, the U.S. National Oceanic and Atmospheric Administration. It was termed: *the Bloop*.

The consensus for years was that it was the sound of ice sheets calving thousands of miles away. But there were the skeptics, and one was NOAA's own Dr. Christopher Fox, who believed the sound was more likely to have come from some sort of massive animal because its signature was an undulation in frequency similar to the sounds already known to be made by large marine beasts.

But there was one crucial difference: sensors up to three thousand miles away detected *the Bloop*. That meant it must have been far louder than any whale noise, or any other known animal.

Matt tapped the chart with a knuckle. So, the obvious question was: *is there some creature bigger than a whale lurking in our ocean depths*? He straightened, still looking down at the images. No matter how much he wracked his brain, he also couldn't think of anything past or present that fit the physical signature he was seeing here.

"How would I know, anyway?" he whispered.

He crossed to the final map that looked like another bathological production, a recent one, but this time, there were handwritten notations all over it. Janus Anderson had laid out maps showing the Mariana Trench, the famous crustal rift that ran for over fifteen hundred miles and plunged to depths of between thirty-six thousand feet and "unknown depths," because the sensors couldn't find a bottom in one of the obscure sections.

Janus' handwritten notification drew attention to the fact that the trench bottom hid something else, a rift within a rift, that continued on down. Also, that the water down there was warm, not the usual abyssal cold of the stygian depths.

Matt guessed the inference—if there was something large in the ocean, these days, satellite scanning made it hard for anything to hide. That was unless it had a bolthole.

"Knock knock." The meeting room door pushed inward.

Matt turned.

Janus Anderson entered, smiling broadly and with arms wide. "Hiya, Matt, how's it going?"

Matt nodded and smiled. "It's going good. Just looking over your maps and trying to make sense of what I'm seeing."

"Excellent." Janus' lips curved into a small smile, and he walked toward the table edge, folded his arms, and looked down at the maps, reports, and satellite images. "Pieces of a puzzle… that are all coming together."

He sighed. "But we need to get moving now, as the salvage season will be with us soon, and the southwestern Pacific only stays calm for a few months. After that, summer typhoons can turn the place into a devil's cauldron."

Janus' phone buzzed and he lifted a finger to Matt then answered it. "Okay." He looked at Matt as he spoke, a smile spreading on his face. "Yes, send her up."

"What is it, yet more pieces to the puzzle?" Matt asked.

"More like more people to the puzzle." Janus continued to smile. "Many hands make light work and all that."

There was a knock on the door.

"Come on in." Anderson stepped back from the desk.

Matt turned as the door swung inward. He saw it was a woman, probably mid-thirties and attractive in an outdoor, athletic kind of way. She had a no-nonsense set to her jaw.

"Jane," Janus exclaimed. He turned to Matt. "Matt Kearns, paleolinguist and adventurer, meet Jane Baxter, biologist and might I say, also an adventurer."

Matt held out a hand. "Nice to meet you."

She shook it, her handshake firm. He noticed then that she had some sort of lesion on the back of her hand.

She noticed him staring and she withdrew her hand, sticking it in her pocket.

Janus' grin never slipped. "Jane can also claim to be one of the few people on the planet who has traveled to the center of the Earth."

"Is that for real?" Matt fished in his pocket for the gold coin and held it out flat on his hand. "Did this really come from there?"

"Where did you get that?" Her eyes carried a mixture of shock and barely contained anger. "Who the hell…?"

"I don't know, honestly. It came in the post, and just with this note." He handed her a small piece of paper.

"From the lost city in the crystal cave. At the center of the earth."

Jane sighed and dropped her arm. She glanced at Janus. "Mike again?"

He shrugged.

"Mike?" Matt asked.

"Mike Monroe is Jane's… good friend. He's also the other person to climb from the center of the Earth." He looked down momentarily. "He's also dying. Like Jane is."

"What?" Matt asked. "Of what?"

"A form of aggressive skin cancer," she replied. "We are using interferon to slow it down, but it'll eventually overtake us." She gave him a crooked smile. "And it's from the intense radiation down there."

Matt spun to Janus. "You never told me this. You can shove this up your…"

Janus held up a hand. "They were both there for many months. We'll only be there for a few days, a week or two at most. No problem."

She shook her head. "We only planned to be there a few days or weeks as well. But you know what? Shit happens. Bad shit." She turned away.

Janus sidled closer to Matt. "You never asked why Mike would send you the coin. And involve you."

"You tell me," Matt asked.

"Because there is a natural compound down there that can treat them. And the race of people who were its, *ah*, custodians and creators, could not be communicated with. A new race, Matt, a new language, a new civilization—we will have limited time, and we need to understand them, and them us, quickly. We need an expert for that—the best expert." Janus lifted an eyebrow at Matt. "You."

"Whoa." Matt felt a little giddy.

"*Whoa*, is right." Janus nodded slowly. "Bottom line, Mike wants to save them both." He smiled crookedly. "Not an unreasonable objective."

The room fell to silence for several moments until Janus Anderson clapped his hands together like the crack of a gunshot. "Okay, good, now that the introductions are over and ice broken, let's see where we are up to. *And*, I have more to share with you."

Matt glanced at Jane, who still seemed to be simmering.

"Let me share some of the initial impressions and observations." He also laid out some photographs. "As expected, the water in the area is relatively uniform." He stood aside but kept his hand on the bathological map. "Except for the rift, or cave, or... or tunnel, or whatever it is down there."

Jane folded her arms but leaned forward to glance at the details. "What's with the 'unknown depths' notification you've made here?"

Janus smiled back. "It is what it is. We used several devices like SNAR—Sound Navigation And Ranging sonar—to send out pulses of sound energy and then monitor how quickly the sound travels back." He shrugged. "In those areas, nothing came back. It exceeded our equipment's capabilities."

"Okay." She straightened and turned away. "And that's where you believe there's some sort of large biological entity hiding out?"

"I don't know." He stuck his hands in his pockets. "Maybe. And maybe it's just a geological thing. An upwelling when the rift opened. Or some sort of pumic expelation. Nothing has been confirmed one way or the other."

"If that's the case, then why us?" Jane straightened. "Why bring in our level of expertise?"

Janus seemed to ponder on it for a moment. "I'm successful because I manage risk, calculate the odds, and usually win. So, from a risk management perspective, even if there's the remotest possibility that what you and Mike said you saw is real, then I want people with us who have dealt with this sort of anomaly before who can advise." He lifted his eyebrows. "I've done my homework. Your credentials are that you went, you saw, you conquered, and you survived. I want that experience backing up my crew."

"I've done a little homework on you too, Mr. Anderson." Jane's gaze was flat. "You're an overpaid antiquities dealer. You made your fortune salvaging to sell. And you also aren't shy about selling your services to governments. *Any* governments."

"Sure did. And?" Janus grinned. "That's how I make my money. And I made a lot of it. Is it not better to retrieve lost things, and let others have the right to enjoy them?" He held up two fingers. "I have two primary objectives for retrieval: one, the woman, Ally Bennet. A team is already on route to try and retrieve her. And two, the medicinal compound."

"And?" Jane folded her arms. "Go on."

His face became grim as he slowly held up a third finger. "Three, if there is a large seaborne entity attacking ships, we are to destroy it. This is sponsored by the United States Naval forces with the backing of the International Maritime Authority."

"Holy shit." Matt exhaled through pressed lips.

Jane shook her head and looked away. "You have no idea."

"*Uh*, question." Matt held up a hand. "What am I missing here?"

Janus waved his hand as though dispelling Jane's warning as if it were nothing more than vapors. "Wondrous things, Professor Kearns, wondrous. Look here." He opened a small computer and started up a video.

Matt leaned closer, watching and waiting for a few seconds, and then his eyes widened. "Oh my God. This can't be real."

It was an underwater scene, and as the dark water was illuminated, he saw there were colossal steps leading from a platform surrounded with broken columns and tumbled plinths of titanic proportions, all crusted in slimy growths and mosses.

Janus watched his face. "From one of our deep-submergence vehicles, or DSVs."

The DSV's lights then moved over a vast wall showing carved images of monstrous beasts, some fighting each other, and some with what looked like miniscule figures, but were probably human scale, all marching up a long platform toward the tentacled mouth on one creature that was bigger than all of them.

The submersible continued along the wall and soon came to a broad set of steps all leading downward toward the edge of an immense rip in the ocean floor, and then they kept on going into its impenetrable blackness.

"Are they ruins? Because they look like ruins," Matt gushed. "Where is this?"

Janus nodded. "Yes, they are ruins, Professor. And they're at the bottom of the Mariana Trench, some 36,000 feet, nearly seven miles below the surface. And their size is astronomical." He smiled into Matt's face. "Who built them? *How* did they build them? And where are the builders now?" Janus held his hands wide. "So many interesting questions."

Matt looked spellbound as he stared at the small screen. He glanced over his shoulder at Jane. "This is... something else." He turned back and then his brows came together, and he tilted his head as he tried to make sense of another image that was appearing out of the gloom. "What's this showing us?"

Jane snorted softly. "They're floating stones."

"Floating? What are they made of?" Matt asked.

"Granite, sedimentary sandstone?" Jane shrugged. "It doesn't matter. What their composition is, is not the right question." She turned to Janus. "It's a gravity well."

"Yes, that's what we think." Janus nodded. "Now watch."

The DSV continued to film as it headed down past more of the ruins toward the impenetrably black hole.

"Stop," Matt exclaimed. His brows came together as he lifted a finger to point. "On that wall—there's something written."

Janus paused the film. "Oh yeah, I never noticed that as I was so focused on the well." He turned. "Can you read it?"

"I've been working on the language for days." Matt fished in his pocket for the gold coin and quickly examined it. "Yes, it's the same form of writing." His eyes ran over the symbols. "Mostly obscured, but..."

While his eyes moved over the glyphic images, Jane took the coin from his open hand, and looked deeply into the gold—the side with the three-faced royal rulers—and flipping it, she saw the monstrous image on the back. It gave her a jagged feeling in her chest.

"Something like, *the living god*, maybe." His lips moved. "*Sleeper or slumberer*, I think." He straightened. "Can you clean it up?"

"Probably," Janus said. "But I think we know who or what that is referring to." He turned. "Right, Jane?"

"Dagon," she whispered.

"The Lovecraftian legend, like on the coin. The god of the deep?" Matt chuckled. "You mean *that* Dagon?"

"No legend." She snorted. "Very real."

"Enemy number one," Janus replied. "And Jane talks from

experience."

"You've seen it?" Matt asked, brows shot up.

Jane folded her arms and walked a few steps away from the table.

"Was there any more footage?" Matt asked.

Janus nodded. "Just a little more."

Jane turned to watch as Janus restarted the film.

The camera followed the ruins down toward the dark hole in the ocean trench floor. It moved past some of the floating rocks and then actually entered the massive hole.

At first, it was moving slowly, and even though the feed grew a little grainy, it was still good clarity. Then there came the motion of speed. Faster and then faster again, until the feed totally whited out with static.

"That's it. We lost communication with the DSV at one hundred and twelve thousand feet. We estimate they were traveling at close to three hundred miles per hour when they fell off the radar." Janus folded his arms.

"Did they return?" Jane half turned.

"No," Janus said. "Or not yet anyway."

"They must have been pulverized by the pressure," Matt said.

"Jane? You like to field that one?" Janus smiled.

She turned and stared at the paused image on the computer screen. "There's no pressure in the gravity wells. It's like a fast-moving river… all the way to the center of the Earth."

Janus' smile broadened. "There's your answer, Mr. Kearns. That's how we will be traveling. We have two modified DSVs and a specialist team of scientists and security personnel." He smiled as he raised his hands. "What an opportunity."

Matt faced Jane. "Seriously?"

Janus checked his watch. "*Whoops*, I've got to step out for a few minutes to take a call. I'll have coffee brought in. You two finish looking over the material and rewatch the film if you like."

He headed toward the door and turned with his hand on the door edge. "And, Professor, the intellectual reward will be great, and you may bear witness to the opening of a dialogue with an entire new race, civilization, and I dare say, *world*. What a thing to tell your kids."

He turned to Jane. "We have a small window of opportunity, and a fast chopper departing for the support vessel tomorrow morning. I want you and Mike to join us but will understand if you don't."

"Mike?" Her brows came together.

"Oh, he's already committed." Janus saluted the pair and left the room.

***

Matt and Jane watched the door close and then she turned to Matt. "Well?"

"Well, what?" Matt asked. "About the mission, what might be down there, or…?"

She scoffed. "I know what's down there, Matt. I've been there. I meant the mission. My gut feeling is to say no."

Matt hiked his shoulders. "I don't know. This is the most intriguing thing I've heard in years."

She shook her head while staring at him. "You have no idea what's down there. This is no field trip to the everglades or hiking into some small cave in the Appalachians to look at wall paintings. This is serious."

Matt nodded. "I've been around, Jane." Matt's eyes were dead level. "I'm like you. I've seen things—strange, horrifying, and monstrous things. Things from the depths of the ocean, and in dark jungles. Things that had no right to exist. I've just come out of six months therapy after my cousin was killed by this swarm of creatures from somewhere below the earth. For all I know, they were from the same place you visited."

"You're *that* Professor Kearns?" Her brows shot up.

"Yeah, that one." He gave her a broken smile. "The one with a curiosity that borders on being suicidal."

"So why are you doing this? You can't really have a death wish, surely?" she asked.

Matt turned away to run the images on the screen again and spoke as if in a trance. "Knowledge is an addictive drug. But there's something else I was told by a special team of soldiers who are tasked with defending the world against these sort of things…" He turned to her. "We save lives. Lots of lives. And people never know."

She grunted, not yet convinced.

Matt tilted his head. "Do you know how many people vanish at sea every year?"

She shrugged. "Hundreds?"

"Thousands," he replied. "We might be able to save some of these people just by stopping this… *thing*."

"Dagon," she added.

"Yes." He nodded. "…just by stopping it from surfacing. But there's something else. Imagine if the cure you and Mike need really can treat cancer. That would be mind blowing." He blew air between his lips. "Yeah, I just want to make a difference."

"I'm sorry. I'm sorry I sound like a coward. I'm not, but I'm scared." She lifted her chin. "How do you do it? Where does the courage come from to keep going and confronting these things over and over? Why aren't you scared?"

He smiled. "I never said I wasn't scared. I am, every time. But I'm an optimist, and I always imagine I'm coming home." He grinned. "And I just tell myself, I'm excited, not scared."

They laughed together, and she thought the guy with the long hair and surfer looks was the bravest and most noble guy she had ever met.

"Courage is contagious. When a brave man takes a stand, the spines of others are often stiffened." She smiled.

"That's pretty cool. Who said that?" Matt asked. "Was it a soldier?"

"Nope, Billy Graham," she replied. "It's been good to meet you, Matt." She held out her hand. "Okay, let's save some lives." She shrugged. "One being Mike's. The other being my own."

***

In the building's security monitoring room, Janus sat back and smiled. "Got 'em." He focused the camera in a little closer on their faces. "You have the magic touch, Professor."

Janus knew he might not be able to convince Jane to go back down, but she might listen to someone she thought was honest and independent—enter the famous Professor Matt Kearns.He lifted a phone. "Marco, get the team ready. We'll have two extra passengers for rapid disembarking eight am, sharp." He paused. "And don't forget to send a fast chopper to pick up Mike Monroe. Tell him Jane Baxter is all in."

He disconnected the call, and then closed his eyes for a moment, thinking through his plans. They needed to find the race of people Mike had referred to and secure samples of the salve that could be worth a hundred billion worldwide if it had the cancer-treating properties the man suggested.

He'd also need to get an update soon on how the rescue and retrieval mission was going in Russia. At least that was costing them nothing.

Plus, there was the bounty on the head of this large entity that was attacking their ships, if it was even real. But just in case it was, they'd be packing several armaments that could put a hole the size of a train tunnel in anything they chose.

"We can do this," he whispered. "And everybody wins."

He rose to his feet. If this job panned out, he'd go from millionaire to billionaire in a week. Janus whistled as he headed back to Jane and Matt.

CHAPTER 07

The deep caves, 6 miles northeast of the Kola Borehole – 4 months earlier

Ally Bennet's eyes were wide, but she saw nothing in the Tartarean darkness. But what the darkness took away, it gave back in other areas—her sense of smell and hearing were now acute. She learned to block out the odors of her own waste and finally the smell of blood as well.

A few months back, another caver had been dragged in and staked out close to her. She could only guess at the time as days, weeks, or months had no meaning without any of the circadian change of light and darkness that signified days and nights.

It was a woman, Russian, and a professional spelunker. She spoke a little English, and sadly, she was already tipping into insanity from her predicament. Ally should have as well, but her specialized military training meant she could endure things that most normal people could not.

She learned the woman's name was Anya, and her caving team had been attacked by the slimy, pale creatures in the darkness a few days before. Her friends had scattered in the caves with the things chasing them, and she held out hope that they were still alive and would come find her. Ally kept quiet, knowing that the sounds of feasting she heard would be all that remained of her team.

When the creatures came back, Ally took herself from her own body and dreamed of blue sky and fields of green grass dotted with wildflowers. The worst part of it was the things trying to mimic the women's pleading and screaming.

"*Остановка*!" Anya had screamed over and over, which Ally found out later meant "stop."

Then the things mimicked her—it wasn't the same exactly, but with practice they were getting better. It was fun to them, as their primitive brains still enjoyed playing, and to them, the people were nothing but toys and food.

When the creatures had finished with them, and their bodies were covered in blood, bites, and the grease of perspiration, Anya had whispered her plan.

"I am be dead," she said.

"No, we're not dead yet," Ally replied softly.

"No, *ah*, I mean, I play be dead," Anya had clarified.

"You're going to play dead?" Ally asked.

"Yes, so they leave me. Sorry." She sobbed. "I must try."

"I don't think it's a good idea," Ally urged.

So, then Anya had refused to eat, make a sound, or even move when prodded, bit, or scratched. She kept it up for maybe days.

On the third day, they ripped her from her bindings, breaking her arms when they pulled her free from the straps. Then they took her out and Ally heard them tear her to pieces, ripping her apart, stripping the meat from her bones, wasting nothing.

A fresh dead body had value, as protein. Ally tried to block her ears but couldn't. She finally turned her head to scream. "*Help me*! My name is Ally Bennet. I'm here!" she screamed, over and over. "*Help me, help me, help me.*"

The echoes bounced away for miles in the cold stone labyrinths miles below the ground.

CHAPTER 08

Help me!

Zhukov held up a hand and the group stopped at a junction in the caves. He turned to his second-in-command, and the big man nodded.

"I heard it too," Vlad said softly.

Zhukov clicked his fingers. "Mister Yuri, get a direction on that voice."

Yuri Chaika drew forth an instrument that looked like a flare gun that quickly unfolded into a cone at the end and pointed it into each of the caves.

Help me!

He panned the device around for a few moments and then shook his head. "All over the place. The stone is bouncing the sound everywhere. We need to be closer."

"Doctor," Zhukov said, calling up the female scientist. "What lives down here?"

"Down here, in the caves at this depth?" Dr. Valentina Sechin's mouth turned down. "Nothing other than some methane-ingesting bacteria." She shone her flashlight around. "There is nothing to survive on. No food source, no sunlight or heat source. It is a dead zone."

She then smiled up at the Russian captain. "And yet, I heard the voice too."

Zhukov patted her shoulder. "Then we're not going mad after all." He turned to his group. "Anitoliy, send a pulse into each cave and let's see which one is a dead-end and which one is the way forward."

Anatoliy Serdyukov nodded and aimed the pulser into the first cave that would send a sonar pulse and read the returning wave. It would then decode the information and tell them how deep, and even how big the opening was.

After another moment, he read the screen. "Five hundred and twelve feet. No branching."

"Next," Zhukov ordered.

The man did the same with the larger one and at first looked about to respond, but then: "Wait…"

"What is it?" Zhukov demanded.

"I thought it was blocked." He frowned down at the device. "But seems to have unblocked. Must have been a glitch. There was no return pulse, which means the wave continued for over a thousand feet without hitting an obstruction." Anatoliy moved to the last cave, and after a moment shook his head. "Shallow, it narrows, and ends in a squeeze choke."

Zhukov walked toward the large cave and put a hand on the edge. He quickly drew it back and looked at his gloved palm in the glare of his helmet light. His fingers glistened, and he rubbed his thumb and forefinger together.

"Doctor." He held out his hand.

Vlad joined them and his nose wrinkled in disgust. "Looks like snot."

Doctor Valentina took hold of his hand and examined his fingers closely. She then reached into a pouch at her waist and lifted free a magnifying glass that had several lenses. She pushed them together for maximum magnification and studied his glove once more.

"Very interesting. It might be biofilm—basically, millions of bacteria all clinging together in an excreted gel." She looked up. "And forms the basis of a food chain."

"I thought you said there was nothing living down here?" Zhukov lifted a single brow.

"I did say that. And I meant it. But nothing is absolute all these miles down because we just don't know enough. Only a few years ago, a group of scientists from the University of Ghent in Belgium discovered live nematodes two miles down in a disused ore mine." She smiled. "They were living on biofilm."

"Yech." Zhukov wiped his hand on his pants. "Nematodes are just little worms, yes?"

"In shape only," she replied as she stepped forward to examine the rim of the new cave. Doctor Valentina moved her light over it. "Nematodes are one of the world's oldest survivors and possibly date back a billion years. They're extremely hardy, able to cope with extreme heat, cold, and dehydration. If any animal could live this deep inside the Earth, it would be them."

She turned. "One more thing—the scientists found that the deeper they searched, the larger the worms."

"How much larger?" Vlad asked.

"Well, they found one close to eleven inches long."

The man snorted.

She smiled. "But the largest found on Earth lives in the belly of a whale and grows to twenty-three feet. Be interesting to see how large they grow down here at the 10-mile depth." She checked her kit. "I must take some samples back."

"Better you than me." Zhukov watched as she scooped some of the slime into a small jar, and then turned to his team. "Mr. Fradkov, prepare to take us in."

***

The team moved in a procession of bobbing lights, and although cool, dry caves have little odor, Zhukov could detect the smell of the granite around them and was conscious of the fact that above his head were billions upon billions of tons of rock.

The cave the group traveled within soon became just a crack between two vast walls, and the men with the broadest shoulders began to scrape and were eventually forced to turn sideways. Zhukov thought they'd soon have to slide, and he hoped that after moving within their chosen cave for an hour they wouldn't need to turn back and find another way forward.

From up ahead, Fradkov yelled his discovery and the echo of his voice had an open quality to it and not the enclosed bounce-back they got within the rift-crack, but then they found out why—the young Russian soldier stood on a ledge.

"It ends here," he said and turned to lean out and point his rangefinder downward. He shook his head. "No return pulse, so could be a thousand feet deep or ten thousand." He leaned out a little further and pointed his finder upward. He read the information on the tiny screen and snorted softly. "Possibly half a mile."

Zhukov stood beside him and pointed his flashlight. They seemed to be on one side of a massive rip that had torn the earth in two, maybe by some earthquake many eons ago, or even a crustal shift. To his left and right, the massive cliff wall disappeared without end. And below them it seemed bottomless.

"No, the cave doesn't end." He pointed his light straight ahead and across the dark void.

About thirty feet across, there was an opposite wall, and matching their own cave, there was another just like it.

"Seems our cave was split in half at some time." Zhukov narrowed his eyes. "We need to cross this chasm to continue. Volunteers?"

His second-in-command elbowed Fradkov in the ribs, eliciting a grunt from the young man.

"Thank you, Mr. Fradkov, your brave offer is accepted." Zhukov grinned as Fradkov spluttered, and the other men laughed.

Doctor Valentina joined him. "How would the American woman get across?" she asked.

"Maybe she didn't have to. Maybe she came from the other side." He turned to the smaller woman with his brows raised. "Or she was carried."

Fradkov muttered as he dropped his pack and began to extract carabiners, ropes, and expansion pins. He checked each one closely and then hung them from his belt.

Vlad handed him the loaded harpoon gun, and the young man threaded his rope into it. The foot-long device was a little like a spear gun in that it ejected a high-speed projectile. But instead of using a rubber launcher, it used compressed gas and fired a tungsten-tipped dart with such velocity that it embedded into solid rock.

The other feature of the caving tool was that the bolt upon striking its target immediately expanded within the stone, locking it in place. In addition, its normal break-and-strain level was close to five hundred pounds, so a single man even with fully loaded kit should have had no problem.

Fradkov lifted the gun, aiming just to the side of the opposite cave mouth. "Fire in the hole." He pulled the trigger and with a sound of high-pressure air, the dart flew across the chasm taking the rope with it and struck the opposite wall with a solid *thunk*.

Fradkov tugged on the rope. His final task was to secure his end high in the cave they waited within, and he hammered in a spike to then tie the other end off on his rope. He yanked on it, then hung from it for a few seconds.

He saluted Zhukov. "Bridging line achieved."

"Well done. Proceed," Zhukov replied. "And don't fall. I don't want to have to tell your mother." He cuffed the young soldier's shoulder.

Fradkov replaced his pack and secured it tightly to his body. He then took hold of the line, reached up to clip a shorter line from his waist to the rope, tested it one last time, and then began to cross, one arm over the other.

He avoided looking down and just kept his eyes on the opposing cave mouth. In just a few minutes, he was nearly there. Zhukov smiled, now having a better impression of the young man after his initial fuck-up over Pytor.

When Fradkov got to the end, he swung himself into the cave and dusted his hands down.

"Easy," he called back. "Next."

"Well done," Zhukov called. "Wait there, and when…" He turned and nodded to Yuri Chaika, "…Mr. Chaika joins you, I want you to reconnoiter the cave for two hundred feet. Then double straight back and report."

Fradkov nodded. "Sir."

Chaika immediately hooked his line to the rope bridge and started over. He moved quickly and surely and in only a minute was across. Fradkov helped him into the mouth of the cave and then bumped fists with the big man.

He turned to give Zhukov the thumbs up and then he and Fradkov disappeared into the new cave's depths.

Then, one after the other, the men went across the rope bridge. The only challenge was Vyrin Andropov, the largest and heaviest of them. The man's Slavic eyes never blinked as he reached up for the cord and gradually pulled down on it. There were a few pops and creaks as the elasticized cord took his weight as he began his crossing. It sagged more than with the others, but as expected it held and he was eventually across.

Finally, there was just Zhukov and Dr. Valentina Sechin. He turned to her and saw she looked pale in the glare of his light.

"Okay?"

She shared a watery smile. "Did I tell you I don't like heights?"

He leaned closer. "Did I tell you I don't either?" He winked.

She nodded and turned to look up at the rope.

"We'll go together. The rope will easily take our combined weight."

She nodded again and her lips were pressed into a tight, bloodless line. She looked like she didn't want to speak in case her voice trembled and gave her away. Zhukov helped her hook on.

"You go in front, one arm over the other, just like when you were a kid at the playground."

She looked back over her shoulder. "I used to fall at the playground."

"Not this time you won't. I won't let you." He rubbed her shoulder. "Go."

Valentina got up on her toes to grasp the rope. Zhukov reached up and pulled on it, bringing it down another few inches so she could get a good grip.

Both of her gloved hands worked on the soft rope for a moment, and she sucked in and blew out air twice like she was about to dive into icy water. Then she lifted her legs and threw one hand out to grip the rope a foot further out from her position.

"Well done. And again," he said.

She did the same, swinging her arm out, gripping, getting her balance, and then repeating the process. He waited until she was a few feet over the chasm before he gently pulled down to begin his own crossing.

Zhukov didn't want to be so close as to cause the rope to jump in her hands but also didn't want to let her get too far ahead if she...

She fell.

Valentina screamed as she hit the end of her waist tether, six feet down from the rope bridge. She had thrown a hand out, but this time her grip was on nothing but thin air. Her single arm wasn't enough to hold her for long.

From the other side of the chasm, Yuri went to climb out to meet them, but Zhukov held up a hand and stopped him.

"Stay calm," he said to her. "Breathe easy and keep looking at me."

He moved out to be on top of her and gripped her tether. Looking down, he saw her eyes were wide with fear, but he could tell she trusted him. That was good.

He smiled calmly. "I'm going to pull you up to me. When you're close enough, grab my leg and climb up my body. Then onto my back. Okay?"

She nodded vigorously.

Zhukov then gripped her tether rope and lifted it. He then wound it around his hand, and did the same again, slowly reeling her in while holding on above his head with one arm.

Soon she was close enough to grab his leg, and she used his pants, belt, pack, and everything else to grip onto him and then climb up and around him.

"Good," he said calmly.

When she was at his back, she looped her arms around his neck.

"Sorry," she whispered into his ear.

"You're safe now," he said and easily scaled the rest of the way across, barely feeling the woman's extra weight.

When Zhukov got to the cave opening, Vlad reached out a hand to grab the front of his caving suit and pulled the pair of them into the cave. The big man leaned forward.

"You could have carried me you know." He winked.

Zhukov slapped his friend's shoulder. "You, I would have dropped." He turned. "Are you okay?" he asked her.

Valentina nodded. "Yes, but I feel a little stupid."

"Don't. You, and I, would have felt a lot worse if you had dropped." He turned. "Before we leave here, there will be more *first* mistakes, by all of us. The second mistake is when you don't ask for help. That's the one that is usually fatal. We're a team, remember that."

Zhukov walked a few paces into the new cave. "Where are Fradkov and Chaika?"

"Not back yet," Vlad replied. "We were focused on you."

Zhukov growled as he stared into the cave depths. "What part of come straight back do those fools not understand?" He shook his head. "Okay, rest, take coffee, cigarettes, then we go after them."

***

Fradkov and Chaika crouched beside the pile of empty clothing. It was little more than rags now, and Chaika lifted the remains of a boot. He saw that even the leather sole was rotting down.

"This is a Russian boot," he said. "But it must be over a hundred years old." He then lifted an ancient caving piton, which was heavy, forged iron, with a spike at one end and loop at the other.

"There were other people down here?" Fradkov asked as he got to his feet. "A hundred years ago? They were dumber than we are."

"Maybe." Chaika looked up at the young soldier. "Notice something missing?"

Fradkov looked around and then shrugged.

"The owners of the clothing. Where are the bones?" His forehead creased. "Did they strip off and go running off into the dark, naked as a skinned bear?"

"Maybe they went mad." Fradkov glanced at his watch. "We better get back or we'll be the ones getting skinned, by the kapitan."

Chaika tilted his head, listening.

"What?" Fradkov asked.

"Something." He rose, still holding onto the boot and staring off into the darkness. "Two more minutes, I think there's something else up ahead."

Fradkov scoffed. "Well, you get to tell Kapitan Zhukov why we're late."

Tock.

Chaika paused and looked over his shoulder. "Did you hear that?"

"Water dripping?" Fradkov suggested.

"Maybe," Chaika responded softly.

Help me.

The pair of them spun to the voice, their eyes staring into the stygian blackness.

Finally, Fradkov swallowed and broke the silence. "The woman." He turned slowly to his colleague. "Coming from just up there, I think."

"She's alive," Chaika breathed.

"She sounded strange," Fradkov whispered.

"So would you if you'd been down here for nearly a year." Chaika pulled his handgun.

"We should get the others," Fradkov urged.

Help me.

Chaika pointed with his weapon. "She's just up ahead. Come on."

The two men crept forward, guns up and flashlights held firmly in their other hand. Chaika led them, and in a few more minutes they entered a larger void.

"*Phew,*" Chaika said. "Shit hole."

Fradkov moved his light around the walls. There was little to see but some of the rocks glistened as though spattered with something putrid that looked exactly like what it smelled of: shit.

Help me.

Chaika walked forward. "Where are you?" he boomed. "We're here." He turned to his young teammate. "What was her name?"

Fradkov shrugged. "Ally something."

Chaika nodded. "*Ally!* Where are you?"

Tock.

Fradkov spun back.

Tock.

Tock. Tock.

"I don't like this," Fradkov whispered. "That's not water dripping."

Tock, tock, tock.

"Come on, let's get out of here." Fradkov gulped noisily.

"Shut up, I'm trying to think," Chaika demanded. He turned back to the darkness. "Ally. American. Where are you?"

Tock, tock, tock.

All around them the smell got worse.

"Where is she?" Chaika demanded.

Help me. My name is Ally, help me.

"*Where are you? We're here!*" Chaika roared and walked further into the large cavern.

A few tiny pieces of gravel bounced off Fradkov's shoulder. He slowly lifted his light beam. Higher and higher.

Then he saw them—dozens of glistening white, almost translucent bodies clinging to the ceiling. He frowned, confused, but his heart rate immediately kicked up.

Their bulging sightless eyes quivered and long ears ran all the way down the side of their heads.

One of the creature's mouths moved. "*Help me,*" it said, but in a woman's voice.

"*Ab, ab.*" Fradkov's mouth wouldn't work. He pointed his gun. "*Ab... above us!*" he screamed and began to fire.

The bodies dropped down on them.

*** *** ***

The sound of gunfire had all the soldiers immediately on their feet with weapons drawn. Zhukov spun to his second-in-command.

"Vlad, double-time."

Vladimir barked orders, pushing the large frame of Vyrin Andripov to the front, and then in seconds they were on their way.

The gunfire sounded again but seemed in two distinct bursts: one fairly close to them now and another far away.

Then came the screams.

"Faster!" Zhukov yelled.

The men began to sprint, determined to rescue their colleagues from whatever hell was being rained upon them.

In the next second, an ear-splitting screech came from just up ahead.

"The sonic device," Zhukov remembered. Each man had one affixed to their belt. He thought at the time it was nothing more than a talisman or a joke being played on them by the Americans. But soon, he would see.

As they rounded a bend, there came gunfire that exploded rock chips back at them and the huge form of Yuri at the front flattened himself against the wall and held one large arm out to stop the advancing team.

"*Cease fire, cease fire!*" he yelled.

The gunfire shut off.

"Kapitan?" the shrill voice asked from the darkness.

"Shut off the screamer!" Zhukov yelled back.

The irritating screech stopped, and the men eased out to see a lone soldier jammed into a crevice, his back to the wall and gun barrel extending.

"*Fradkov,*" Zhukov said and turned about. "Where is Chaika?"

"They took him." The young man put a hand over his face.

"What is that smell? Shit?" Vlad frowned.

"Get to your feet, soldier!" Zhukov roared. "Where is your partner?"

The young Russian stood. "They came out of the walls and dropped from above. Too many of them."

The group shone lights above them for a moment or two, then brought them back down on the young soldier.

Zhukov ordered two men to keep watch above and their lights went back to the vast ceiling above them.

"Calm yourself." Zhukov stepped right up in front of the young man, grabbed the front of his shirt, and shook him a little to focus him. "Tell us what happened."

Fradkov swallowed. "We found some old clothing and caving gear, very old, maybe over a century old. Then we heard the woman. Or we thought it was the woman." He grimaced. "*Help me*, she said."

"You heard the woman? The American?" Zhukov shook him again as his eyes began to dart.

Fradkov nodded. But then shook his head. "We thought it was. Chaika wanted to check it out. But I wanted to wait until we had back up." He swallowed again, noisily. "We came in here, this stinking place, but saw nothing. Until we looked up."

His eyes went wide, and he gripped Zhukov's forearms. "There was no woman. It was them. They were calling for help. Tricking us."

"Who?" Zhukov shook the man and his face contorted in distress. "Make sense. Who was calling for help?"

"The creatures. The dog people, like skinned dogs with the faces like gargoyles. They were everywhere. So many of them." He shook his head and shut his eyes. "They took Chaika away. I heard him screaming."

Zhukov pushed the young man off his arms, but Fradkov clung on.

"The sonic device, it worked. I turned it on and they fled," Fradkov almost pleaded.

Zhukov looked at the young man for a moment more before turning away. "So, it seems the stories are real."

"And the woman is not," Vlad added.

The group stood in silence for a moment or two until it was broken by his second-in-command. "If the woman is not real, then…?"

"We don't know that, yet," Zhukov replied. "And we still need to find our man, and quickly."

Zhukov turned to seek out Viktor Sobyanin. "Mr. Sobyanin, find my missing soldier."

Each man had swallowed a small capsule that contained a small tracking device before departing. The device would stay in their system for up to a week, as they were designed to loiter in the alimentary system before being finally excreted.

Sobyanin held out the tracker and it showed each of the team members signified by a red dot and an identifying code. By entering Chaika's unique code number, they could just focus on him.

"Got him," Sobyanin said while staring down at the small, illuminated screen. "He's still on the move. But not far away."

"This may work in our favor," Vladimir said.

"I know. If the things have him, then maybe they will take him back to where the woman is." Zhukov circled a finger in the air. "Mr. Sobyanin, plot our course, and Mr. Ludzkov, you are promoted to point man."

Zhukov faced the still-trembling Fradkov. "And you pull yourself together. We have work to do. Let's move, double-time," Zhukov said.

The group ran on into the caves.

***

Deep in the caves, it felt the vibrations from the trampling boots of the men. Its fifty-foot-long body pressed against the walls of the cave that were covered in a lubricating mucous. Tiny hairs prickled as they passed the vibratory signals back to the creature's brain stem.

Movement meant food, which was hard to come by in the deep caves. Its bulk surged forward, sliding as it pulsated forward using a peristaltic motion.

The monstrous nematode was little more than a mouth on the end of a giant pipe of muscular flesh. But it and its kind had lived in the dark depths, miles below the surface, for millions of years. And they lived solely to eat and reproduce.

The vibrations were coming closer. It increased its speed to catch its next meal.

CHAPTER 09

Mike Monroe, Jane, and Matt sat across from Janus in the Sikorsky SB1 helicopter. Mike thought Jane looked tired, or pissed, or both. He guessed it was understandable on both counts as they had just come off a high-speed jet into Guam, and then been ushered straight onto this chopper. Plus, he knew she didn't want either of them to be here. Truth was, if circumstances were different, he would have made sure they'd both run a mile. But circumstances weren't.

She caught him watching her and her mouth quirked up a little at the side and she shook her head. He could tell what she was thinking—for months, she had wanted him to be more active and not retreat, but this wasn't what she had in mind.

He loved her so much he was prepared to do anything to save her, and if that meant traveling back to hell to find that medicinal compound, he'd do it a thousand times in a thousand lifetimes.

He looked across to the young professor. Matthew Kearns was their puzzle solver. Mike figured that if Katya wasn't alive—and how could she be—then they couldn't waste time trying to find out how and where the salve came from. Speed was the key, and Kearns was their shortcut.

Kearns looked up and gave him a goofy smile. Mike nodded in return. With his long sun-bleached hair, he looked like someone straight out of the surf. But Janus had shown him the guy's background report, and he was one of the sharpest linguistic minds on the planet.

Mike sat back. They had a good team and plenty of brainpower. He glanced out the small window. Now to meet the muscle.

***

The helicopter was whisper-quiet, and their destination was a ship already over the Mariana Trench. Supporting their vessel was the USS *Bainbridge*, an Arleigh Burke-class guided missile destroyer.

In another half hour, they were preparing to be lowered to the deck of their ship. It was unusual in that it was extraordinarily large, and Janus had told them it was for launching underwater vessels.

"Military?" Jane asked.

"Yeah, one of the new line of vessels owned by our naval forces but not exactly broadcast. It's designed to covertly launch prototype DSVs with the advanced propulsion systems." He turned and grinned. "Of which we get to trial two of the latest models."

"Prototype DSVs?" Matt Kearns asked. "They're safe?"

He chuckled. "Yep, safe as all DSVs traveling to over 35,000 feet are."

"Modern submarines are fairly reliable," Mike said. "But as there can still be accidents, if they happen at depths, well, you can't exactly get out and walk away."

"Yeah, that's what I thought," Matt replied glumly.

"They're the future of warfare, at least naval warfare. While the missile and missile-defense systems are crossing swords in the air, below the water, DSV craft will be seeking to advance positions at all depths." Janus turned. "The faster and deeper we can go, the better we can hide."

In several minutes, they were hovering over the ship. Matt was strapped into the drop harness first and gave a small salute as he was lowered away.

Jane watched him drop and thankfully there was little breeze, so the harness and tether didn't swing at all.

"Hard to believe," Mike said and turned to her.

"What is?" she asked.

"That below us is the deepest water on Earth." He stared down at the blue water. "You could drop Mt. Everest in there, and it'd still be nearly a mile and a half below the surface."

She looked back at the warm, azure water that seemed so calm on the surface. It was deceptive, inviting almost, but something had been coming up from the deep water and attacked ships, and for all they knew it was the same thing that had been dragging vessels down for centuries.

The idea of it filled her with dread, and she couldn't trust her own sanity for coming back. "We know it hides a lot more than just deep water down there." She turned to him. "Don't we?"

"Yeah," he said softly. "Yeah, we do."

She reached out and put a hand on his shoulder and squeezed. "In a few days, it'll all be over. And I'll have saved you." She smiled.

"That's weird, 'cause I thought I was saving you." He grinned, took her hand, and squeezed it.

Matt reached the deck, was grabbed, and then quickly unstrapped from the harness. It was then immediately hauled back up.

"Who's next?" Janus asked.

"Ladies first," Mike said quickly.

"My hero." She laughed. "Piece of cake. Besides, this is the easy part."

Jane sucked in a deep breath as the harness arrived. In seconds more, she was strapped in and her experience in caving and mountain climbing meant she secured the straps herself. She nodded to the winch operator, winked at Mike, and then stepped out.

Heights never bothered her. How could they and she still be a caver when she had dropped down rifts in stone walls that were half a mile high, free-climbed vertical peaks in Colorado, and of course, floated down gravity wells that dropped for tens of thousands of miles.

As she neared the ship's deck, she felt her excitement kick up a little. She didn't want to go, and oddly, now she did. Many people led lives that were unremarkable and when they left this world, a few days later no one even remembered them or what they did. She didn't want to be like that, and she knew neither did Mike.

She guessed they were both hostages to their curiosity and spirit of adventure. She remembered an old saying by the legendary actress, Mae West: *You only live once, but if you do it right, once is enough.*

She smiled, liking the sentiment. If she could leave this planet after doing something good, then her life had been worthwhile.

As she touched down on deck, she was roughly grabbed and hands quickly unbuckled her. Even though she was vastly experienced, she knew the drill—get it off and get away quickly. The worst thing that could happen was while you were half in, half out of your gear a sudden gust of wind shifted the chopper, just a few feet. But the tug and jerk on the line could be enough to catapult you over the side or lift ten feet in the air to then drop like a sack of sand to the deck.

She joined Matt, whose eyes sparkled with excitement. He bumped fists with her and then pointed to a group of military men watching them and raised his eyebrows.

"Our fellow crew members?"

Jane looked across to see the brutally fit-looking crew. There were a few women among them, and they looked as rugged as the men. The group stood with arms folded, scrutinizing the pair as much as Jane and Matt did to them.

"They look tough and competent," Matt said.

"They better be," she replied.

The pair then shielded their eyes and watched as Mike first then

Janus were lowered to the deck. As Janus finally touched down and then was released, he turned to give the chopper a thumbs up. Its nose dipped for a second in salute and then turned in the air and headed northeast, back to the Guam base.

An intense-looking man with a thin, straight nose with a dent in it halfway up that was obviously evidence of a former impact he hadn't bothered fixing approached them. He was dressed in combat trousers and T-shirt that displayed a formidable set of arms.

Janus nodded. "Captain Loche." He turned to Mike and Jane and thumbed over his shoulder at the squad. "Captain Loche and his team are Navy SEALS on loan to our mission. Joshua here is English, but don't hold that against him." He sniggered.

Loche's eyes slid to Janus for a moment and then returned to their group, appraising each of them.

Janus then pointed from Jane and Mike to Matt. "This is the pair I was telling you about: Mike Monroe and Jane Baxter. Also, the eminent Professor Matt Kearns of Harvard University."

The man looked at each, continuing to scrutinize them down to the bone.

"Joshua Loche." His voice was deep and with the British accent still running through it. He smiled and held out a hand to shake. "I've read your files. I must say it's going to be a pleasure working with you." He eyeballed Jane and Mike. "Especially you two. Your experience with the inner world will be invaluable for the mission ahead."

"We have files?" Jane scoffed. "Then I hope in real life we can live up to our profiles."

"We'll know soon enough." Loche turned to Janus. "Craft and crew are ready and awaiting your orders, sir."

Sir? Jane was a little surprised. Seems the little guy does pull some weight here.

"Good," Janus replied. "Final briefing and then we can launch immediately after."

"I'll gather the team in the mess hall," Loche said, saluted and headed off.

"You're military? You have rank?" Matt asked.

Janus shrugged. "Yes and no. I'm not military, but this operation is primarily military-based. Overall, the project management and leadership is being overseen by us four." He tilted his head. "In fact, they report to all of you as well. We're more than just advisors here,

Professor."

Janus pointed. "Let's grab a coffee, meet the team, and then get ready to jump."

"Jump?" Jane laughed softly. "Yeah."

The mess in the large ship was a good-sized hall. The usual crew carried on their duties, but they were easily distinguishable from the large and fit-looking SEAL team members that now crowded the room.

Janus poured them each a coffee from the large urn into mugs with a naval crest on them. He poured himself one, and then walked to the front of the group as he sipped.

Jane was impressed by his calm demeanor and air of authority among the much bigger soldiers. Even though he wasn't military, it was obvious to the team that the small, dapper man was in charge. At least up here.

Janus put his coffee down on the table in front of him and looked along the faces of each of them. A small smile formed on his lips. "Today is the day."

The room silenced immediately.

"I expect the submariner crews to have read their briefing report. Some of you may not believe it, but you better be ready for it."

He briefly turned to Mike and Jane. "With me, as expected, is Professor Matthew Kearns, one of the, if not the, leading paleolinguists in the world today—that means he can speak or read over a hundred and fifty languages, live or dead. If you like, Matt will be our spokesman if that's what we need.

"Also, we have Mike Monroe and Jane Baxter, who recently returned from the center of the Earth. And importantly, have encountered and engaged the, *ah*, adversary, we may encounter."

There were murmurs and nods of greeting.

Janus then half turned so he could face the soldiers, as well as Mike, Jane, and Matt. "Let me introduce our military members who, with you, will make up the Mariana Trench Mission team. You've already met Captain Joshua Loche." He smiled. "He'll happily answer to captain, Josh, or Loche."

Loche gave them a small, friendly salute.

Janus turned back. "Then we have lieutenants—Maxine Archer, our chemist, who will be assessing the viability of any compound we recover."

Jane noticed the blonde crewcut woman. Even though she was a scientist, she was still quite formidable looking, and she gave them a casual nod.

Janus continued. "Our other dive master is 2nd Lieutenant Nina Masters, second-in-command to Captain Loche, and an anthropologist." Janus turned to Matt. "I expect she'll be of great value to you, Professor, if or when we find the race of indigenous folk down there."

The black woman smiled at Matt. "It's an honor, Professor Kearns. I read your work on the proto-Sumerian alphabet—it was riveting."

A few of the other soldiers groaned, but Matt looked delighted to have a like mind on the mission.

"Thank you, Nina." He grinned and returned her salute.

Janus then introduced the muscle. The guys who were the weapon tradesmen—Rick Croft, the hawk-eyed marksman; Lawrie Williams, the explosives specialist; and Chris Angel and Chuck Watts, demolitions and heavy weapons, and both with the size to match. Also, Joe Edison, smaller and bespectacled, and appropriately in communications.

Janus held an arm out to the last two members of the group. "Last but not least, our submersible pilots, Albie Miles and Joni Baker."

"We'll get you there and bring you home, count on it." Joni Baker flick-saluted them with two fingers.

Jane thought they were a likeable bunch. But she needed them to be ready, and likeable or unlikeable, she doubted they were yet ready for what was to come, or what they might face.

She tapped Janus on the shoulder. "Do you mind?"

"No, please, go ahead." He took a step out of the way, and then turned to the soldiers. "Listen up, people."

They focused on Jane, and she folded her arms. "How many of you read the briefing report?"

All hands raised.

"Good." She nodded. "Now, keep your hand up if you believed everything you read in it?" She looked along their faces. "Be honest. I'm here to answer questions."

Most of the hands came down.

Jane nodded. "Yeah, that's what I expected. And if I was you, I probably wouldn't believe it either." She looked along each of their faces. "We have all heard of a place called Hell. From our schooldays, church, or movies. It's supposed to be a place of infernal heat, red skies, and full of demons, right? And it has its ruler, a devil, or *the* devil."

Some nods, mostly flat stares.

"Well, let me tell you something that might keep you all alive.

Believe me when I tell you that Hell is real, and we're going there." Jane lifted her chin, daring them to challenge her. "And the devil and its minion are real."

The group shifted, some looking uncomfortable as they probably wondered at Jane's sanity.

"We are limited by what we know, and can see, and perhaps, imagine. But consider something that is beyond your imagination." She smiled, but with little humor. "Let me ask another question—how many of you have ever heard of giant sea creature legends, like the leviathan?"

Janus smiled as he watched her.

Nina raised her hand. "The leviathan was a biblical beast," Nina said. "It's a myth about a giant creature that either comes from Hell or guards the gates of Hell."

Captain Loche nodded "That's right. I remember reading once that Herman Melville's Moby Dick was inspired by the legendary creature."

Janus Anderson nodded. "When the gates of Hell opened, the first beast through was the Leviathan." He smiled. "That's from a clay tablet recovered from a tomb in Babylonia and dates to around four thousand years ago."

"You're referring to *Dagon*, aren't you?" Matt Kearns asked. "The slumberer below."

"Yes," Jane said.

Janus turned to Matt. "Professor Kearns, have you come across reference to this, *ah*, creature, in your research?"

"Many times," Matt replied. "It's one of the most ancient deities, and some of the first recorded references were from the Mari texts in ancient Syria, some 4,500 years ago." Matt seemed to search his memory. "The Babylonians dreamed of Dagon continually. Interestingly, it was the Babylonians who first depicted Dagon as the fish god, the sinker of ships and eater of men."

The room was quiet for a few moments.

Jane went on. "The bottom line is, Dagon is mountainous in size, intelligent, carnivorous, and we don't even know if it lives for a hundred years, or a million. Or even if it can be killed at all."

"But by your own report, you said you wounded it," Loche replied.

Jane nodded. "We only think so. We certainly scared it off."

"If it fears physical harm, then that is because it can be hurt, and therefore, killed," Loche replied.

"We'll deal with whatever comes at us. That's why we're paid the big bucks." Janus lifted his chin. "Any other questions?"

There was silence.

"We took your report seriously, Jane." Janus nodded slowly. "Why don't we take a tour of our vessels, and maybe that'll give you some assurance that we can deal with whatever we encounter down there?" He held out an arm. "This way, please."

***

Loche and his team stayed up in the mess, while Janus led Jane, Mike, and Matt down to the bowels of the ship.

After passing through a final watertight portal door, they beheld why the ship was so vast—inside wasn't filled with cabins or storerooms but a single cavernous room, and at its base were two crafts, each about seventy feet long and more torpedo shaped than the usual pill shape for DSVs.

They stood at a railing, looking down as technicians crawled in and over the two crafts.

"Meet Abyss-1 and Abyss-2." Janus shrugged. "But A1 and A2 is fine."

"They look fast," Matt observed. "Not something I expected to see on a deep watercraft. What's their depth tolerance?"

"They're designed with an internal ovoid steel matrix that actually increases in strength the deeper we go. The design means we can carry less steel and therefore be more maneuverable and more, *ah*, reactive when and if we need to be."

"They've been to the bottom of the trench?" Matt asked.

"No, but we've tested them in the laboratory to ten tons per square inch. The water pressure at the bottom of the Mariana Trench is eight tons per square inch. Or about a thousand times the atmospheric pressure at sea level. We'll be more than safe." Janus smiled

He looked back at the two crafts. "And other than the slim and liquo-dynamic shape, there's something else you wouldn't expect to see on a DSV." He turned. "Torpedo tubes."

"Warheads?" Jane asked.

Janus nodded. "We have an arsenal of four miniaturized, high-impact warheads, also two nukes apiece. They're low yield but pack enough punch to destroy a city block. That should afford us plenty of underwater defensive capabilities. And that's not all." His brows went up. "The turbine engines can be supercharged to deliver a shock either over the entire skin of the vessel or throw out a pulse for a hundred feet in all directions."

Jane was impressed. "And above water?"

"We have a range of armaments onboard, from small arms to rocket launchers. Plus, several of the crew were selected for their marksmanship and overall skill with weaponry." He smiled. "Jane, I can't put my hand on my heart and tell you nothing will go wrong. But we have prepared for what we know, and what you described."

Jane nodded but turned her gaze back to the craft. They were matte-black but with a red-striped camouflage. *Another instance of them paying attention to the red environment they'd encounter,* Jane thought. Together, they looked like a pair of metallic, tiger-striped sharks, with a single large eye at front, which was their view screen.

"Nothing will go wrong," she repeated softly, more to herself as a talisman.

But Janus took it as her vote of confidence in him and his preparations.

"Then good." He checked his wristwatch. "We depart in fifteen minutes. Grab your stuff and then we can begin to load up."

EPISODE 12

Deep into that darkness peering,
long I stood there, wondering, fearing, doubting,
dreaming dreams no mortal ever dared to dream before – Edgar
Allan Poe

CHAPTER 10

Matt was first to drop in through the Abyss-1 hatch and Captain Joshua Loche took his pack from him.

"Thanks." He turned about. The craft was small inside, and he had to crouch. He was in a single large room with seats all facing forward toward the front window that Matt had been told was unbreakable, eight-inch-thick glass.

There was a slight smell of ozone that he expected, as he'd been in submersibles before, and it came from all the electronic equipment packed into the vessels. There were banks of screens all around them that would display feeds from the outside cameras dotting the length of the DSVs. There was even a small area below them, the lower deck, but this was for weapons storage.

Abyss-1 was the command craft and would house Matt, Mike, Jane, Captain Loche and Janus, the chemist Maxine Archer, as well as the pilot, Albie Miles.

The other craft held the muscle, as Matt liked to think of it, and its crew would be Lt. Nina Masters, Rick Croft, Lawrie Williams, Chris Angel, Chuck Watts, and pilot Joni Baker.

Matt didn't envy that craft, as the last two guys with their bulk would make it feel real crowded inside.

"How long until we reach the bottom?" Matt asked.

"Captain." Janus turned the question over to Joshua Loche.

"Normally, it takes between six and eight hours to get to the bottom of the trench, but these craft are built for speed and strength, so we'll drop at about 23 knots." He bobbed his head. "It'll still take us nearly an hour to get to about 36,000 feet, then we'll slow as we get close to the rift hole," Loche replied

"The gravity well," Jane added.

"That's right," he agreed.

"One question," Mike asked.

"Sure, Mike." Janus raised his eyebrows.

"It's an obvious one, I guess." Mike exhaled. "Those images taken of the ruins around the breach, *er*, gravity well entrance, by the craft that ventured inside… what happened to it?"

"We don't know," Janus replied. "It's been nearly a week and we've had no response." He shrugged. "But that's to be expected."

"Why?" Jane frowned.

"Well, for a start, and according to your own report, it takes between twenty-four and thirty hours to descend in the well, and then, ascend. Plus, the pilot would have had no idea what was happening. So, after spending that amount of time caught in the gravity well to finally pop out in an underground sea, and a red one, might have been a little confusing."

"He'd be disorientated, maybe lost. Plus, standard comms would be useless over that distance anyway," Loche added.

Mike nodded.

"For all we know, he might still be there, waiting for us," Janus said.

Mike glanced at Jane, and he bet she knew what he was thinking—the likelihood of that was less than zero.

Janus looked around. "Any more questions?"

"Hundreds, but here's hoping they'll be answered by the mission," Matt said.

"I'm sure they will." Janus nodded to Loche. "Captain, load 'em up, lock 'em down, and let's ride."

"*Yes*, sir." Loche organized the two teams. "Okay, people, find your seats, and then I want an update from our pilots before we drop. Let's hustle."

Jane, Mike, and Matt followed Janus' instruction on where they'd be seated—thankfully, close to the front and the view window. But everyone also had a small screen close to them.

Loche spoke softly to Albie Miles, the Abyss-1 pilot, who quickly and expertly ran through his pre-launch procedures, and then patched in Joni Baker on Abyss-2 so Loche could talk to his second-in-command, Nina Masters. After he confirmed they were all ready, he turned. "On your word."

Janus smiled and faced forward. "And the words are *open doors*."

Loche spoke into the headset to the command ship's operations room and the whine of heavy machinery could be heard. Immediately, the hull began to fill with water, and the two crafts powered up. After a few moments, the cradles were lowered in the water to below the hull and then disengaged.

The two crafts gently dropped away. Jane felt her stomach flip a little from nerves, and she had the urge to scratch at one of the scabby sores at her hairline that tingled madly.

She noticed that Matt Kearns' face was lit blue by the glow from the sunlit ocean via the large, glass view panel. She smiled; he looked like a long-haired kid about to enter a theme park.

Mike reached out and grabbed her hand, and she turned and smiled. Even though there were the familiar red blotches on his temple and chin, in the dimming light, he was his familiar, handsome old self whose eyes sparkled with curiosity, enthusiasm, plus a little tension.

"Angle down at forty degrees, ahead 10 knots, continuous scan for UOs," Loche said softly.

"UOs?" Matt asked.

Albie repeated Loche's commands as he carried them out, and the captain turned in his chair. "UOs, underwater objects. You'd be surprised how many large objects there are on the first few hundred feet down, from shipping containers to basking whales. Once we're past the top layer, we'll open it up to greater speed and take her down in a giant corkscrew all the way to thirty-six thousand feet."

"Thirty-six thousand feet," Matt repeated with a smile. "Do you know that if you dropped a penny from the top of the Empire State Building, it would take nine seconds for it to hit the street. But here, if you dropped that same penny into the Mariana Trench, it would be drifting down for over three and a half hours before it hit the bottom."

Mike chuckled. "You sure know a lot about pennies, Matt."

Matt grinned back. "Of course. How do you think they pay me?"

Janus eased back into his chair. "Might as well get comfortable, folks. Gonna take us forty-five minutes before we get close to the floor, and once we lose the sunlight, there'll be little to see."

"We might spot a cetacean or two, but we'll be traveling down without our lights on, so it'll be black," Loche added. "As we near the ten-thousand-foot mark, you might spot an odd flash of bioluminescence, and that's likely to be one of the deep-sea varieties of life. Or even a colossal squid."

He went to ease back but seemed to have another thought. "We'll also be lowering the cabin lights to reduce our luminescent profile. Like Mr. Anderson said, might as well just take it easy and relax."

"Good." Jane knew then that they believed her about the massive entity and going dark might give them some cover in the abyssal depths.

She and Mike eased back in their seats as Matt Kearns had his head under a towel as he looked at something on a small screen.

Jane heard Loche talk softly into the microphone as he coordinated with the other craft on the way down. His sonorous voice was almost hypnotic, and it allowed her mind to drift. She wondered about the small red people, and the lobster-like arthropod creatures who were the minions of the horrifying beast they'd seen in the massive inner world sea. And she also wondered about the Russian woman, Kayta, and whether she survived. Unlikely, but she hoped so.

Minutes passed and then more minutes, and then it seemed time sped by as soon Loche announced that they were just five minutes out from arriving at the trench floor.

Janus turned in his seat. "Professor Kearns, you may want to get a front row seat for the view coming up."

"You bet," Matt said, pulling the towel from over his head and then pushing long hair back off his face.

Janus left his seat and Matt sprung up front to take it. Jane and Mike watched by occasionally leaning forward but also using the set of controls they had to change the angle of the small external camera feeds.

So far, there was nothing but black on blackness, and as long as the silt wasn't stirred up, it was so clear as to appear like the nothingness of outer space.

"Five hundred feet," Loche intoned. "Slow to three knots."

They all felt the craft slow in the water, and then saw the beginning of the trench bottom. Or rather, the beginning of the ruins.

"Holy *fu*..." Matt jumped forward in his seat, his eyes wide.

Columns rose to greet them like colossal fingers in the darkness. It was astounding to see them, and to see them at this depth, but what was truly alarming was the sheer size of them. They had to be two hundred feet high and fifty around.

The raised dais came next, and the stones fit together with absolute precision and in strange geometric shapes of some sort of Euclidian design, with each being the size of school buses.

There was also what could have been a huge tabletop, fifty feet in length, toppled beside a rounded stone plinth, obviously its base, and on its surface was etched other worldly whorls and lines.

It was made all the more eerie by the absolute stillness surrounding the ruins and the darkness, which was like they had come across some alien civilization in the dark void of space.

"Can we get a little closer?" Matt asked.

Loche nodded. "Abyss-2, hold your position. We're going to take a closer look."

"Roger that," Joni Baker replied.

Their DSV eased forward, down to about two knots. The massive columns rose around them and as they approached the fallen altar, something like a long, flattened eel, that may have had legs, slithered away into the darkness.

"A little more to the left, I mean, *ah*, port side," Matt whispered.

Abyss-1 swiveled in the water.

"Stop here." Matt leaned forward, his mouth an open grin. "There's writing. A little like on the coin."

"Can you read it?" Janus asked from behind.

"It's picture glyphs, like a mix of Egyptian and Mayan. Each image could be a word, an entire sentence, or perhaps an expression." He half turned. "And no, not fully yet, but I expect so soon."

"Would you like us to take some shots?" Loche asked.

"Sure, yeah, you bet," Matt replied eagerly.

In seconds, some hard copies were being produced, and Loche handed them to Matt.

"Why are they so big?" Loche asked.

"I don't think they were made for human beings." Matt shrugged. "Maybe they were made *by* humans, but I think they might have been designed in deference to their gods and with them in mind. After all, look at the size of the pyramids."

"If they were made by humans, then how the hell did they get to be thirty-six thousand feet down?" Janus asked. "Even with our current technology, we'd struggle to be able to build this."

"If it was us, we'd build it by assembling it first, and then transporting it down," Jane said. "Matt said they might have built it but not brought it here. Someone or something else did that."

Jane's reply had everyone looking back at the ruins in silence.

"Look." Albie Miles switched on the high-beam lamp. Immediately, a few more hundred feet of the ruins and surrounding landscape was revealed.

"Skeletons," Loche said. "And by the look of the size, I'd say whales."

"Normally, if a whale dies and sinks to the bottom, it's devoured quite quickly by isopods and a number of other abyssal scavenger species. Even the bones are broken down in just over a matter of months," Matt said. "But these bones look intact, and some are old." He squinted. "All look like they've been chewed, like by a large predator. And there seems to be several carcasses all jumbled together."

"Whales don't have a communal graveyard, you know, like elephants, do they?" Janus asked.

Loche shook his head. "Nope, something brought these here." He swung to look at Mike and Jane. "Something big enough to grab a whale and bring it back for a snack."

"Lots of whales," Matt added.

"We've seen enough," Janus said. "Captain, prepare to take us into the rift."

"Wait a minute," Matt urged. "We need to see more here. There could be vital clues for dealing with the Dagon entity."

"Matt, we're in tin cans, six miles down, and with limited oxygen. You've got your pictures. Work with those," Janus replied flatly. "Captain."

"Yes, sir." Loche ordered the pilot to swing around toward where the hole in the ocean floor was meant to be.

On their way, they moved along a wall of colossal proportions.

"Look, wait, *wait*!" Matt jumped up. "Ah… pan to starboard."

The pilot looked to Loche who nodded, and the man slowly swung the craft around. There was the huge glyphic writing style again, and this time there were carved images.

Jane saw Matt's lips moving as he took in the eon's old language.

"Can you read it?" Jane asked.

"Some of this, yes," Matt said without turning. "And I'll know more as I study it." He took in more of the fifty-foot-high inscriptions and images.

"*Beyond, beyond, and below*," Matt whispered as he translated. "*Beware to those who dare wake the slumberer beneath*."

"That's uplifting," Captain Loche said.

"There's more… can you …?" Matt asked the pilot.

"Sure. I've been recording it. Do you want hard copy, or the entire image thread?" he asked.

"The thread—send it to my device." Matt gave him the address, and the pilot forwarded the entire wall image scans. "Thank you. Thank you." Matt sat down, staring at his tablet.

In seconds more, they were hovering over a massive dark hole in the bottom of the ocean trench. There were rocks floating over its dark void just as they'd seen up in the command ship.

The group sat in silence as they collectively stared into the stygian dark nothingness of the massive hole.

"Abandon hope all ye who enter here," someone whispered.

"Stow that talk," Loche ordered.

"From Dante's Inferno." Jane snorted. "But Hell is right; just wait until you see the sky."

The two craft hovered over the dark entrance to the gravity well and Loche sat back. "Mr. Anderson, your orders?"

Janus took a deep breath and let it out slowly. "Ladies and gentlemen, this is why we are here—to defeat two monsters: one is cancer, a disease that has plagued mankind forever. The other is to confront an adversary that is the nemesis of global shipping." He strapped himself in. "Captain, lead us in."

"Yes, sir." Loche half smiled, perhaps at the little man's bravado, and then opened the mic to the other craft to gave them final instructions. The pair of vessels then approached the massive hole in the ocean floor with several rocks and other debris hanging over it like a kid's helium-filled balloons at a birthday party. They nosed through them.

"All clear on sensors, sir," Miles said.

"That's what I want to hear, Mr. Miles." Loche leaned forward. "Hang onto your hats, people. All ahead, slow."

The pair of craft entered the dark void and then the rush of acceleration took them.

CHAPTER 11

Kapitan Viktor Zhukov held up a hand as they entered the larger cave. The group gathered around him.

Sobyanin quickly wiped his greasy brow with a forearm and then held the tracker up. The glow from its tiny screen painted his face in a ghoulish, green tinge as he panned it around.

"Mr. Sobyanin?" Zhukov asked.

"I think close by, but…" He bobbed his head from side to side.

"We have multiple routes forward. Give me a bearing," Zhukov ordered.

He looked up briefly, then back down, frowning at the small device. "Strange. It says Chaika is here. *Right here.*"

"There must be a malfunction," Vlad replied.

Sobyanin nodded. "Maybe, but when I switch to group, everyone else shows up. With our missing Mr. Chaika included."

Zhukov cursed under his breath. "Spread out, in twos. Eyes and ears open. Doctor Valentina, with me. Double-time."

The groups quickly paired up and spread out in the cathedral-sized cavern. Its roof was out of sight in the darkness above them, but it wasn't a dry cave, in that they heard water dripping from somewhere away in the darkness.

The larger cave had multiple exits, some at ground level and some of the side caves forty feet up from the cave floor. Zhukov stared up at one, contemplating if they'd need to climb and investigate every hole big enough for their missing man to fit into.

"Can you smell it?" Valentina asked.

"Yes, methane," he replied without turning.

"It's possible that methane is naturally occurring. We know that volcanoes, vents in the ocean floor, and methane hydrate deposits that occur along continental margins are an example of natural methane. Especially at this depth." She lowered her voice. "But I don't think they are the primary source here, do you?"

He turned to her. "No, because I can smell shit as well."

"Me too." She turned slowly. "And that worries me."

Zhukov clicked his fingers. "Mr. Sobyanin…"

"Got something," the man said, and quickly crouched. "I think."

The team started to converge. "Stay alert," Zhukov ordered and the team went back to scanning the cave mouths.

Zhukov approached the man. "What have you got?"

Sobyanin didn't respond but just shone his wrist light at the ground. Zhukov and Doctor Valentina crouched beside him.

"Could that be what I think it is?" Sobyanin asked.

"The tracker." Zhukov sighed. "That was inside our man."

There was a blob of blood and mucous, and in among it a tiny, pill-shaped object. Zhukov rose to his feet. "Look for a blood trail, and everyone be ready for anything."

"How did this happen?" Sobyanin rose to his feet. "Chaika was a big man. He would have fought back, hard."

"We'll soon find out," Zhukov replied.

The team started to move out and around the cave.

"Here." Fradkov had his gun light pointed at the ground. He slowly lifted the muzzle, tracking something. "Goes that way."

"Let's go, people, while the trail is fresh." Zhukov organized his team, sending the huge Andripov out to point.

They moved across the floor of the huge cavern until the blood trail led to a cave about five feet up from the ground and little more than three feet wide.

Zhukov peered inside, and beside him Vladimir Ustinov pointed a motion tracker into the hole. After a moment, he shook his head.

"Cold as a witch's tit." Vlad pulled the device back. "Small cave—how big were these creatures supposed to be?"

"The report said around human-sized," Zhukov replied.

"Could it be their nest?" Fradkov asked.

Zhukov's mouth turned down momentarily. "Maybe it is. Maybe this cave has an exit or they liked the small size because it's defendable."

"Defendable? Down here? Against what?" Vlad asked.

"Who knows. We have to go in, but I don't want us strung out." Zhukov turned about. "I'll take Fradkov, Andripov, Igor, and Doctor Valentina. You, Serdyukov, and Sobyanin keep our exit open."

His second-in-command nodded. "Remember, our communications are limited down here. Once you pass through a few twists and turns, we'll lose our link."

"I know." Zhukov smiled flatly. "But our man was taken in there, or what was left of him. We have to see." He turned. "Mr. Fradkov,

Andropov, take the lead. Doctor Valentina, behind me, and dear comrade, Igor, bring up the rear. Let's go."

***

Outside the cave, Anatoliy dropped his arm holding the tracker. "Lost them. Must have gone around a bend."

"We expected that," Vlad replied. "But keep watching and keep that movement tracker on. I want to know the second anything moves in there."

He looked about in the massive, dark cavern. "Lev, keep your eyes on this cave. Nothing creeps up on us today, yes?"

The soldier nodded.

"And your first task... cover me while I take a piss." Vlad moved off about a dozen feet along the cavern wall and unzipped his fly.

He pissed long and hard, the smell of his urine finally masking the strange animal scent in the air.

Vlad zipped up and paused, tilting his head. He turned to Lev who still covered him with his gun. "You hear that?"

Lev turned away to listen for a moment and then shrugged. "Just heard you pissing. Sounded like the fire department."

Vlad concentrated. "No, after that." He was sure he heard a low sound, like someone dragging a sack or heavy rug across the ground. He shone his light about for a moment before giving up.

He hoped the kapitan wasn't long, as everything about this mission unsettled the shit out of him.

***

"Getting tighter," Andripov said from deeper in the cave.

He had to get down on his hands and knees, his large shoulders only just making it through the narrowing tunnel.

Zhukov prayed that they moved into a more open space soon, as it was now only large enough for them to move in a single line, which was a terrible defensive proposition. But they had no choice.

"Keep talking," he said into his mouthpiece. Normally, he'd have ordered and respected radio silence, but if the reports were correct, these things hunted by sound and smell so probably already knew they were coming.

"Opening up a little more just up ahead," Andripov said. "Holes in the walls, cracks. Stinks even worse up here."

After another few minutes, they began to pass by the holes or side caves, some only inches across and some over a foot. The men leaned away from them, as inside the smell was miasmic.

When Fradkov was passing by one, he stopped, spun, and pointed his light inside.

"I heard…" He squinted into the dark.

Help me.

"There. Did you hear?" He turned back to Zhukov, his eyes bulging wide.

"The woman?" Zhukov asked.

Fradkov shook his head. "Yes, no, like when Chaika was taken."

The young soldier turned back to the small side cave to listen again and leaned closer, just as a grotesque head appeared from within it.

Fradkov had an impression of a gargoyle-like face, with flatted nose slits, sightless eyes, and large ears running up the side of its head. The being was greasily pale to the point of being transparent.

It lunged forward, mouth open and displaying a set of sharp, chisel-like teeth that fixed on the young Russian's shoulder.

Fradkov screamed and beat down on the head, which worked furiously for a moment before pulling away in a spray of blood. It vanished backward into the hole like some sort of foul jack in the box being rewound into its tin.

Fradkov howled and covered his shoulder.

In the glare of his light, Zhukov could see a chunk of flesh missing from the shoulder and thick blood pulsed between the man's fingers. He had no time or room for panicking, and they still had another man missing.

"Shut up," he ordered.

Fradkov grimaced, eyes watering, but clamped his mouth shut.

"I must tend to that," Valentina urged from behind him.

"Not yet." He turned back to the young soldier. "Patch that. We'll see to it when we pull back." Zhukov slid forward to grab the man's boot and tug. "Understand, soldier?"

From up front, Andripov cursed and fired several deafening rounds, as from the small side caves, clawed hands shot out, grabbing clothing, flesh, anything they could dig their talons into.

Zhukov knew they were in a kill box and strung out so much they couldn't get into a defensive position. His soldier's instinct was to fight or die with and beside his men. But then he remembered what he had been told and quickly reached for the small box on his belt, slipped the cover off, and depressed the button.

Immediately, an ear-piercing shriek filled the claustrophobic cave, beating at his ear drums and making his back teeth hurt. But the effect on the creatures was as instantaneous as it was dramatic—they clawed at their heads, writhed in pain, and then they pulled back into their tunnels, abandoning their attack.

Zhukov waited a few more seconds and then switched it off. Silence reigned for another moment.

"Sound off!" he yelled.

Thankfully, his team were all there. He looked back at Valentina who grimaced but nodded.

"I think I lost some hair." She touched a red spot on her scalp. "I guess they were our dog people."

"Orders, sir," Andripov yelled from the front.

"Continue on. Their lair must be up ahead." He looked past the doctor. "Igor?"

"Yes, sir. All clear back here."

"Good. We move, and…"

"*He-eeelp.*"

Zhukov turned back.

"It's those tricking bastards," Fradkov said through pain-gritted teeth.

"I'm here. I'm Ally… *help me*," the voice said again. But this time, weak and strained.

"No, not this time," Zhukov said. "Andripov, move quickly. Find that voice."

The big man elbowed forward, and the group struggled after him. In moments more, they emerged into a cave that was so foul it made their eyes water.

"This must be their nest," Valentino said and held a hand over her lower face.

"Seems our sonic blast cleared them out in a hurry," Zhukov replied. He lifted his head. "*Helloo!*" he yelled in English. "Where are you?"

"*Here, help me,*" came the reply.

He pointed to a small side cave. "In there."

Andripov hunched his shoulders and kept his gun barrel up as he charged into the smaller cave.

"Valentina, with me. Fradkov, Igor, you stay alert out here." Zhukov quickly followed the big man with the female doctor on his heel.

There came a scream from up ahead.

"Here!" Andripov shouted.

They burst into the smaller cave and saw the woman staked out on the ground. She was in a terrible state, naked, lying in excrement that had long dried, and had festering wounds all over her dark brown skin. And her hair was like a halo of mad wire around her head.

She screwed her eyes shut.

"The light," she gasped.

"Point them away," Zhukov said and knelt beside her. "Are you Ally Bennet?"

She nodded and tears began to run down her cheek. "Is this a dream?" she whispered.

Zhukov pulled a knife. "No, we were sent to rescue you. Can you move?"

He cut the binding, and she slowly pulled her limbs in. She nodded. "They took me out for exercise. I'm weak, but I can move."

Zhukov helped her sit up, and she held onto him. "Give me a second."

She drew in deep breaths, and Zhukov tried hard not to be repelled by the smells coming off her.

"Up you get, Ms. Bennet. We need to go, quickly."

She got unsteadily to her feet and rubbed the raw marks on her wrists. Doctor Valentina draped a thin blanket over her shoulders and Ally held it closed.

"What day is it? The date?" Ally blinked but kept her eyes as slits.

"December 15. You've been missing for eight months." He remembered what the report said they would have kept her alive for. "Are there... are there offspring?"

She shook her head. "No, I can't have children due to a childhood accident." She faced him without opening her eyes but gave him a brown-toothed smile. "They would have killed me soon when I didn't produce. Then eaten me."

As they eased her out of the small cave, Fradkov's mouth dropped open.

"*Fuck*... she's alive." He frowned. "Barely."

Zhukov growled. "Shut up, fool."

Valentina began to press the American woman's arms and feel her pulse.

"No time for that." Zhukov clicked his fingers at Fradkov who turned quickly and then grimaced from the wound in his shoulder. "The spare clothing, quick now."

Fradkov shunted his pack to the ground and pulled free a drawstring bag which had a caving suit, like the ones they wore, as well as boots. They'd already known her size from the American notes. But Zhukov knew with the weight she had lost, it would still swim on her.

"Get this on, quick now."

"Wait." Valentina quickly pulled a face-wiping rag from her pack and doused it in water. She quickly wiped the woman's face, under her arms. "Turn around," she said.

Ally did as asked, and the doctor splashed more water on the rag and wiped her bottom and backs of legs free from most of the dried excrement.

"That'll have to do." Valentina flung the rag away.

"Thank you," Ally said softly as she took the suit. She began to slide a leg into it. "I want a gun as well."

Zhukov tilted his head. "Are you sure you're—?"

"Yes," she shot back, and then looked up, her eyes now open and seeming to shine silver in the darkness. "I want to kill them all."

"I think we will leave that for another day, yes?" Zhukov replied. "At least with the sonic alarms we can keep them at bay. We should be okay for extraction."

"Maybe." Ally quickly finished with the clothing and bent to pull on and lace the boots. "When they walked me, they were always on guard," she said. "There are other things down here even they fear. And it isn't us."

"Captain," Igor said and pointed his light at the ground. "There were others."

On the ground were more stake marks and human-shaped stains on the cave floor.

Ally nodded. "Other people would be found." She shook her head. "The ones who go missing in the deep caves when spelunking. It seems not all of them fall off cliffs or get lost in the labyrinths. Many are captured by the monsters and the women kept here... at least for a while."

"Did you see, *ah*, I mean, did you hear others when you were a prisoner?" Valentina asked.

"Yes." Ally straightened. "In the end, they were all eaten... alive."

"Oh." Valentina looked away.

"This is why I don't do caving as a hobby," Fradkov commented.

Zhukov exhaled. "We're done here. Let's back out to re-join the rest of the team, and immediately evac to the surface."

Ally took a step in the boots and stumbled a little. Valentina caught her. "Are you okay?"

The American woman nodded. "Just… just, the thought of going home makes me feel strange. A little scared, that I'm going to wake up and find I'm still here, tied down." She exhaled and shut her eyes again. "I had the rescue dream so many times."

Valentina rubbed the frail American woman's arm.

Ally's jaw set and she straightened. "If we are attacked, kill me. Do not let those freaks take me again." She turned. "And, Captain, I'll take that gun now."

"When we re-join the others." He turned. "Igor, lead us out if you please. Andropov, cover our rear."

The big man nodded. Fradkov rolled his damaged shoulder, waiting on his instructions.

"Okay?" Zhukov asked him.

"Nothing a week at the Black Sea can't fix." He grinned but looked pale.

Doctor Valentina approached and stuck a needle into the meat of his shoulder near the wound.

"Ow." He looked away.

Zhukov snorted. "Russia's bravest."

"Antibiotics, and a painkiller," Valentina said. "Keep the bandage on it, and I can stitch it when we have more time."

"Igor, you're up." Zhukov motioned forward with his head.

Igor turned and got down low to begin maneuvering his way back through the cave. Then went Fradkov, Ally, Valentina, Zhukov, with the huge Andropov at the rear.

Halfway through and they began passing by the smaller side caves again. From the rear of the group, Zhukov noticed the American woman lift her head to sniff the air—and then he knew why. Just then, from one of the caves a grotesque head lunged at Fradkov, again, and the young man yelled his fear and shrunk back.

The American woman, teeth bared, was already crawling over the top of the screaming man, and as she went she snatched his gun from the holster, fired several rounds into the thing's face, and then lunged in after it, screaming her fury.

The rapid gunfire in the small hole was near deafening and between the blasts he heard the woman screaming, *die, die, die,* as she fired.

Someone—Igor, he thought—engaged their screecher, and Zhukov felt insanity creeping in as the cacophony of noises shredded their nerves. He sucked in a huge breath and then roared, "*Get her out of there!*"

Fradkov grabbed the woman's ankles and yanked her back. Ally then reappeared, her face dripping with blood. She panted heavily with her bloody teeth still bared.

She nodded as she handed Fradkov back his gun. "I wish I had more bullets."

"*Don't do that again!*" Zhukov yelled. He then winced. "And shut that off."

Igor stopped the screecher, and except for the group's heavy breathing, silence returned. Igor kept the box ready; however, it seemed the screech-blast had obviously sent the grotesque creatures far into the dark labyrinths, as there was no sign of them.

The group sucked in breaths, waiting for nerves to settle. Zhukov saw Ally looking back at him, a small smile on her lips.

"Don't... do that again," he ordered.

She continued to stare. There was no apology, but after another second there was a slight nod. Zhukov lowered his brow for a moment, sighed, and then lifted his head.

"Okay. Ludzkov, continue, please."

Igor turned to the front and continued to burrow on through the dark cave.

Within twenty minutes, they were approaching the exit.

Zhukov tried to raise Vlad but got nothing but dead air. *Must be too many twists and turns*, he thought. He was looking forward to seeing the looks on the face of his second-in-command when they emerged with the American woman—*a successful mission*, he thought with relief, even though they had lost some good people on the way. But during his initial high-level meeting, the mission risk profile estimated a twenty-five percent attrition rate, so he was well under that.

In a few more minutes, Igor exited, jumped down, and turned to let Fradkov pass by so he could assist Ally. Doctor Valentina jumped down, followed by Zhukov and Andropov.

"What the hell?" Zhukov frowned and engaged the comms system again. "Vlad, where are you?"

He looked one way then the other, seeking out any dots of light of his team's lanterns, but the huge cave was empty and coal dark.

"Here are their packs," Fradkov said and reached down to search their contents. He immediately jerked his hands back and straightened, looking at them. "What the fuck is this shit?"

Zhukov turned and shone his light at the young man. He held his hands out and they glistened. Zhukov then panned his light around them and saw the cave floor and some of the rocks also shone as if they were covered in glutinous oil.

"I don't like this," Valentina said.

"Me either," Zhukov replied evenly. He lifted his chin. "*Vladimir!*" he shouted.

The word bounced away and then echoed several times before the cave fell again to stillness. The group stayed silent for several seconds after the shout, concentrating on trying to pick up even the faintest response. But nothing came back.

"*Volloch.*" Zhukov threw his hands up. "And the only one who had the personnel tracker was Sobyanin." He cursed again. "Okay, spread out." He turned to Valentina and Ally. "You two wait…"

"*No,*" Ally shot back. "I'm not staying by myself. Not ever again."

"*Ach,* okay." Zhukov didn't have time for arguments. "Go through the packs and grab some other armaments, and then stick with me. Everyone keeps their weapons and screechers handy."

The captain pointed. "Igor, over there. Fradkov, down there. And we'll take this quadrant. Yell if you find anything."

The team split and headed out quickly.

Ally put a belt around her waist, and that included a firearm, ammunition, and screecher. Then she loaded a pack with more ammunition, water, and dried food. She slowly put it over her shoulders, and she wobbled a little from the weight.

"You don't need that now," Zhukov said, but she ignored him.

"Yes, I do." She approached, steadier on her feet now. "I'm ready."

Valentina, who had been crouched beside a smoothed rock examining something, slowly got to her feet. She caught up with them and had something between thumb and forefinger. She rubbed them together and then sniffed and frowned.

"What is it?" he asked.

"I think a type of biological mucous," she replied.

Zhukov turned to Ally. "Any ideas?"

She grabbed Valentina's hand and sniffed the fingers. "My night vision is probably much better than yours now, but the gargoyles operated in total darkness, so I never saw anything. But there were times when we were out, that they retreated, fast, as something was coming, something big. I never knew what it was, but it smelled like that." She pushed Valentina's hand away and stared away into the darkness. "Like I said, those foul things that captured me aren't the only predators down here."

"Great. So much for our fast extraction." Zhukov noticed Valentina still staring at her fingers, her forehead furrowed. "What is it now?"

She slowly looked up. "Remember what I told you when we were higher up? About the nematodes living undisturbed in the cave depths?"

He nodded.

"And how I said they seemed to be larger the deeper they were found?" She held out her hand, displaying the glistening slime. "I think this is the same excretion that coats the nematodes."

He snorted. "Big enough to chase off Vlad and the men? No. I think it was more likely that the creatures we repelled in the cave ambushed them." He turned away. "Let's find them before we lose them."

***

Fradkov was at the west end of the cave, and to his left he could make out Igor's bobbing light as he checked along the southern side wall.

As the young Russian edged along, he kicked something metallic that skidded along the cave floor. He bent to pick it up and found it was a Russian flashlight and once again coated in that same greasy shit.

"*Yech.*" He let it drop and wiped his hand on his pant leg.

There were multiple openings in the wall and roof of the large cathedral-sized cavern, and far too many shadows for them to quickly investigate. He could only think that the missing men must have felt the need to take shelter for some reason. But he wondered why they would go so deep to be out of radio communications.

Fradkov came to one cave mouth, stopped before it, and held his light up. There was an impenetrable darkness inside.

"Vladimir?" he called softly.

He waited and was about to pull back when there came a small sound, a little like crunching gravel. He dropped his hand to his belt to feel the screecher there and also pulled his gun.

His shoulder still ached even though the doctor had pumped it full of painkillers and antibiotics, and he had no desire for any more wounds down in the labyrinths. Getting one on an extremity might mean an infection before he could return, and a field amputation was not a way to end a career.

He took a few more steps inside. "Vla…" He stopped himself as he couldn't bring himself to say the officer's name out loud.

Fradkov swallowed noisily and eased forward, even slower now. There was something up ahead. He took a few more steps and could just make out the end of the cave at a wall—or what he thought was a wall—in the flare of his light that seemed to have a strange, spongy texture. And he was sure it was moving. Or pulsating.

He stretched his arm out, holding the light closer.

The wall shifted, lifted, and readjusted itself. Then what he thought was a wall moved and at its middle was something that reminded him of his late grandfather's toothless and puckered mouth.

"What is…?"

Fradkov felt the hair on his neck rise, and he took a step back. At that moment, the thing surged forward, perhaps at the detection of his retreat.

Fradkov went to step back again but skidded on a small pool of slippery mucous and suddenly fell to the side, just as the puckered hole ejected a stream of fluid toward where he had been standing. The stuff spread wide to open like a net but only ended up catching one of his legs. But it stuck.

The webbing then began to be hauled in toward the doughy-looking hole in the wall that started to bloom open. Fradkov pointed his gun and fired into it, but the mass seemed to just absorb the bullets with little effect.

He held on, but as his stuck leg was pulled, he felt himself begin to slide on the slime as he was reeled in.

"*Help!*" he yelled.

"Fradkov?" came the faint reply from Igor somewhere outside the smaller cave.

"Igor, in here, *help me!*" Fradkov screamed as he leaned forward with his knife and began to saw at the web that was now piano-wire tight as the thing ate it back into what was obviously its mouth.

He had no desire to be dragged into that maw, and he sawed harder at the sticky bonds. He began to cut them through just as Igor arrived.

"What is this?" Igor yelled, lifting his gun.

"*Fire, fire!*" Fradkov yelled.

Igor did as requested and sprayed bullets into the thing. In that moment, Fradkov cut himself free, rolled and got to his feet, and immediately began to run, leaving Igor behind.

Igor stood his ground, rifle pulled in tight to his shoulder, and delivered a stream of rounds into the thing. Fradkov turned at the cave mouth to yell for his colleague, but perhaps in response to its prey fleeing, the thing surged forward at astonishing speed.

Fradkov could only stare open-mouthed as in one second, Igor was before the abomination, firing a weapon, and the next, the thing lunged forward, bloomed open from top to bottom, and totally enfolded the man.

Fradkov stared with his mouth hanging open. His friend screamed and then his shouts became muffled. But he *still* screamed as the mouth closed to return to its puckered state with his teammate now inside.

"Igor?" Fradkov backed up.

The thing wasn't finished and pulsated forward in a sort of peristaltic motion.

"*Help!*" came Igor's faint, wet, and muffled cry from inside the revolting mass. And then. "*It burns.*"

Fradkov's bile rose in his throat. He'd seen enough and turned to run. *It just ate Igor alive. And he was still alive in its gut*, he thought madly.

As Fradkov ran, he turned his head to eject the contents of his stomach onto the cave floor.

***

Kapitan Zhukov heard the gunfire.

"Quickly." He began to sprint. Ally and Valentina tried to keep up.

Without giving it a second thought, he flipped the lid from his screecher and pressed the button, allowing the ear-piercing shriek to fill the cavern. He spotted Fradkov coming out of a side cave, and he switched it off as the young man spotted him.

"It's coming!" Fradkov yelled while pointing the way he had come.

"What? What's coming?" Zhukov switched on his muzzle light and held his gun up.

"I don't know, I don't know." Fradkov grimaced. "It ate Igor."

"*What?*" Zhukov grabbed the young man and dragged him closer. "What the hell...?"

Just then, over the sound of grinding gravel, the monstrous worm surged from within the side cave. It continued to disgorge itself, revealing a long, glistening, black body, six feet around, and covered in red streaks.

"Nematode gigantica," Valentina whispered as she backed up.

Already the thing was a good twenty feet out of the cave, but it still trailed inside. It lifted its head as though sampling the air as it tried to locate the humans. Zhukov punched down on the screamer button again, once again fulling the cavern with the agonizing scream, but it did nothing.

Ally had her hands pressed over her ears and yelled over the screamer, "It doesn't hunt by sound."

Zhukov shut it off as the creature disgorged another twenty feet of itself and slid across the cave floor.

"Carnivorous," Valentina said. "Now we know what happened to Vladimir and the rest of your men."

"This must be the thing the freaks were frightened of," Ally said. "I heard it moving but never saw it. I know it's fast and boneless, so can fit itself into smaller caves. We need to get out of here."

Zhukov pointed. "Our way back is that way." He began to move to the side.

The cave they originally came in through was on the other side of the worm, and the more it piled out of the cave, the more their way was blocked. It seemed to catch the scent or vibrations of the humans and it began to pulse forward.

Fradkov pulled at Zhukov's arm. "It fires a sticky web. Wanted to trap me."

Zhukov tried to work out a path around the worm or find somewhere to hide and wait it out. But just then the worm surged forward, fast, curling around a tumble of huge rocks and bearing down on them.

"Run!" he yelled.

The two men and women turned to flee, but Ally hobbled, the muscles in her legs still very weak from just occasional exercise. There came a loud splat, and Valentina screamed and then was pulled backward off her feet.

Zhukov turned to see a long, sticky cord that ended in a mesh-like blob stuck to her pack and trailing all the way back to the front of the creature. The worm began to eat the cord back in while coming forward. At the same time, Valentina was dragged backward on her ass.

There was no time, so Zhukov jumped for her and ripped the pack from her shoulders. "Leave it," he said and dragged her up by the arm.

In an instant, the pack was hauled in and disappeared into the toothless maw.

Ally was gasping hard and stooped to pick up a fist-sized rock. "Stop. Everyone, *stop*." She threw the rock fifty feet to the other side of the cave.

The group froze as the rock struck the ground and bounced into the mouth of a cave no more than three feet wide, and then kept going. The giant worm swung to follow the new vibrations as the group dragged in huge gulps of air.

"Ah, shit," Zhukov breathed out. The front end of the worm elongated and compressed, and it pushed its head into the cave.

"Yes," Valentina said. "Without bones, it will be able to follow us into the smallest of caves."

Zhukov looked up and then cursed again. "There's been a cave-in here before, so using explosives might bring the roof down on all of us. We need to get around it. Or hide from it."

"You can't hide from it," Ally said. "The freak creatures sometimes barricaded themselves in their nests for weeks when I could smell the worms outside. We don't have that amount of time. We'll die of thirst."

"We throw more rocks to distract it," Fradkov urged. "Then we sprint to the way out. No choice."

"No good. The American woman can't run." Zhukov was determined not to leave Ally behind.

Fradkov looked about to burst into tears. "I saw it eat Igor." He shook his head. "I'm not…" He clamped his mouth shut.

"We'll make it. Just stay where you are, soldier," Zhukov ordered.

"No, I can make it." Fradkov looked up, his eyes round. "I'm fast." He turned back to Zhukov. "I can go and get help."

"You hold it together, soldier," Zhukov warned.

Fradkov took off his pack and handed it to Ally. "For you."

Zhukov frowned. "What are you doing?"

Fradkov then brought his hands together as if beseeching his superior officer. He started to back up on his toes. "I can make it. Promise."

"Hold your damn position. That is an order." Zhukov's voice was low and menacing.

"I'll get help," Fradkov whispered, nodding. He then reached down to snatch up a rock in each hand. He turned. The worm was just pulling its head from the cave, its body once again fattening to its former size.

The young Russian threw another rock and began to run, his destination around the back end of the worm and along the western wall.

His throw was a good one and the solid rock bounced once, twice, and then into one of the smaller caves. The worm immediately swung its head after it and fired a jet of white liquid into the cave.

The young Russian ran fast, but lightly, keeping up on the toes of his boots. He was halfway there when the worm began to pull away again. Fradkov threw the second stone, once again the heaviest vibrations attracting the huge, glistening nematode.

"He's going to make it," Valentina said.

Fradkov slowed a little as he approached their exit cave and just as he went to cross in front of another large void, from within its impossibly dark depths a jet of white sprayed out to cover his head and shoulders in a sticky mesh.

"I knew it," Ally breathed out. "There's more of them."

The young man screamed and planted his boots as he wrestled with the mesh that was solidifying around him. Zhukov could see him begin to be reeled in, and then from inside the cave the monstrous head of the new worm appeared.

Its puckered end opened and Fradkov was drawn closer as it bloomed open, waiting to accept its prize.

Then from another cave, another worm's head appeared—it seemed Fradkov's bouncing rocks had attracted more worm attention than he expected.

The wrestling man raised his rifle and fired several rounds into the thing, but even though he couldn't have missed the gigantic pillowy body, they had no effect.

"*Shit*." Zhukov went to run to the young soldier's aid, but Ally grabbed his arm.

"There's too many."

"I have to save my man." Zhukov pulled a grenade, knowing the risks, but it was his last option.

Before he had a chance to deploy the explosive, Fradkov skidded on some gravel, immediately losing his tug-of-war with the giant worm. Without his pull back, the cord leading to the worm maw was quickly reeled in. The man was dragged along the ground, picking up speed, as the fleshy end fully opened to accept him.

Valentina looked away as the screaming young man went headfirst into the pillowy mouth. Another worm appeared from another cave and pulsated its way out, and then lifted its gross head in the air.

"It knows we're here and is sensing for us," Ally whispered.

Fradkov was then pulled fully into the thing's mouth and his muffled cries continued but already seemed far away.

"There's too many. We can't outrun them. We can't hide from them or get around them. We need a damn exit. Now," Zhukov said and turned to Ally. "Well?"

She watched as several of the huge things began to snake toward them. Ally looked back over her shoulder briefly.

"You heard of Winston Churchill?" she asked.

"Of course. Wartime English leader," Zhukov replied.

"He had a saying for times like this…" She began, "…when you're going through hell…"

"You keep going," Zhukov finished.

Ally sighed. "I know one place that the worms won't follow. Or the freaks." She turned. "But it really is hell."

"We don't have a choice. Anything is better than here," Zhukov shot back.

Ally stared at him for a moment before turning to the dark caves behind them. "This way."

***

Ally ran back to the cave, which led to the gargoyle-like creature's nest. At the entrance, she quickly ripped open one of the other dropped packs and started to pull out what she needed.

"Carry as much as you can," she ordered.

Zhukov grabbed two, and Valentina another. Then they climbed into the hole, but after a few minutes she took a different route from the nest destination and crouch-ran as fast as she could manage.

Her legs screamed in agony from all the sudden use they were getting, but she knew that there was no option, and while she felt pain, she knew this was no dream. And besides, pain was something she had become accustomed to.

Every second now, she revelled at being free. Her only disappointment was she wouldn't be able to slaughter every single one of those damn demons after what they had done to her.

After another moment, the cave opened up a little and they could move upright. She pulled Zhukov and Valentina past her and stopped to stare into the darkness. Her eyes were better dark-adapted then either of her companions, but there was still nothing but an impenetrable blackness beyond them.

After her eight months suffocated by total darkness, she had other developed senses, which she now used. She could smell the worms coming and hear the crush of stone as the gross bodies pulsated along after them. *How much time did they have?* she wondered. *Seconds, minutes, more? No, not even that,* she guessed and turned away.

"Hurry, they're coming fast."

In another few minutes, she reached her destination and the small group exited into a cavern that was perhaps fifty feet around. There were multiple exits, but the only thing of significance was the massive dark hole in the center of the cave floor.

Ally stared at it, feeling a sense of dread.

"Now what?" Zhukov asked.

She continued to stare at the pair. "Do you know where I came from? Where I had been before those freaks captured me?"

Zhukov glanced at Valentina and then shook his head. "No. I thought you had been caving, and then those things found and took you. It wasn't relevant to the rescue mission."

She spoke without turning. "Believe me or not, I had been on an expedition to the center of the Earth. My team traveled there via one of these things called a gravity well. It transported us all the way there and back." She finally turned to the captain. "This is one of them."

"To the center of the Earth?" Valentina swallowed. "This is not possible. Maybe you dreamed this while…"

Zhukov exhaled loudly. "Really, Lieutenant Bennet, I think you…"

Ally held up a hand and turned to the cave they had just exited from. "It's nearly here. It won't stop chasing us until it corners us or runs us down." She snorted softly. "Or we simply run into another form of predator." She smiled at the doctor. "Or maybe I'm still in a dream now."

They could all hear the approaching worm now as there came the sticky sound of something pressing itself into their narrower cave.

"Then I am in the nightmare too." Valentina grimaced as she kept her eyes riveted on the cave behind them.

Ally turned and stepped to the void's rim. "This hole does not have gravity in the same form as we know it. We will float, *fly,* all the way down to the center of the Earth, and it will take us an entire day." She looked up and gave them a broken smile. "The worms won't follow, or the cave freaks. We can hide out there, for a day, or week, or however long…" she lowered her voice, "…we can survive this."

"I'm not jumping into some bottomless black hole in the ground. That's suicide," Zhukov said and raised his gun, turning back to the exit.

"Staying is suicide." Ally picked up a rock and tossed it over the pit. It floated in the air.

"Look," Valentina said.

Zhukov turned back and could only stare.

From within the cave, there came a crush of gravel, close, and then a jet of sticky, white fluid shot out to strike the soldier's arm.

Ally lifted the gun she held and fired a deafening stream of rounds back into the exit cave and across the mesh snaring the soldier, cutting it.

"Take my hand," she yelled as she let the gun hang from the strap over her shoulder.

Valentina took her left hand and shut her eyes tight. Zhukov took her right.

"*Now.*" She pulled them both in with her.

CHAPTER 12

Matt Kearns floated and dreamed.

He had tried to stay awake watching the nothingness pass by the tiny porthole windows in the submersible, but after an hour, the occasional blue fleck of unknown luminosity from the dark and weightless depths had become monotonous, and then hypnotic, and then his eyelids had drooped.

He had been overwhelmingly excited about the prospects of meeting a new race. He dealt with ancient and long-dead languages, and was undoubtedly the best in the world at his craft, but the idea of finding an unknown language, one not developed on the world's surface, and the race of people still alive who spoke it, was astounding. How did their language evolve, what were its roots, and were there other dialects? Plus, as it had a written form, were there books, records, or libraries? So much to see, so much to learn.

He had wondered then about the crustacean-like creatures that had been referred to in Mike and Jane's report. Were they intelligent enough to be communicated with? The questions had dazzled his mind and then after staring at the small window trapped within a fog of his own thoughts, he had finally let it all go and slipped into a slumber of nothingness.

And then the nightmares began. In the dark space of his mind, there was the huge, hulking form of something with glowing red eyes like pinpoints at the heart of a fire. It probed his mind, and it knew him, and worse, it awaited him down in those depths far below them all.

Hours slipped by. Then more hours. The two DSVs moved together at speeds of up to three hundred miles per hour.

Then just twenty-nine hours later, it was like reverse thrusters had been applied as they came to the floor of the well and the gravity surge eased to first slow them and then to stop among a field of other floating debris of rocks, huge bones, and metallic debris that might have once been a submarine.

Captain Loche and Albie Miles in Abyss-1 were already awake, as were Joni Baker and Nina Masters in Abyss-2.

"Proximity sensors, geographic sounding, and sonar mapping,

double-time," Loche said. "Let's wake 'em up." He pressed a small button, and the lights of the craft came on, as well as a gush of cool air.

The soldiers were immediately alert, and gradually Matt, followed by Jane and Mike, sat forward, blinking several times.

"Are we there yet, Dad?" Matt asked and leaned to the side to see out the large front view port. His mouth dropped. "Holy shit."

The portholes and the front viewing window were blood red. All red. And the deep-red twilight glow coming into the craft made the inside of their submersible look like it was some sort of gothic hell house.

"Depth, two-twenty feet. No obstacles, no large underwater signatures within one mile in all directions," Albie reported. "However, I do see some metallic forms on the grid... possibly a debris pattern."

"Show me," Loche said, then waited.

Albie scooted them toward the bottom where there were the edges of something sticking from a flattened sheet of bright yellow steel that could have been cloth. Or flesh.

"I think we now know what happened to our missing DSV." Loche sat back.

"It's flattened," Albie remarked. "Those little guys can take up to 5,551 psi, around 378 atmospheres. What could do that?"

"What indeed." Loche looked over his shoulder to Jane and Mike.

"I can see things swimming out there," the chemist, Maxine Archer, said almost reverently. "I think they're fish."

"They might be. Or might not," Jane replied.

As if in response, one of the things swam closer and then right up to Matt's porthole. Its head *clonked* against the glass.

"It's hard, covered in a bony exoskeleton," he observed. "Like a primitive fish of the surface ocean's Devonian period, I think."

Mike craned forward. The thing lifted its head as it tried to taste the glass and instead of a mouth, there was a set of hard, furiously moving mandibles. From underneath a shelf-like bony brow, eight small, black eyes peered in at them.

"Or not a fish at all, but an arthropod," Mike said.

Something around six feet long zoomed out of the red twilight to snatch the smaller shelled fish, shake its head a few times like a dog with a bone, and then kept going in a cloud of dark blood and bone fragments.

"Rule of tooth and claw. Just like home," Loche said.

The pilot listened to his comms for a moment. "Roger that, Joni."

He half turned. "Abyss-2 and crew at optimal and awaiting orders, sir."

"Miles, find me my coastline."

Albie pinged the western distance, sending out a radar wave. It bounced back almost immediately.

"Less than one mile, west southwest, sir," he replied.

"Good." Loche nodded. "Send up an airborne drone and let's take a look."

"Yes, sir." Albie worked the controls for a moment, and then pressed a button that lifted a small panel and joystick. "Airborne drone-1 away."

Above the craft, a pod sped to the surface, where it bobbed for a moment before opening. The bird-sized drone lifted off and immediately the small screen on the console came to life.

"Putting it up on view," the pilot remarked and each person's small screen displayed the camera's visual feed aspect.

The drone continued to lift for two hundred feet and then hovered. Above them, the sky was a cauldron of fire—no sun, no clouds or serene blueness, just what looked like violently boiling magma... exactly as it was.

"Panning left." Albie moved the airborne drone in a slow pivot. There were a few dots of things flying in the distance, but without any further information, they could have been gull-sized or airplane-sized. Then came the towering column of the gravity well they had just arrived within, which looked like a massive tree trunk, miles wide, and rising from the sea to vanish up into the seething redness above them.

"Take us to shore, all ahead, ten knots," Loche said.

"Surface, sir?" Albie asked.

"Yeah, let's do it," Janus urged.

"No, let's stay down for a while longer." Loche overruled him as he stared hard at the screen. "But we'll rise to one hundred feet and send the drone ahead."

The drone that had been hovering over the top of the submerged craft now sped away, throwing back images of the placid red ocean below it. It crossed over a pod of long-necked creatures swimming just below the surface and also something hundreds of feet wide that moved like a carpet being pulled over the ocean bottom. Jane wondered whether it was a single organism or thousands of small creatures all moving tightly together.

Then there came what first looked like reefs, but as the water shallowed a little more, it could be seen that those "reefs" had straight lines and angles and what could possibly be cobbled laneways between them.

"Water shallowing rapidly, sir," Albie observed.

"Take her up to negative ten." Loche rubbed at his chin. "Anything else airborne?"

The pilot checked and shook his head. "Small signatures, bird-sized, but nothing to concern us."

"Okay, let's slow to three knots." Loche glanced at the drone's image as it now passed over the shoreline. "And there it is." He turned. "Your city."

Mike and Jane nodded as they watched the images appear, and Matt also seemed transfixed.

The drone dropped to about a hundred feet above the city. The shapes were eerie, nightmarish, and bore no semblance to any architectural standards that human beings knew.

"Could not look any more alien if they tried," Janus observed.

Some of the buildings were recognizable as a habitable structure. But others were of no Euclid design employed by mankind, and their angles and even proportions just didn't make sense. There were more that didn't look built at all, but more grown, or excreted, as if some sort of hard resin had been used.

"Take it lower," Janus requested.

Loche dropped the drone down to hover just over the tallest building. Though the drone was near silent, it still gave off a faint whine like a giant mosquito and should have at least brought something out to investigate.

"Can we take it inside one of the dwellings?" Janus asked.

"That's why we use the drones, Mr. Anderson. Taking her in." Loche lowered the drone to street level and headed toward a section where the ancient, cobbled street met in a form of intersection.

He turned the tiny craft in a full rotation, and then approached one of the squat buildings with a dark oval opening.

"Here goes nothing." Loche switched on a powerful light on top of the drone and maneuvered it in.

The craft floated into the fifty-foot-wide room and hovered in its middle. There were oddly shaped items scattered about, but it was impossible to discern their function.

"Is that supposed to be furniture or objects of art?" Janus asked.

"No, there, on the wall...*that's* their art," Matt replied.

The drone approached one side of the room and there, pinned to the wall, were shells of creatures, skulls, as well as animal hides. The drone pulled back a few feet and panned the camera along the mounted remains.

"*Ah shit*," Matt breathed out.

There was the small skin of a human, still reddish-brown, but it even had the facial features, as if the skull had been removed, cleaned, and then later sewn back into it. There were no eyes, and the mouth was just a gaping toothless hole.

"Perhaps it's the trophy room," Loche said softly.

"Monsters," Mike grimaced.

"Just different to us," Matt replied.

"No, Mike is right, they *are* monsters," Jane replied.

Loche swiveled the tiny craft in the air.

"Over there, what's that?" Matt sat forward.

There was a block of stone that was acting like a bench with objects upon it. But as the drone approached, they saw it was dried food scraps and the makings of a stone knife.

"There's nothing. No writing, no cuneiform, no pictures, nothing. A very primitive culture. And yet they built these structures." Matt snorted softly. "Maybe it's simply hive learning."

"Let's try another building," Mike suggested.

Loche pulled the drone out, and they checked several more of the small houses, but they held little clue as to what happened to the crustacean race of beings.

"It all looks abandoned now," Matt observed.

"Maybe only the surface dwellings. The creatures were at home above and below the water—after all, they were crustaceans," Mike replied.

"Okay, if they might be in the structures below the surface, then we need to keep an eye on them as well," Loche said.

"I suggest we don't dock at the city, and perhaps find somewhere up or down the coast from it," Jane added.

"That's the plan," Janus said and turned to Loche. "Right?"

The captain nodded, and then took the drone controls and maneuvered it higher for a few moments to turn slowly, surveying the coastline. About two miles on the southern coast, there was a river whose mouth opened in a wide estuary.

"There," he said. "Water looks deep enough for the DSVs to enter."

Albie checked the instruments. "Sure is. Deep trough, around a hundred feet, more like a harbor mouth." He half turned. "Take her in?"

"Yeah, nice and slow, mid-water." Loche leaned forward, staring out at the red-tinged water as the pilot kept the submersible at around fifty feet and relayed the instructions to Abyss-2.

Above them, the drone lifted and from a height of about five hundred feet, it looked down at the water and could just make out the two seventy-foot-long crafts moving into the estuary mouth like a pair of killer whales gliding in formation.

Jane licked her dry lips. "Careful, estuary mouths are where predators lie in wait for things to try and cross from salt to fresh or vice versa. Especially if there are any sort of migrating species."

"Got it," Loche replied. "Keep all sensors focused on that river. You too, Abyss-2."

Albie nodded. "All clear so far."

As the team watched, they saw several new species of sea creature—it was hard to call them fish—swim up closer to the craft. There were a few things that might have been like lampreys or other species of parasitic fish, eight feet long and like long, grey bags with a round sucker shape on their heads that looked like they wanted to latch onto them, but a brief shock pulse repelled them from getting too close.

Another creature that looked like a ragged bird but was probably a giant form of water beetle flapped its chitinous wings toward them as it seemed to fly under the water. It was around twenty feet in length and stayed close to them for several moments, checking them out, before peeling away into the red gloom.

Albie pulled back a little from his screen. "Sir, got something, I think, on sonar. Like a shadow and can't quite get a hard fix on it. It seems to be ghosting us. It's big though."

Loche leaned in closer to the images on the sonar screen. "Could it be debris?"

"Maybe." Albie shrugged. "Might be a malfunction, but I don't want to call it a bug, not in this place..." he chuckled, "...but whatever it is, it's there but not there—most of our sensors are passing right through it. Weird."

"It's moving," Loche observed.

"Yeah, maybe getting out of our way," Albie said.

"Okay, keep an eye on it. Proceed," Loche replied.

They continued mid-water and Loche took the drone over the stretch where the strange object had appeared, but there was nothing visible below the surface, not even a shadow.

The two craft were about fifty feet apart, gliding silently through the red water and observing the variety of arthropod creatures mixed with near normal-looking species of aquatic life.

"We ate many species of local fish," Mike said. "Tasty, and no ill effects."

"What about the bugs?" Matt asked.

"Yes, we did, when we had to. And we're pretty sure that the indigenous red people cooked some of the arthropod people for us to eat." Mike raised his eyebrows. "Delicious."

"Right, so who're the monsters now?" Janus chuckled.

Albie exhaled and shook his head. "Captain, that thing ghosting us…"

"It's back?" Loche asked.

"It never left. It's closing on Abyss-2. Seems it moved aside, but only so it could come at us from behind." Albie shook his head. "Increasing speed."

"Typical ambush behavior. Strap yourself in, people." Loche opened the comms to their sister craft. "Abyss-2…"

"Yeah, we see it," Nina replied. "Or rather we can sense it, but still see nothing yet."

"Hold your position, we're coming around." Loche nodded to their pilot who turned the sleek submersible in the water.

"I can see it now." Matt rose from his chair. "Holy crap, it's enormous."

Everyone stared. Though the electronic sensors still couldn't make out the mass in the water, they could see the thing now as it bore down on their twin submersibles.

"A freaking jellyfish. A giant freaking jellyfish," Jane said. "Why not?"

The massive bell-shaped creature must have been a hundred feet across and thirty thick. It trailed long electric-looking streamers beneath it, and by the look of the fluorescent colors of them, Jane bet they were packed with stinging nemocytes.

As if in a current, one of the thicker tentacle-like streamers almost lovingly reached out to caress Abyss-2.

"Better back up a little, A2," Loche said.

Nina acknowledged and the submersible began to ease backward in the blood-red water. But invisible to them was that some of the enormously long tentacles had already wrapped around the craft and began to pull the huge bell of its head toward them. Abyss-2 was reeled in, and the bell bloomed open to envelop them.

Nina's voice came over the speaker. "Not much solid mass to this thing, but going to give it a little shock, just three seconds at half power, as I don't want those tentacles fouling our propulsion exhaust."

Loche frowned as he watched. Jane could tell the man was worried. And if he was, she was as well.

The image of the submersible distorted for a moment as the electric pulse emanated from the craft. But afterward, there was no pain response from the monstrous jellyfish and instead the entire bell continued to enfold the submarine. Then the tentacles started to fluoresce.

"I doubt those stinging nemocytes will cause the vessel a problem. However, all jellyfish digest their food with an enzyme in their multiple stomachs." Jane grimaced. "I don't know for sure, but something that size might just have enough gut acid to do some serious damage to the hull."

Loche engaged the mic. "Try again, Nina," Loche said. "Give it a ten-second blast this time—seventy-five percent."

"Roger that," Nina replied.

The image distorted once again, for longer this time, but when it returned to clarity, the massive thing was still there.

"Damnit," Loche whispered. He turned. "I'm betting if I tried to use a standard torpedo, it'd probably pass right through."

Jane nodded. "And then it'd simply regenerate."

Loche thought for a split second. "Okay." He turned back. "Nina, full power pulse. Keep it going for as long as you can."

"Josh, *ah*, sir, respectively, that'll drain our batteries pretty quick," Nina said.

"No choice." Loche sat forward. "If that thing damages your hull or fouls you, you might not have a craft. Or crew. Do it, *now*."

"Yes, sir. Going full pulse," she responded.

The entire image on their screens whited out for a second or two and when it returned it was still jagged with interference. But they could see the bell of the jellyfish begin to glow and then there seemed a milkiness surrounding the massive creature.

"I think some of it is being boiled away," Jane observed.

"Good," Janus responded.

Then, as if being spat out, the submersible was freed, and the jellyfish began to unwrap its tentacles and pull away. There were cheers from inside Abyss-2, and Loche exhaled.

"That did it," he said.

"Sure did. But we're down to 10 percent power," Nina replied.

"Yeah, we'll need to take to the land and allow you to recharge. We'll find a place soon." He turned to Albie. "Ahead, three knots."

"And, sir?" Nina asked.

"Yes, Nina?" Loche replied.

"Next time, it's you guys' turn."

Loche laughed softly and half turned to Albie. "I just want you to know that everyone onboard Abyss-1 appreciates you guys being the guinea pigs for us, okay?"

Nina chuckled. "You're welcome."

"Give me a few minutes to do a little more drone investigation, and we'll find somewhere to pull in, over and out." Loche then took control of the drone and sped down along the shoreline.

As the small drone headed into the estuary mouth, Loche dropped it down below a few large, leafed trees that hung their branches over the red-tinged water. He hovered there, looking along the waterway. The dense tree canopy trees made it like a cave inside. He took the drone in and switched on the small craft's lights. As he did, there was movement in the branches above him, and something he only just glanced snaked away from the lights.

"Got movement," he said. "Checking it out."

The drone lifted and he pivoted the light beam into the foliage above. The branches shivered a little more, but nothing appeared.

"I'm not seeing anything in there," Janus remarked.

The dense growth hid everything, and just as Loche began to pull back, the entire branch moved.

The revealed creature was a miracle of camouflage evolution in that it was a long, stiff body, with its armor plating the color of bark and a few gnarled segments mimicking branches. But even beyond that, on the fake branch tips there were some smaller scales or scutes that were a deep green to mimic leaves.

"Whoa." Loche tried to pull the flying craft back, but a long sticky tongue darted out from the creature's now open mouth parts and shot toward the small drone... that was, until it hit the rotors.

It knocked the drone off balance, but the sharp, spinning propellors seemed more than a match for a soft tongue and blood flicked away, and the tongue was rapidly reeled back in.

"Ouch." Matt grinned.

The fake branch shuffled off, and without trying to hide anymore, they could now see the twelve-foot-long, log-like body, and flat face with compound eyes.

"Like some sort of cross between a chameleon and stick insect," Maxine Archer commented.

"Except a hundred times bigger," Matt added.

"Nothing down here follows the rules of evolution as we know on the surface," Jane said. "We must be prepared for that when we set foot out there. Every step we take, every inch we cover, we must be on guard, because a stick might not be a stick, or a rock might not be a rock."

"Yeah, I think that's the plan, Jane." Janus shared a condescending smile with her.

"Okay." Loche turned back around in his seat. "Let's take her in, slowly."

The drone still hovered over the estuary mouth and the captain swiveled it to look at the landmass once again.

"Beachhead coming up with enough water for us to get close to the bank for disembarking. We'll bring the drone in for recharging, as I want it as our eyes in the sky for as long as possible."

The two craft slowly and silently headed in toward the estuary mouth, rising from deeper water as it followed the contours of the river mouth into the shallows.

"Surfacing," Albie announced as the craft breached and then sailed the last fifty feet in toward the bank. Right behind it, Abyss-2 came up and also pulled in.

The drone came down and a small hatch opened on the nose of the craft for it to drop into, with the hatch quietly closing behind it.

Loche used the external cameras plus the front view screen to examine their surroundings.

"Movement or heat signatures?" he asked.

Albie bobbed his head. "Lots, but nothing significant. Just like any normal forest." He turned and grinned. "But not."

"Good enough for me." The captain spoke over his shoulder. "Kit up, people. This is where the fun starts."

"We're here." Janus leaped up and rubbed his hands. He spun to the group. "We did it."

"Jane, Mike," Loche called. "From what I gleaned from your report, you traveled the equivalent of two full days before you arrived at the desert zone where the red people had their hidden city. Think you can find it again?"

"We can find where it was. As long as it's still there," Mike replied.

"And as long as they're still welcoming us," Jane added.

Janus thumbed toward Matt. "And that's where Professor Matthew Kearns will be using his magical linguistic powers for us." He grinned at Matt. "Right?"

Matt scoffed. "The magic will be if we can find them. And then they want to communicate."

Loche stood and looked down at Jane and Mike. "You guys ready?"

Jane nodded. "Just butterflies." She looked at Mike. "You?"

"Pelicans." He smiled back.

Loche stood in a crouch in the cramped vessel. "Okay, people, line 'em up, and let's pop the hatch. Albie, while you have the drone in range, you'll be our eyes and ears so stay on comms. Understood?"

Albie saluted. "You got it, sir. I'll take good care of you and our fish." He saluted. "We'll be here waiting for you."

"Good. All efforts on defense." Loche saluted back. "Don't want to have to walk home."

Mike popped the hatch and immediately a gush of warm and humid air rushed in that smelled of plant sap, scented flowers, and brackish water from the estuary.

Loche went up the ladder, paused with his shoulders out for a moment, and then kept going. The others quickly followed.

Jane felt her heart beating rapidly, and Mike put his hand on her shoulder and squeezed. "We'll be fine."

"Of course we will." She took a deep breath and then climbed the ladder.

The crew wore foreign legion-style hats that covered their ears and necks, but the heat still hit her hard as she climbed out and leaped to the bank from the top of the craft.

Jane squinted up at the boiling ceiling above them. "And at last before me, I behold the hot red hell from my nightmares."

"Appropriate," Loche remarked. "Is that from Dante?"

"No." She shook her head. "From Captain Raymond Harris who led our last expedition."

Jane could tell Loche wanted to ask her what happened to him but didn't. Instead, he nodded and turned to the group.

"Okay, people, weapons, comms check, and supplies. Double-time." He then lifted his chin and saluted the approaching tall, black woman leading the crew of the second DSV.

"First Lieutenant Nina Masters, how was your voyage?"

Nina saluted and then broke into a grin. "Walk in the park, sir. A little rocky right at the start, and a few locals tried to get a little too cozy, but I can announce the submersible armaments checked out."

"That they did." Loche turned. "Well, according to Mike and Jane's notes, we have around two days trekking ahead of us, and at a standard three miles per hour, taking into account rest and heavy jungle, we'll call it around sixty miles to cover." He looked up at the sky and pulled his dark glasses over his eyes. "And we sure don't have to worry about losing daylight down here."

"Is this real?" Janus had his arms wide, and his face turned to the red sky. "I mean, I read about it, and I sort of expected it, but this is beyond amazing." He lowered his head to look at several of their team members. "Are you not knocked out by all this?"

"And all been hiding beneath our feet for billions of years. And we never knew," Matt added.

"Exactly." Janus pointed at Matt's chest. "And if it wasn't for that old mad Russian, Arkady Saknussov, we might still not know."

"I wish we didn't," Mike said.

Janus spun to him. "Why? This is the biggest scientific discovery, like since forever." He grinned. "And it's all ours."

"That's why," Jane said. "Because it'll either kill us, or guys like you will kill it."

Janus shook his head slowly. "No, Jane, exactly the opposite; we'll preserve it."

"I'll believe it when I see it," Mike replied.

"Let's leave those questions to the politicians. We've got a job to do. Let's form up, people." Loche organized the team with Janus, Matt, Mike, and Jane at the center, Chris Angel, one of their heavy weapons guys, leading them in, followed by Rick Croft, their resident marksman, and then his second-in-command, Nina Masters.

Then came Loche, and bringing up the rear was their comms guy, Joe Edison, Lawrie Williams with their explosives, and their other heavy weapon's guy, Chuck Watts.

Albie Miles and Joni Baker would stay with the DSVs, and Albie would work the recharged airborne drone overhead as their scout and continually feed the info back to him for as long as he could.

Loche felt he had assembled a good team with the best skill sets available. He also felt he would have been happy taking it into any hot zone anywhere in the world. He looked again at Mike and Jane, Matt, and then Janus. The physicality and brains of the team wasn't in question, but the mental state of several might become an issue. Places like this tested even the strongest of them. And a "below Earth" mission was something he and his soldiers had never experienced.

Time would tell, he knew. And that time began now. "Okay, let's move it out."

The group headed out along a natural trail, two abreast. Many of the soldiers used movement trackers and an array of other sensory equipment as they trekked. Loche moved up closer to Jane and Mike.

"Yell out if anything is worthwhile noting to us."

"Don't worry, we will," Mike said and turned. "The problem is, we were some miles to the west of here, and even then we were on the run, so we were moving fast. Therefore, we didn't have much time for sightseeing."

"Understood," Loche said. "But even impressions are valuable."

"Here's one impression," Jane replied. "When we were in this area, we found it vacated of all animal life. We guessed later that it was because we were entering the domain of the *Y'ha-nthlei*; the deep, old ones..."

"The shell people?" Loche asked.

"That's right," she replied. "But now that they're gone, I expected the wildlife to have repopulated the area."

"And I'm betting that's not a good thing?" Loche asked.

Jane looked at his face for a moment. "You read my notes about some of the flora and fauna we encountered, right?"

He nodded. "Yeah, don't worry, I'm not going to underestimate anything."

"Good." She turned away. "Because we lost an entire team of professional soldiers and scientists to horrifying things that sometimes came out of nowhere. Everything we step on, brush against, eat or drink, should be regarded as potentially lethal."

"Got it." Loche smiled and then leaned a little closer. "We'll just do our jobs and get the hell out. How's that sound?"

"Sounds like what I signed up for," she replied.

He saw she continued to watch him. "Something else?" he asked.

"Yeah..." Jane half smiled and shrugged. "I'm not really a hard ass. I'm just scared. For myself, for Mike, and everyone else. This place eats you up. I've seen it."

"I know, and I know you have a right to be scared. But I want to thank you and Mike for coming. We need you, and it showed real courage," Loche replied.

She sighed. "I don't feel courageous."

He nodded to his team. "My guys are courageous for coming, but that's their job. However, you're well beyond that for coming back when you know what horrors exist here." He smiled down at her. "Remember what Mark Twain said: Courage is not the lack of fear. It is acting in spite of it."

"You know Mark Twain?" She grinned.

He shrugged. "I think I read it on a beer coaster." He winked.

She laughed softly. "Thank you."

"You're welcome." He touched the brim of his cap and went to catch up with the leaders.

***

Jane had at first been watchful for everything and anything, with numerous small creatures frightened away from their approach, and only a few larger creatures that seemed to be bovine-like herbivores that stared at them with large and liquid-looking sets of eyes crowding hard and angular faces.

Then, after the hours began to accumulate, she felt the heat and humidity start to suck the energy from her muscles. She sipped at the already warm water in her canteen but knew she was losing more than she was consuming and her temples started to pound under her hat.

The travel would be over several days, but rather than have a long down-time for sleep—as there was no nighttime—they would march around the clock and take breaks every few hours for short bursts of rest and food. Already, Jane desperately wanted a rest but would rather fall down and die before she'd be the first one to call for it.

Thankfully, just twenty minutes later, it was Loche who pointed at a huge tree with spreading limbs that offered them some respite from the red, boiling heat from overhead.

"Croft, Angel, check it out," Loche ordered and also ordered Albie to fly the drone over the top to ensure there was nothing lurking in the upper canopy.

The group waited while cradling their weapons as the two men trotted in and under the impressive, spreading limbs. There were no sounds of approach or escape from the limbs overhead, and in a few minutes, Croft came out of the tree's shadow and gave them a thumbs up. Albie also gave the all-clear.

"We'll take a rest break here for fifteen minutes," Loche announced. "I want everyone to stay alert, and I want two people on perimeter watch just inside the shadow line."

He picked two men, and the rest of them moved in under the tree. There was appreciated respite from the blasting heat from overhead, but the humidity never went away.

Croft pointed upward. "Anyone else want an apple?"

Everyone looked up to see some rounded red balls looking like Christmas decorations or candy apples higher up in the tree branches.

"I'm having one of those." Croft pushed his gun over his shoulder.

"A word of warning," Jane said. "Last mission, one of our people decided to taste something that smelled and looked like a giant strawberry. They nearly lost their tongue and lips."

"You heard the lady, knucklehead," Loche said.

"Thank you, boss." Croft grinned.

The group settled down, and a few of the soldiers laid out straight, put their heads on the packs, and pushed their hats down over their eyes.

Jane was amazed to hear some of them begin to snore almost immediately. She guessed that years of training taught them to catch sleep anywhere and fast—recharge their batteries when they could.

She settled back on one elbow, and Mike smiled at her. "Penny for your thoughts." He raised his eyebrows.

"Next holiday, I want us both to go somewhere cool, with snow, and ice-cold schnapps, and fondue, and…"

"…and bearskin rugs and a roaring log fire." He wiped his brow. "Okay, maybe not the fire." Mike lay back, still holding her hand. "We'll get there."

"I know, I know." Jane lay back and glanced up at the dappled red light as it cascaded through the leaves. She could just make out the fist-sized fire engine red balls that really did look like juicy, crisp apples. And she would have loved to bite into a cool, crisp apple right now.

She closed her eyes. She doubted she'd be able to sleep with all the snoring. But in a few seconds, she had already drifted off.

***

In the tree directly above the group, one of the ripest-looking apples jiggled a little on the branch.

Then it bloomed open.

The exhalations from the people below had wafted up toward the red bulbs and excited them. But it wasn't a fruit at all and if anyone looked closer at the bulb, they would have seen a tight mass of coiled thread-like organisms, some no thicker than a human hair.

They quested in the air, tasting it and searching the direction of the warm breaths. Finding it, one by one they disengaged from the bunch and began to drop down. Many would only find the ground and starve or be eaten by other minor predators.

Some might land upon a body, but it will find the external shell or skin was inaccessible to the tiny, weak worms.

But then others, the lucky ones, might land in or close to an open orifice.

***

Lawrie "Lozz" Williams always snored loudly, and with his mouth open. Most of the time his buddies would either nudge him in the ribs or if they were out on mission, threaten to shoot him.

This time, they simply gave him some space as they only had a few minutes down time, so many had learned to sleep anywhere, anytime, and even been trained to lay out in the open during thunderstorms, in snow, or up a tree.

Lozz never felt a thing when the hair-thin, blood-red worm floated down and landed on his upper lip.

Either end of the thing was pointed and either end could act as its head, as both had the tiny bundle of cells that controlled its senses, and either end had the tiny dot of a primitive eye on its tip.

It immediately found the source of the warm, wet exhalations and slithered up to travel into his left nostril. Lawrie Williams snorted and slowly reached up to wipe the tickle in his nose.

Of the bundle of thread-like animals, only one in a thousand might find a suitable home. This one found Lawrie Williams.

***

Within fifteen minutes, Loche had them all on their feet again. Only Williams looked a little bleary-eyed. He groaned and pinched at the bridge of his nose with thumb and forefinger.

"You okay there, Lozz?" Croft asked.

"Yeah, yeah, just this damn heat-headache, I guess." He squinted up at the red sky for a moment. "Yeah, gotta be the heat."

"What heat?" Chuck Watts grinned as he brushed things like dried red hairs from his jacket. "I hadn't noticed."

"That's because you need a brain to feel things." Williams flipped him the bird, and then pulled his shaded glasses onto his face and his hat down lower.

The group got organized with the heavy weapons guys at point with the marksman, Croft. Then came Loche at front with the civilians, and Nina Masters with the rest of the squad at rear.

Albie, back in Abyss-1, still worked the drone and it was their constant companion hovering just above and ahead of them. Loche had authorised Albie's updates to be sent to all their comms systems, so they were receiving real-time information about what threats or opportunities lay ahead.

Often, they had to skirt around areas where huge beasts seemed to lay in wait for an ambush or take cover as some sort of land leviathan with six column-like legs the size of redwoods made the ground jump as their footfalls thumped down. Then another time they had to wait as a pack of predators followed them, perhaps hoping to pick off some of the smaller beasts in the herd.

Albie did a great job of keeping them safe, but he also had to call for assistance as some sort of insectoid raptor came swooping out of the red sky to try and pick the drone out of the air. The thing was the size of a large dog with eight legs spread wide and membranous wings with chitinous talons poised—that was until the marksman, Croft, put a single round through the thing's head.

He scored a direct hit with the high-caliber slug, but the flying oddity still winged away after delivering a stream of screeches that was probably a string of center-Earth obscenities that would have turned a Barbary pirate's face red.

Loche slowed to walk beside Mike and Jane. "Looks like you were right about this place repopulating itself now that the *Y'ha-nthlei* have vanished."

She nodded. "They captured everything and fed it to the great beast, Dagon. I saw it happen."

"A nightmare."

"Mike." Matt Kearns caught up to them. "You said in your report that one of your group, the linguist, tried to communicate. It didn't go well, right?"

"You could say that," Mike scoffed. "They tore his tongue out and staked him out. I just hope he was already dead when they did it."

"Horrible." Matt nodded, thinking. "But that tells me they didn't see him as a peer. But more an anomaly. They might have wanted to understand how he could talk, rather than understand what he was saying."

"No shit," Mike shot back.

"Mike, don't misunderstand me," Matt replied. "It means they have some sort of base intelligence but might have just been surprised by the talking mammal. After all, did you know that most people don't think fish feel pain? They do, but they just can't tell us they do."

Jane scoffed. "For chrissakes, Matt, please tell me that you don't still want to communicate with them?"

Matt shook his head. "I'm not misty-eyed on that potential. But modes of communication tell a lot about the logic patterns and thinking of a clan grouping. If we ever need to anticipate their strategy, it'd come in handy."

There was murmuring from the group behind them, and Loche stopped them and turned. "Second lieutenant, all right back there?"

Nina Masters was staring up into Lawrie Williams' face as he held his head and swayed on his feet.

She half turned. "Might have some heatstroke here, boss."

"Take five. Croft, Angel, on guard." Loche headed back down the line.

Jane could see that Williams' face sweated profusely and his expression was one screwed in pain. Captain Loche came back to stare into his face before leading him to a rock and sitting him down.

"Something he ate?" Janus remarked.

"Unlikely." Jane grabbed Mike's arm. "Come on."

Matt tagged along and the trio headed back to where Williams sat on the rock looking dazed with his mouth hanging open. Loche was down on one knee trying to talk to the young man, but he just sat there now, staring vacantly straight ahead.

Jane came closer. "Ask him did he eat or drink anything here."

"I doubt that he—" Nina began.

"I *know* but ask him," Jane cut in. "Infected water killed one of our previous team members in just a few hours. And another of our guys ate a berry that nearly killed him. Ask him."

Loche nodded.

Nina exhaled through clamped teeth but turned back to look deep into the man's face. " Williams, did you eat or drink anything down here that was not part of your stores?"

The man just sat there, staring at nothing, and as Nina looked about to ask him again, a hair-thin trickle of blood ran from his nose down to his top lip.

Jane stared. No, it wasn't a trickle of blood, as the thin line of red changed course and passed from his nose into his mouth.

"*Did you see that?*" Jane pointed.

Lawrie Williams rose to his feet.

"Easy there, big guy," Nina said, trying to hold his arm, but he shrugged her off.

The man then walked stiff-legged, zombie-like, toward the trunk of the huge tree close to them.

"Hey, mister..." Loche began, but Lawrie Williams walked straight past the team and then when he got within a few feet of the large tree trunk, he reached out his arms and embraced it.

"What's up with your soldier?" Janus asked Loche.

"Damned if I know." Loche followed him, his jaw jutting. "Williams..."

Williams ignored him and leaned in real close to the tree. He then began to grind his forehead into the trunk. Then harder and harder.

"Stop him," Jane said as she saw the skin on his forehead begin to abrade.

Loche turned to Chris Angel. "Angel, pull that man back a step."

"Yes, sir." Angel pushed his gun up over his shoulder, stepped forward, and placed his arms on Williams. "Come on, big guy, one step back." He began to tug.

But the man held on tight, with his head now smacked in hard against the bark. As they all watched, Williams' hair looked like it began to grow.

"What the hell's that?" Angel released him, his hands up as though he had just touched something dirty.

Then they saw that the top of Williams' head wasn't growing longer hair, but instead something else was growing out of it. Something alive, that wasn't Williams.

"What the fuck is going on?" Angel backed up.

Williams then began to grind both his head and face further onto, or into, the tree.

"Goddamnit, get hold of him!" Loche yelled. "Stop him."

As several of the soldiers approached, Williams' head grew, and expanded, and then even more rapidly, deflated. But in its place thousands, or millions, of red, thread-like worms burst from the top of his scalp.

"*Fuck!*" Croft exclaimed as the men fell back.

To the horror of the group, the man's head emptied like a bag and the worms began to make their way up the trunk into the treetop. While Williams still clung to the bark, his fingers now hooked in deep, the entire top half of the man began to also be evacuated.

"What the hell is happening here?" Nina Masters yelled.

"Stay back," Loche ordered.

Some of the crew had their guns up and were beginning to pan them around, as if looking for some sort of adversary to take out their fear and anger on. Loche's eyes were wide and his jaw set.

"Everyone get back," he said. "Hold the line, people."

Jane knew that he really meant *hold your nerve*, as the group of soldiers were horrified to the point of panic—even for hardened combat vets.

In another few seconds, Williams' clothing sagged, his hands dropped from the tree, and the remnants of the escaping worms, probably in the millions, were moving up the trunk into the higher branches like a red river.

The group watched with eyes bulging and mouths hanging open, as many of the worms began to coalesce into groups, and in the next moments, they began to form into shapes, turning themselves into rounded masses like glistening Christmas decorations, or…

"Apples," Croft said, his mouth tight in a fear rictus. "They were never fucking apples, they were balls of worms."

Janus shook his head. "Did that asshole eat one?"

"I don't think so," Jane said. "Everyone get back. Get out from under this tree."

The group did without hesitation.

"What just happened here?" Loche asked her.

"We took a rest under that tree that was hanging with these things. Somehow, Williams got infected," she replied.

"More like infested," Loche said. "They were parasites. I've never heard of something like this before." He grimaced. "That poor sonofabitch."

"It's more common than you think," Jane replied, her eyes still on the flattening pile of clothing.

Janus scoffed. "What? We don't have crap like that topside."

"We do," Jane sighed. "Take the African horsehair worm. It emerges as a tiny thread-like worm from the edge of a pool of water or pond and is eaten by a grasshopper or cricket. But then the horsehair worm begins to develop inside the insect, growing huge and filling its body after it has ingested the organs. Then, when the worm is in its final stage of development, it needs to get back to the water so it makes the cricket search one out and go and drown itself—where the adult worm bursts free."

She turned to him. "Or how about a species of flatworm that…"

"*Shut up!*" Croft yelled.

"Keep that talk behind your teeth, soldier!" Loche yelled back. He turned to Jane. "But I think we get it."

Janus overheard and stepped closer. "Ah, could anyone else be infested?" His brows were up.

Mike shrugged. "I don't know. But I kinda think we'd know by now if they were."

"Fine, then how about we get *the fuck out of here*?" Janus looked around momentarily before back to Loche. "Captain?"

Nina pointed. "What about Williams?"

Loche shook his head and looked from the now-empty pile of clothing to the newly formed red bulbs above what was left of him.

"It's over. He's gone." He turned and circled a finger in the air. "Let's go, people."

Mike glanced at Jane. "One day, one down."

EPISODE 13

"If at every instant we may perish, so at every instant we may be saved" — Jules Verne, Journey to the Center of the Earth

CHAPTER 13

A small smile curled Ally's lips, just a little, as she dreamed. Even though she was heading back to the hellish interior of the Earth, it didn't worry her a bit. She had spent eight months being beaten, raped, fed, watered, and walked like a dog by creatures from a lunatic's nightmare. Her only respite was that the total darkness had rendered her blind to what they looked like. Whatever was in store for her now, she knew it was preferable to that living hell.

Ally floated and dreamed some more: in her dream, she held under one arm an M249 light machine gun—it was powerful and had been one of her favorite weapons. She also had half a dozen grenades strung around her belt. She sprinted through dark labyrinths and ran down the gargoyles who had trapped her—she shot them, many times each, decimating them and showing no mercy. And when she bailed the rest up in a dead-end, she filled their cave with grenades and obliterated them. She inhaled the burning bloody stink and her smile widened.

Time meant nothing to her now. In a world without days or nights, hours stretched or maybe went past in the blink of an eye. The priority was staying alive, not counting minutes.

The impact after deacceleration wasn't hard, but it still knocked the wind from her and jolted her from her slumber. She knew from her experience that there was no time for drowsiness and to survive, you needed to come alert instantly.

She shot to her feet and stood, listening to her surroundings. Beside her, Captain Zhukov groaned and rolled over, and Dr. Andrina Valentina lay still, breathing groggily on the cave floor. In the air hung some rocks, bones, and there was even an ancient, rusting storm lantern used for caving in the 1800s.

Zhukov sat up. "Where are we?"

Ally flung out a hand, flat. "*Quiet.*"

She turned slowly. The cave was in a blue twilight as the crystals shone like fluorescent lamps, and many were unpolished and sunk in the rock. It was a raw cave, untouched, and she remembered how the crab people had taken them all from the previous cavern they had arrived in. Maybe that meant this one hadn't been discovered yet.

She relaxed a little and dropped her arm. "I think we're good." She turned. "Is Valentina okay?"

Zhukov shifted over and knelt beside her. He lifted her hand and then helped the doctor to sit up. He nodded. "Just still dazed. She had a soft landing."

"Wha...?" Valentina's eyes blinked open. She looked around. "Where...?"

"Good question," Ally replied. "Captain, do you have your GPS?"

He nodded and felt in his pack for a small box which he pressed and slid switches, illuminating a small screen. He shook his head.

"I don't think it's working. It says we're below Japan." He looked up. "Impossible."

"Nope. Very possible. Down here, the size of the geography is vastly different. A thousand miles on the surface is just a day's walk down here." Ally began to move about, keeping her footfalls soft. "We need to move. Above us is now blocked so we need another way out."

Zhukov helped Valentina to her feet, and the doctor walked to the wall and grasped one of the rod-shaped crystals. With a dry *crack*, she pulled it free. It lit her grimy face a pacific blue. "Where is this place?"

Ally snorted. "Welcome to the center of the Earth."

***

Zhukov did a quick weapons and supplies check. He was glad they each grabbed packs so they had plenty of food, ammunitions, and were moderately well armed. For now.

He wasn't yet sure exactly where he was and was not inclined to believe the tall, black American woman, with wild hair and even wilder eyes. After all, she had been held captive by inhuman monstrosities for nearly a year and he bet that it had created some severe psychological trauma for her to deal with.

Ally approached him with a grim expression. He smiled. "So, I'm hoping you know another way out."

"Yes," she said. "And one that's still viable, especially as we have the screechers now." She smiled. "We just need to get there."

He looked around at their cave and its multiple exits. "We first need to find our way out of *this* cave."

Valentina rubbed her head. "What a nightmare this has become for us."

"Nightmare? It hasn't even begun yet." Ally walked closer to the shorter woman. "You need to steel yourself, lady, because we will be tested down here like at no other time in our lives." She turned away for a moment, but then paused. "And just something to bolster your spirits—your objective was to find me." She held her arms out. "And look, here I am. Mission accomplished."

"Mission accomplished?" Zhukov scoffed. "Mission is accomplished when we get you home. And one more thing. I am part of a two-pronged mission. We were sent to find you, but there is another mission being sent to the bottom of the Mariana Trench, I assume to find their way down here as well. Something about searching for red people, and a cure for cancer." His brows rose. "Does that make sense to you?"

Ally laughed softly as she began to nod. "Yeah, a lot. It's wonderful news. And it just changed our plans. That's where we will go to find our way home." She walked past several of the cave mouths and then at one she lifted her head and sniffed. "Here."

Zhukov and Valentina joined her and inhaled.

"I can't smell anything," Valentina said.

Zhukov also shook his head. "Dead air."

Ally turned back and inhaled again with closed eyes. "I smell plants, heat on rocks, and the tang of ozone—this is our way out."

Zhukov scoffed softly. "Really?"

Ally nodded. "When you can't see, you learn quickly to rely on other senses."

"How far do we need to go?" Valentina asked.

Ally shrugged. "We head southwest and hopefully I can pick up some landmarks." She turned to face the pair. "Look, comrades, I will be brutally honest. This is the deadliest place I know. Everything is strange, oversized, and wants to kill you. If we can find the others, our odds of survival will improve enormously. If not, then I give us a twenty percent chance."

Zhukov laughed. "While we are alive, our odds are always good."

Ally nodded once. "That's the spirit." She turned away. She knew that if they didn't find the other people, then they'd need to locate a different gravity well. And that meant traveling up into the labyrinths by themselves. And even though they had the screechers, they'd have to navigate around eight miles of climb in the darkness—she suddenly thought she might have been optimistic about that twenty percent chance.

Valentina still held onto her rod crystal, and Ally pointed. "That reminds me, grab more of the crystals. We can use them instead of running down our flashlight batteries."

In moments more, they had several each loaded into their packs and also held one of the rod crystals in their hand that fluoresced a magnificent cerulean blue.

"Okay, follow me. But remember, move silent and move fast. We've just become tiny morsels of meat in a very big and very hungry food chain." She stopped. "Questions?"

"I don't know where to start. So, I'll stay quiet, learn as I go, and keep up." He nodded to the female doctor. "Valentina?"

She just shook her head.

Zhukov shrugged. "After you, Lieutenant Ally Bennet."

Ally turned to the darkness, tilted her head, listening for several moments for the tiniest scratch of claws on rock, or breath, or scent of a beast, and then after a few moments, satisfied, headed in.

***

Ally could tell that these raw caves were uninhabited. They were dust-dry, and there had been little geological movement, as there were no tumbled rocks to navigate or rips in the walls from shifting stone.

After around an hour, she began to leave the coolness of the dry cave behind and started to enter an area of thicker, hotter air, and soon the glow of her crystal was paled by a stronger glow from up ahead.

Ally slowed and spoke over her shoulder. "Everyone be ready, we're coming to the exit. That might mean the external area of the cave may be inhabited, and remember, the world here is a very primordial place."

Valentina wiped a streaming brow. "How long did you say we need to be in it?"

Ally chuckled. "I'm guessing, but we may need to cross up to fifty miles. If we can do ten miles a day, that'll get us there within a week."

Her expression softened when she saw the horror on the Russian woman's face. "Don't worry, we survived months down here."

"But you said you all died—and *you* were captured," Valentina shot back.

"Well then, let's hope we can learn from their mistakes," Zhukov added.

Ally pointed at the screecher on Valentina's belt. "We already have." She turned back to the red glow from outside. "Come on—the sooner we start, the sooner we're home."

***

Ally saw that their cave never opened up to have a large entrance. In fact, it ended as just a rip in the stone only about a foot and a half wide, and with the blood-red light streaming through it, it looked like a fresh wound. The upside was it meant that nothing big could have made the cave its home.

A few creatures looking like ten-foot-long millipedes with feathery antenna and grasping hands instead of hundreds of feet scurried from their path, and Ally was first to lean out of the crack. The Russians followed.

"*Svoloch.*" Zhukov placed a hand over his eyes. "It's so... *red.*"

Before them was what looked like a desert landscape with spartan, scabby forest that stretched as far as the eye could see before it curved beyond the horizon.

"I feel like I landed on Mars," he whispered.

Ally squinted in the red glare as she looked for imminent threats. There were trees, twenty feet high and sparsely clumped together, with their tiny foliage so tight and dense they looked like brains on a single stem. Below them were plants that might have been fleshy cactus, spindly reeds, and lumps of dark, purple rock.

"It's going to be hot," Ally sighed. "We'll need to protect ourselves from the direct light. Make hats."

Zhukov held a hand to his brow as he looked up at the boiling red cauldron above them. "This... this was beneath our feet the whole time. This entire world?" He lowered his head to turn slowly. "How could we not have ever known about this? With all our science?"

"That's a joke, right?" Ally laughed darkly. "Want to know something really funny? You guys knew about it first. Some damn Russian fool by the name of Arkady Saknussov found his way down here over five hundred years ago. No one believed him. Then another group of damn Russian fools scaled down here in 1972 by following old Saknussov's notes. Only one woman escaped alive from that expedition by the name of Katya Babikov."

"I heard that name whispered in our briefing," Valentina said.

"And then you damn American fools came, yes?" Zhukov raised his eyebrows.

"No, my team came to stop more Russian assholes blowing up the world from down here." Ally grinned like a death's head and leaned toward the man. "But this place ate them all before we could get to them. And kill them."

"Politics," Zhukov grunted. "I hate it."

After a moment, Ally leaned back and nodded. "Yeah, you and me both, Boris."

"Viktor," Zhukov replied.

"Whatever." Ally turned away.

Valentina stepped out of their cave mouth a little. "Is this... like when you were here?"

"No, we had to deal with a jungle." Ally also eased a little further out of the crack and looked up the rock face. "The upside? Nothing big is going to be able to sneak up on us." She pulled back. "The downside is that even the small things here can be deadly. Plus, we got less shade. And the light and heat here is a killer."

Zhukov checked his GPS and then held an arm up. "That's the direction of the ocean trench. If their well is in the same place, then that's where we will meet them."

Ally nodded. "It's also the place where Dagon and his followers live."

"Dagon?" Zhukov turned to frown. "The fish god?"

"Yeah, I can fill you in as we travel." She stepped back into the small cave and shucked off her pack to then rummage through it. All she could find was a small cloth that might have been for self-cleaning; it'd have to do. She wrapped it around her head, making sure one end dangled down over her neck and then tucked the front up a little so it jutted on her brow, making a little shelf to guard her nose and face. It'd have to do.

Zhukov and Valentina watched her and set about doing the same, and in moments the trio looked like a small squad of foreign legionnaires.

Ally checked her weapon, ensuring it slid easily and rapidly from her holster. She took a deep breath.

"Ready?" She didn't wait for a reply and headed out.

In only a few steps, the heat felt like a hammer blow, and she knew that crossing the desert when they were already fatigued and with little supplies or water meant they would have to forage. She hoped that the cactus things were like the surface variety, and they'd be able to suck water from them. If it turned out to be deadly, well, then they were as good as dead anyway.

She led them down the rocky front of the cave to the ground. Small lizards scurried from their path, and things like stick insects on stilts with high polyp eyes like those on a snail watched them from the shade of the purple rocks.

Zhukov chanced another look up. "It's like boiling fire. Like the surface of a sun that never sets."

Ally also glanced up at the fiery ceiling. "Yeah, the last group of scientists told us it was the molten core held back by a layer of volcanic glass hundreds of miles deep. This inner world, the solid core, has been here perhaps nearly as long as the surface world. Somehow, back then, the ocean poured in and then life sprang up. But things took a different path when it came to evolution." She smiled at him. "Think dinosaurs, but not like those we are familiar with, but from the insect kingdom."

"That's insane," Valentina replied. "I'm a medical practitioner and biologist with extensive troglodytic flora and fauna experience, and I know my evolutionary theory—insects only grew large on Earth because of the lack of predators and also due to the higher percentage of oxygen in the primitive atmosphere." She inhaled deeply. "And the oxygen levels seem normal here."

Ally smiled at the woman. "You'll get used to it. But one theory my team, my former team, came up with was the constant radiation had an effect." She lifted her hand, palm up to the red light. "Feel that? That's a form of radiation constantly bathing the environment. You can bet something like that will cause mutations after a few hundred million years." She shrugged. "Anyway, believe what you want. Our travels will educate you."

Zhukov turned about. "We can trek for about four hours and then take a break. But we should keep a look out for anything edible and a water source. We can try the cactus, but I don't really want this to be our first option. Some cactus contain chemicals that can destroy your liver."

"Agreed." She extended her arm for Zhukov. "You get to be first out at point. I'll take next." She glanced at the small Russian female doctor. "You can bring up the rear."

"Is good." Zhukov checked his weapon one last time and headed out.

The ground was red dust with small balls of something like pumice that crunched beneath their boots like popped rice. Ally tried to keep watch at all quadrants and felt like a heel for sending the Russian guy to lead, but this way, she could assess their risks, and if anything jumped out, it'd be at him first, giving her an extra second to react, as she bet she would have lost her edge.

Still, she got a knot in her stomach when she thought about what they may encounter. The fauna down here mimicked the biological niches up on the surface, so if there were flat plains with plenty of open space, there would be creatures built for speed—herd animals—as well as predators. And those predators might have a whole range of different camouflage techniques—for all she knew, those weren't purple rocks at all. She scoffed at the thought, and then gave the next large purple lump a hard stare for a few moments.

To his credit, Zhukov kept his head up and showed no signs of tiring at all. Ally looked over her shoulder at Valentina and saw she was already twenty paces behind and falling further back every minute.

"Keep up," Ally urged.

The woman nodded but didn't look up. Not a good sign. Ally knew they'd need to take a break soon, but by the look of the way the Russian woman held her canteen, it meant she was drinking too much fluid too quickly, and therefore, wasting it.

They were just passing under another of the weird trees that had bark-like smooth skin and leaves that were fat, each the size of a hockey puck. Ally had been eyeing the spikeless cactus things previously as a water source, and she guessed it was best to try them now when they weren't desperate. She still had some water to wash her mouth out if need be.

"Captain," she said. "Hold up."

Ally reached up and grasped one, squeezing it with her fingers. It felt firm, but not rock-hard firm. She used her knife to cut it free, weighed it in her hand for a moment, surprised by the weight. She then sliced the end off.

Ally crouched as a clear sap ran from the slice and she let some drip onto the back of her hand. She waited a few seconds to see if there was a tingle—there wasn't.

That's level one test passed, she thought and then steeled herself, remembering Martin from their last expedition who nearly burned his mouth off.

"Here goes," she said as she eyed the spots of thick liquid on the back of her hand.

"Good luck, Comrade Ally." Zhukov grinned and gave her a small salute.

She licked the drops from her hand but just held the liquid in her mouth for a second or two. There was no fizz on her tongue, and it actually tasted sweet, sickly sweet, like concentrated cane syrup, but not unpleasant.

That was test two, she thought. Now for the gut test. "Bottoms up."

She held up the pad-like leaf and squeezed a small stream into her mouth, and then swallowed—*test three.*

Ally waited a few seconds and still nothing happened. She smacked her lips together.

"Seems okay. A little sweet, but if it's glucose in there, then that's a bonus energy source for us." She stood. "Let's grab a few and take them with us. If I get sick, we'll toss them, but if not, it'll bolster our fluid supplies." She grinned. "And if I drop dead, you're welcome to eat me."

"Thank you, but I hear American women are too tough and stringy." Zhukov chuckled and then set to cutting free several of the large, fleshy leaves. Even Valentina managed to cut several and place them in her pack.

The captain checked their bearings and they headed out again. In the shimmering red heat haze, they saw nothing but more of the same endless desert with a few spare trees and some long stretches of open, scrabbly ground.

Zhukov pointed. "This way." They struck out again.

Ally kept her eyes to slits; she would have killed for a pair of dark sunglasses or to be in darkness once again. Her hearing and sense of smell was acute, but her eyes were still weak from lack of use in strong light.

She ground her teeth as her headache pounded at her, and she bet it was a mix of dehydration and tormented eyes. She had one more sense that had become super sensitive—and she felt it now.

"*Wait!*" she yelled.

She stood with legs planted, staring down at the ground.

"What is it? You see something?" Valentina whispered.

"Not seeing but feeling. I can sense the vibrations." Ally turned her head, and then quickly crouched and placed a hand flat on the surface. She then threw herself down to lay flat, pressed an ear to the ground, and squeezed her eyes shut for a moment or two. She jumped up and dusted herself down.

"Something's coming." She turned about.

"What?" Zhukov spun about with his gun held tight. "What is it?"

"Not *it*, them." Ally stared into the distance the way they had just come. "There." She pointed.

In the distance, there was the hint of a cloud of dust rising.

"What's coming?" Valentina asked.

"My uncle had a cattle farm," Ally said without turning.

"Sometimes when a storm approached, we'd get dry thunder as the clouds rolled in. It spooked the cattle, and many times enough to stampede 'em. That's what this feels like."

"You could feel it?" Zhukov asked.

"Yeah, feeling was a big part of staying alive in the caves." Ally turned about. "We need to find somewhere to shelter in the event these things run us down." She squinted. "There's some low rocky outcrops—might at least be somewhere to shelter behind. Let's move it."

Ally began to jog, but as soon as she did, she felt the muscles in her thin legs rebel against her and she couldn't lift the pace much past a fast walk.

"About half a mile. We can do it," Zhukov remarked.

Ally looked over her shoulder. "That depends on the speed of those things behind us."

The dust cloud was higher now, and below it she could just make out a line of darker objects. All around them, the smaller pebbles on the ground jumped and she guessed whatever was approaching must have been the size of a good steer. That meant if the things were tightly packed together and caught up with them, they'd be trampled.

"I can seem them," Zhukov exclaimed. He looked back to the lagging Russian woman. "Valentina, your pack."

She looked up, a little confused.

Zhukov dropped back to her and took her pack. He threw it over his other shoulder and took her elbow. "Come on."

Valentina started to jog again, but all three of them were only moving now at little over fast walk pace.

The sound of thunderous hooves now reached them, and it even unnerved Ally. Up ahead just about two hundred yards, there was the first of the rocks.

"Nearly there!" she yelled. "Keep going."

In a few minutes, they had to yell to each other over the din, and they passed the first lump of pebbly purple stone.

The first of the heat-baked exposed lumps of rock were only about a foot high and of no use. Worse, the ground was suddenly becoming soft and more like shifting sand. Each step sucked the energy from their already fatigued legs, and Ally began to feel waves of nausea from the strain.

She plowed on, having to drag her legs up and forward. At least it wasn't wet like quicksand, so it fell away easily from their boots. But it meant their pace was too slow to stay in front of the approaching herd.

The things behind them were in sight now and even glancing back for a moment, Ally could see the wall of chitinous muscle, waving feelers, and bulb eyes bearing down on them.

Just ahead was a bottlenecked area with a three-foot-high line of rocks on either side. The creatures were probably large enough to leap over the stones, as well as pile up in the narrow gap, but it was all they had.

"There!" Zhukov yelled. "It'll have to do."

They used their last burst of energy in a staggering sprint, plodding through the soft sand and around the rock wall. They all immediately dived flat.

Ally took off her pack and put it over her head. The creatures came then, making a squealing-hissing noise, and sounded like heavy sheets of hard plastic rubbing together as they bumped up against each other.

The first ones came through the gap, then like a waterfall, they began to leap over them in waves. Though Ally wanted to keep her head down, she had to see what manner of creature they were and shifted the bag from her head to lift her chin.

The beasts seemed like a muscular form of roach with trunk-like legs and three claws on each. Out front was the weirdest head she had ever seen—a long trunk with tiny eyes right at the tip as if the entire thing was just a proboscis with sight.

She assumed it was for sucking up their food, whatever that was. They made pig-like squealing sounds as they panicked and headed on into the more open area that was like a large pool of sand, and it became clear the shifting grains were going to slow them down.

As expected, they began to get bogged, and the creatures in front had to use their powerful legs and bodies to wade forward as others landed on top of them.

"What's that?" Zhukov shouted.

From one side of the sand pool, something like a forward curved spike approached, cutting the sand exactly as a shark's fin cut the water. Then another and another appeared, and they headed for the first of the struggling beasts.

Ally saw that the hidden creatures had a single large eye on the end of the spike, more like a periscope for finding their prey, she guessed. Then, almost faster than the eye could follow, something launched from out of the sand, long jaws gaping wide to then clamp down on the front half of one of the roach-like beasts and drag it down, with a crunch and crackle of carapace.

"*Shit!*" Zhukov exclaimed and turned about. "This is a kill zone."

It was impossible to move with the huge creatures pouring over the small rock barrier and through the gap between them. They piled up as they waded deeper into the soft sand, and it reminded Ally of the herds of wildebeest trying to cross rivers while crocodiles picked the outer animals off.

One by one, the long, muscular predators sprang from the deeper sand to grab another victim and drag it down. The front animals screamed their fear, but the surging mass of the stampeding creatures kept pressing them forward no matter the danger, and the more that entered the sea of sand, the more the sand predators were attracted to the feeding frenzy.

As Ally stared, one of the things latched on to a larger specimen and had difficulty dragging it under. In a few seconds, it was above the sand's surface. She could see a long and powerful eel-like body with pebbly skin, thin razor-tooth filled jaws of a barracuda, and dozens of short paddle legs running down its side that acted like oars to help it to slither and swim through the sand.

Like some sort of worm, Ally thought, as she watched it shake its head from side to side as it crunched down, severed the prey animal's armor plating, and then tugged it backward below the surface.

The first of the herd of creatures started to make it out the other side, their numbers being far too numerous to be overly impacted by the now dozens of predator animals.

After another fifteen minutes, it dwindled to a few passing along, and then the last few tried to make it across but were attacked and pulled under with their agonized frightened screams being muffled as they were drawn down.

The single eye on the stalk of several of the predator worms still moved through the sand, keeping a watch, until Zhukov sat up. The movement focused them, and just like a school of sharks lining up for the kill, started to home in on the three humans huddled beside the rock.

"Shit," Ally said from between her teeth.

She raised her gun and fired but missed the eyestalk.

She turned. "Quick, up on the rock."

The trio turned, scrambled up on the three-foot-high purple boulder, and pulled their packs up after them.

With the humans gone from the sand, the creatures swerved away but stayed close by.

"Sandworms," Ally said. "Like I said, there's predators everywhere, all the time."

"I think we'll need another way forward," Zhukov replied.

"They are also behind us." Valentina tried to edge a little higher, but their rock was too small.

Ally looked about. There weren't enough rocks close by to allow them to try and leap from boulder to boulder. And right now, they were exposed up on the stone. She also didn't know if the things could reach up out of the sand, or how far. But she bet if they were hungry or excited enough, they might give it a try.

"We've got to move." She shielded her eyes. Just a hundred yards or so to their right, there looked to be hardpacked gravel again, and maybe the edge of the sand sea. There were a few rocks to use, but not many.

"Over there," she said. "I estimate about one-twenty yards—no more than a football field length."

"Football fields are one-thirty at home." Zhukov grinned. "Everything bigger in Russia."

Ally chuckled. "Then this'll be a cakewalk for you."

"We'll never make it," Valentina pleaded.

"She's right." Zhukov sighed. "This is their domain. They'd run us down before we got ten feet, let alone a hundred-twenty yards."

"Yeah, probably right." Ally nodded. "Not a race I want to run."

She continued to stare at the few remaining worm creatures in the sand for many minutes, until she had a thought. "These things were attracted by the vibrations in the sand. Sure, they use sight when in close, but the sounds drew them in from far away."

She began to rummage through her pack. "Do you know what they've found to be a very good short-term deterrent for sharks?" She looked up. "Grenades." She lifted free the two grenades and grinned.

"Might work." Zhukov grinned back. He searched his pack. "I have two as well."

"No, save them." Ally's lips pressed into a line for a moment. "We've only just arrived, and we need to preserve our ammunition for as long as we can." She looked back. "We will encounter things more threatening than these little suckers."

"Little?" Zhukov scoffed.

She turned back. "Ready... Valentina?"

The doctor's brows came together. "To do what? What's the plan?"

Ally pointed. "About one-twenty yards that way, there looks to be hard-packed ground. I don't think these things can't get us there. I'm going to toss a grenade into the sand, and the moment it detonates, we run for it. If more begin to show up, I'll throw another one."

Zhukov nodded. "I reserve the right to throw a grenade."

Ally chuckled. "Okay, but only if needed." She stood. "Get ready."

Zhukov helped Valentina to her feet. Her legs wobbled more from fear than fatigue and he held onto her arm.

"You'll be fine," he said.

"We head for that tract of sand just beyond the two bushes, got it?" Ally said and the pair nodded. "I'll lead us out."

Ally sucked in a deep breath and turned to the sand sea. There was no movement or any sign anything could be living in there, but she bet just below the surface or in one of the sand pools to the side, the predators waited.

She held the grenade up. "And a three, and a two, and…" she pulled the pin, "…a one." She threw it into the center of the sand pool.

"Go." She leaped from the top of the rock and began to run.

There was a muffled *thump* and a gout of sand was blown into the air.

She heard Zhukov and Valentina come down behind her, and the three plodded through the knee-deep sand. It was hard work on already tired limbs, but adrenaline gave them an initial boost, and she felt she was pushing through at good speed.

At a little over halfway, she dared to feel confident and chanced a glance back. Her heart kicked up a few beats as she saw the three fin-like periscopes with eyes on top cutting the sand behind them.

"Incoming!" she yelled, pulled the pin, and then tossed her last grenade.

But it wasn't a good throw and landed too close behind Valentina. The blast blew sand in the air, and the woman over.

Zhukov stopped to help her up, thankful there was no sign of the creatures. Valentina ran on groggily—how long did the things give her last time? 60 seconds? 40? And this time would the sand worms be just as worried by the blast or recognize they had nothing to fear?

Ally powered ahead again, and this time felt the adrenaline fuel tanks running low. Her thighs screamed, and her lungs burned from the effort. Zhukov was literally dragging the Russian woman along with him.

They had just on twenty yards to go—sixty feet—*easy-peasy*, she told herself.

Ally's teeth were grit hard and bared as she used the last of her energy to lift her legs and stomp them down in the sand as the edge of the hard-packed ground neared. She glanced to the side, and then back, and saw that behind Valentina and Zhukov the periscopes had appeared again and cut through the sand far faster than they were moving.

She was about to yell to the man to deploy a grenade, but it might mean a few split seconds of him rummaging in his pack instead of remaining focused.

Fuck it, she thought and pulled her rifle. She tried to run backward and sight on the periscopes as they bore down on them.

Then her heel struck something solid.

"The ground!" she yelled. "Run."

Ally switched to full automatic and fired off dozens of rounds into the sand just ahead of where she thought the things were and at anything that moved close to the Russians.

Zhukov started to lift from the deeper sand and literally threw the smaller woman up onto the hard ground before him.

One of the worms breached close to the Russian captain and then launched itself, its V-shaped jaws lined with razor-sharp teeth opening and ready to clamp down on his raised arm.

"Piss off!" Ally yelled and turned to empty her magazine into the exposed beast. The thing was blistered with holes and flopped back down into the sand to bury itself and vanish.

Ally ran and dove the last few feet to skid up onto the harder ground on her belly. She lay there, panting hard.

Zhukov also rolled onto his back and sucked in deep breaths, unable to even speak. After several moments, Ally lifted her head.

"You okay?"

Zhukov turned his head. "What doesn't kill you makes you stronger, yes?"

She lay her head back. "Funny, I don't feel stronger."

CHAPTER 14

Mariana Trench Mission, US Team – second twelve-hour block

The land became more rugged and for the last few miles, they trudged along an ever-narrowing, but long-dried water course, before their path then took them into a large cave.

So far, in the gloom of the cavern, all they came across were weird three-foot-wide growths that could have been either plant or animal attached to the rock walls and floor that waved feelers in the air as they attempted to net small flying creatures. The odd things seemed benign, and they were relieved to not be bothered by any larger denizens of the inner world.

The huge cave became damper and from up ahead, the background noise they had been hearing rose to become an all-encompassing roar. Loche got a heads-up from the drone pilot that had sped ahead.

"Waterfall," Loche said. "Massive."

"Can we get through?" Nina asked.

"We'll soon know," he replied.

In fifteen more minutes, the group came to a swirling pond and had to narrow their eyes from the spray that filled the cavern. The wall of thunderous water falling in front of them made what lay beyond invisible.

Jane wiped water from her face. "It's too heavy to pass through." She pointed. "Maybe beside it."

Loche nodded as he saw that on one side of the falling sheet of water was a small gap between the rock face and the deluge. They could skirt the pool of water and avoid the falls.

"Okay, everyone, eyes out. We're going to try and edge past the waterfall. Watch that pond there. Not sure if something lives in there, but I'd prefer we didn't disturb it, or it, us."

The rocks were slippery, and small crustaceans leaped from their path into the inky water as the group passed by. In minutes more, they edged out onto a rocky platform that was a series of massive slabs of stone as the water continued to tumble down the slope.

Loche walked to the edge of the slab of stone and placed his hands on his hips as the others joined him.

"Well, I'll be damned," he said softly.

Spread out below them was a deep valley with huge pine-like trees rising hundreds of feet into the air. Curls of primordial-looking mist swirled through the trunks and between the clumps of trees were large swathes of flat green. It was only about a third of a mile wide and traveled for a few miles before bending to the north, so its end was out of sight.

"River valley," Nina said. "There'll be food and game."

Loche turned to Jane. "Is it safe?"

Jane hiked her shoulders. "We never came this way." She turned to him. "But remember, nowhere is really safe down here."

Mike slowly ran his eyes along the deep valley. "If there's water, prey animals will come to drink. And while they're drinking…"

"The predators come out to play," Janus finished.

Mike nodded. "We were further north where it was a little flatter. We could go around, but most places will carry the same risk now."

Loche squinted into the distance. "Where we want to go is at the end of this valley. Looks to me to be the quickest route. Well, nothing ventured, nothing gained." He smiled and called one of his team over. "Croft, what do you see?"

"Sir." Rick Croft pulled his sniper rifle from over his back and lifted it to his shoulder so he could look through the scope. "I've got some avian creatures coming in and out of the tree canopies." Croft panned his rifle around and continued to squint into the scope. "Plenty of vines and creepers so might be tough going down there. Also, some of the trees are moving as if something large is brushing up against them, and… in the open patches, I can see a few grazing animals." He stopped his movement and adjusted the lens for a moment. "And every good river valley should have a, yep, there it is—looks like there's a shallow stream down there, two o'clock."

"Good," Loche said. "That's our destination."

"Along the riverbed? Seriously?" Jane couldn't believe he'd choose that as his trail.

"Yeah, I know, it will be high risk. But like you said, so is everywhere down here, right? And this should cut our traveling time if we don't have to cut through raw jungle."

Loche organized the team, and then took one last look along the length of the valley. He estimated it'd take them a good six hours to get to the bend, and that was only if they didn't encounter any obstacles along the way. *Maybe give it eight hours*, he thought.

According to the positional maps Jane and Mike had created, and GPS, the home of the red people was approximately another five miles beyond that. Loche felt a swell of confidence in his chest. If they were there, and able to be communicated with, he might still be mission-complete and on his way back home in under a week.

"Angel, Watts, heavy weapons to the front. Lead us in, gentlemen. And everyone keep their eyes and ears open, and their wits about them." He waved them on, and they started down.

As they dropped further into the valley, the humidity rose, and by the time they reached the jungle floor, drops of glistening water hung from the end of huge palm fronds and strips of tongue-like ferns.

Loche thought the smells were reminiscent of the deep jungles of the Congo or Amazon basin, and of rich soil, rotting vegetation, sweet-smelling blooms hidden somewhere in among the foliage.

Chris Angel and Chuck Watts moved slowly with their huge guns carried in front. They pushed aside fronds and vines as the group made their way to the stream that was still hidden up ahead. From time to time, they came across stinking, baseball-sized lumps that Jane said were animal droppings. But the shape, number, and the way they were spread in a line were more like those seen left behind on a leaf by a caterpillar rather than the usual animal scat pile in a surface jungle.

Bird-like chirps and trills came from overhead and the canopy shook from time to time as hidden creatures swung through the trees, and scuttling sounds came from the brush as things were fleeing the line of bipedal humans moving through their jungle.

"Was it like this last time?" Janus asked Jane and Mike.

"Yeah, the jungle was." Mike nodded forward. "So, keep your eyes open, even on the ground. As everything everywhere is looking for its next meal." He smiled. "Don't be it."

"Got it." Janus chuckled. "But to be honest, I think this is pretty cool, huh?"

Mike stared back for a second or two. "Lawrie Williams probably disagrees. And remember, eyes open." He powered ahead to catch up with Jane and Matt.

Loche lifted his hand and the group stopped. Up ahead, Angel and Watts went into a crouch with their weapons pointed up into the tree canopy. He immediately noticed the jungle had fallen to silence all around them.

In a few more moments, Jane heard what it was that spooked the men—something was in the trees above them, and in seconds more, whatever it was was right over them. Leaves rained down as things moved like the wind through the upper branches.

"I can't see anything yet," Mike said.

Croft had his sniper scope to his eyes. "Got movement. Camouflaged, agile, movin' real quick."

"The little green monkeys again?" Jane asked.

"That's what I'm thinking," Mike replied.

"Freaking green monkeys?" Janus scoffed. "Awesome."

"Ain't no monkey." Croft moved his rifle and its scope around. "Big, bigger than a man, multiple limbs, fluid movement. Great camouflage, hard to see, several hanging above us now."

"I think they're just checking us out," Jane said.

"Wait," Croft announced. "They're moving off."

Another shower of leaves and then after another few moments, stillness returned, followed by the normal sounds of the jungle. Loche got to his feet.

"Okay." He looked up the line. "Let's go."

Matt kept looking up into the canopy. "What were they? Anyone actually get a good look?"

Jane shook her head. "Unknown. We encountered several arboreal creatures, some with high intelligence. We had a problem with one species that first stole our equipment as we slept, and then later attacked us."

"And they were only a couple of feet tall," Mike added. "Certainly not man-sized."

"Then a new species." Janus grinned. "Who gets to name it?"

Matt chuckled. "You didn't even see it."

Janus grinned back. "Plenty of time."

"Let's go," Loche ordered.

The group continued for another half hour until they encountered the stream. On both sides, the trees grew up to create a tunnel effect, only occasionally opening enough to allow the red sky to be glimpsed above them.

Loche had Angel and Watts lead them in. The stream was shallow so for the most part they could navigate its pebbly bank or even walk in the shallow water.

Jane looked down into one pool to see things like tadpoles flicking about, but their tails were like tiny, segmented machines. She crouched for a moment and used a stick to prod a few other interesting things she noticed.

Nina joined her. "Anything familiar?" she asked.

"With the surface world, or our previous time?" Jane asked without turning.

Nina crouched. "Either, I guess."

"Then both." Jane pointed. "Like tadpoles, but not. And see these…?" She indicated a deeper pool with some disc-shaped creatures swimming about. "They look like normal terrapins, those cute little aquarian tortoises from home, but…" She used a small stick to flip one over. Instead of four legs with tiny, webbed feet paddling away, there were eight, and each one had two long claws. And at the front were a couple of long, wicked-looking pincers.

"*Yeesh*," Nina scoffed softly. "Everything down here is mimicking life on the surface, just using arthropods as its base material."

"Yeah, all niches have been filled." Jane stood. "Wait until you see some of the big guys. Mind blowing."

"I'm not sure I want to." Nina also rose. "I want to do our job and get the hell out."

Jane smiled. "That makes two of us."

"Three." Mike joined them. "Come on, we're moving off."

The trio caught up and fell into their positions. Nina joined the ranks to talk to one of the heavy weapons guys, and Mike and Jane walked beside Matt.

Matt watched them for a while. "Your report made for sobering reading."

"It's a sobering place, Matt," Mike replied. "Which parts?"

"As you would expect, the section on Alistair, the linguist, and what happened to him." Matt sighed. "Terrible."

"They tortured him—the *Y'ha-nthlei*, the shell people." Jane turned to him. "Just because he tried to communicate with them."

Matt nodded and was silent for a moment. "Imagine," he began. "You have several pens of livestock—horses, pigs, sheep, goats—and all of a sudden, one of the sheep starts speaking to you. Its words didn't make sense, but it was definitely making some you recognized." He turned to Mike. "What would you do?"

Mike seemed to think for a while, and his mouth curled up on one side. "Yeah, I see, probably hand it over to the science department."

"That's probably what the *Y'ha-nthlei* did. Except their science department was a lot more primitive," Matt replied.

"The kid was tortured," Jane bristled. "Matt, please don't try and humanize those monsters. They wiped out an entire colony of red people, and I watched as they fed more of them to the monster, Dagon."

"No, don't worry, I won't do that," Matt replied. "And I have no intention of being the next talking sheep." He cocked his head. "But, if the opportunity arises, I will try and understand them. It might be good to know what they're saying. We might need to."

***

The group finally rounded the bend in the river valley and saw that the valley itself broadened but remained as thickly wooded as before. However, there was one huge difference.

"*Shee-it*," Croft breathed out.

"Professor Kearns, your opinion, please." Loche waited, hands on hips and staring upward.

Matt joined him, and his mouth dropped open. "Hol-*leey* crap."

The cliff wall, rising hundreds of feet on either side of them, was carved with the images of statues. The colossal beings looked to be eons old, but their visages still stared out regally over the valley as if they were guardian titans.

"It's as if they're keeping watch on everything that passes before them," Jane said.

The giant figures were human-shaped but were dressed for battle with swords and shields. Their size was beyond anything built on the surface and even massively larger than anything that existed in ancient Egypt. The heads alone were the size of a four-story building.

"Was it for intimidation, commemoration, or power projection?" Matt asked. "There was a conference in 2013 in Guatemala that studied that question. It seemed many ancient rulers wanted to leave an enduring legacy, saying: this is who we are."

"'My name is Ozymandias, king of kings. Look on my works, ye Mighty, and despair!'" Mike whispered.

"Shelley's Ozymandias." Matt nodded. "Yes, very appropriate." The young professor stared for a moment more and rummaged in a small pouch. He drew forth the gold coin with the faces of the kings. "I knew I'd seen that before. Look, the middle figure, the face—it might be the same king." He held it up.

On the gold coin, the face of the *king of the land* of the red people had the same striking features as the middle gigantic statue.

"Could be," Mike said. "According to the red people's legend, there were three kings—one took to the sea, one the caves, and the third to the land. Maybe *this* land."

"Well, there's something living in the mouth of the middle statue. I can see them flying in and out." Croft had the scope to his eye. "Hey, hold the phone." His brow furrowed. "One of them is coming this way."

"Take cover," Loche said.

The group spread to hide behind tree trunks, in among the bracken or just lying flat in the long grasses. Only Loche remained standing, hand on sidearm, with Croft covering him with his sniper rifle.

They watched the tiny dot grow larger as it flew toward them.

"Hold fire." Loche's brows came together. "What the...?" He raised a hand.

The figure drifted lower. It was humanoid-shaped with a greenish color and wings spread out behind it that beat furiously but near silently. The face seemed female, and as it neared, they could see the shape of breasts and swollen hips. It, *she*, wore some sort of tunic and looked anatomically perfect except for the wings and also some sort of extra muscle ribbing at her ribs.

"It's a person," Croft said.

"Not just a person." Watts whistled softly.

It drifted closer and then hovered, its dark eyes fixed on Loche. He half turned. "Kearns, get out here."

Matt scrambled out to stand beside the captain. His mouth split in a grin and he immediately held up a hand. "Hello," he said.

The creature remained motionless a few dozen feet above them as its gaze moved slowly over the small clearing, picking out all of the hiding individuals.

"Maybe it sees thermal and can spot us as clearly as if we were standing naked on a roof," Loche whispered.

Matt stepped forward, both hands up and open. "Hello," he repeated and waved.

The figure dropped toward him, and they could see that the face was quite beautiful, if not tinged with green. It looked to be a young female, no more than five feet tall, but with a muscular chest and back obviously to support the wing structure.

Its eyes were totally black, and the face remained serene. She raised a hand to mimic Matt.

"Good, good." Matt reached out a hand, but the green girl backed away. "Okay, that's cool. Not yet," Matt said. "I'm in no hurry."

"Want to bet?" Loche said.

"Take your time, Matt." Janus had his camera up filming them.

"This is awesome. Try and kiss her." Janus grinned.

"Yeah, right." Matt turned back to the woman and smiled again. "My name is Matt." He tapped his chest. "Matt."

The woman continued to hover, her wings beating so fast they made a soft whining noise. She slowly extended her arm and placed it on his chest. She rubbed it for a second or two and then let it slide up to his face where she felt his features, tugged on his long blond hair a moment, and then even opened his mouth to look inside.

Matt saw her face seemed to have faint lines painted on it. *Some sort of decoration*, he mused. Looking down, he saw a perfect figure, but a small slash of an old scar above one breast. He reached up to touch her hand. "It's cold," he said over his shoulder.

She gripped his hand and began to rise.

"*Whoa*." Matt's arm stretched.

The girl's wings beat faster, and then he began to lift from the ground.

"*No, no, no*," he rushed out. "I can't fly."

"Grab him," Loche said to their communications guy, Joe Edison, who was crouched closest to him.

Edison scurried out and grabbed Matt's legs but their combined weight was too much and the girl lowered him to the ground.

She let go and Edison trained his weapon on her, but Matt placed a hand on the barrel of his gun, lowering it. "No, it's okay. She didn't mean any harm. Maybe she's never met, *ah*, people, who can't fly."

Edison's mouth hung open. "She's beautiful."

The green girl stared down at Matt with her large and liquid, dark eyes.

"I think you've won a heart, Matt," Jane said.

Matt grinned and turned to her. "Do you think they're related to the red people?"

Jane shook her head. "No idea, but unlikely, as they couldn't fly. And flight isn't something that was ever in our surface lineage."

Suddenly, the hovering woman spun in the air, her eyes fixed on the jungle growth. Without another word, she shot into the sky, her wings moving in a blur. And in another second, she was gone.

Matt watched her go. "What the hell just happened?" He turned to their group.

"Armor up," Loche said swiftly. "Something freaked her out. And if a local gets freaked out, then maybe we should get the hell out of here. Matt, Edison, fall back. Everyone else, let's move it, *now*."

The group fell into their positions again, and Matt joined Jane and Mike.

"I've got to tell you, that was pretty cool." He grinned. "And we established base communication," he added.

"I'm not sure I saw it that way," Jane scoffed. "I mean, she tried to lift off with you, sure, but hardly dialogue."

"She mimicked my greeting. That's always the standard opening signal that you want to be friends." He turned to walk backward a few steps as he looked up at the huge figures carved into the cliff wall. "I wonder if they have writing up there. I wonder if it was them that carved these visages or their ancestors."

"If we can find the red people again, maybe we can ask them," Mike said.

"Hey, do you think they *were* the red people, but evolved the jungle camouflage colors?" Matt turned back around. "I need to speak to them again."

Jane and Mike caught up to Loche as he seemed to be giving more orders to his team who had slowed a little to listen.

Then Mike heard it. Or rather didn't hear it. "Hey, jungle's gone quiet."

"Yep, for the last few minutes," Loche said. "And we got movement on our three o'clock. Something's been keeping pace with us for a while now."

"Do you think it might be what scared off Matt's green angel a while back?" Janus asked.

Loche shrugged. "Does it matter? A threat is a threat."

"Just don't shoot until you verify a target," Matt requested. "It might be more of the green people."

Around them, the tree canopy began to shake, just a little, but enough to let them know that something of size was moving through it.

"Whatever they are, they're moving in the trees," Loche said.

"They sound too damn heavy for your angels, Matt," Janus observed.

In a few more moments, they came to the edge of a clearing about two hundred yards in length and breadth to what looked like an ancient overflow plain from the river. The red light streamed down in hot curtains through the mist, making the grass look lush, and there were plump, knee-height grazing animals that vacuumed it up through anteater-type snouts.

Loche stopped them at the jungle edge, staying under cover. "Lot of exposed ground."

Nina momentarily glanced back and then to the clearing again. "We go around, we have to chop through all that undergrowth and that'll take us an hour. Or we double-time it, and we're across in five minutes, easy."

"Agreed. And every minute counts." He turned. "Angel, Watts, left and right flank, covering positions. Everyone else, we're going to double-time it in two columns. Everyone armor up, stay cool and alert."

The captain turned to the opposite wall of jungle across the clearing. "See that largest middle tree trunk? That's where we're going to re-enter the jungle. Ready?"

"*HOOAH*," came the response.

"Let's do it," Janus said.

Loche turned to Mike, Jane, and Matt, who nodded. All three held their handguns.

"Three-two-one... *go*." Loche led out one column at a fast jog.

As Jane ran, she glanced over her shoulder. The jungle remained silent, as if it was waiting to see what they would do—and then it acted.

The two groups were no more than twenty feet out into the clearing when the left-side wall of the deep green erupted in movement—huge things, twice as big as a human, burst from the jungle walls, furiously bearing down on them. Jane immediately thought of an octopus, as there were muscular tentacles and a bulbous head with the large forward-facing eyes of a predator. They were mottled green, as if they were camouflage painted by the military. *No wonder they couldn't see them among the foliage*, she thought.

Nina roared a warning as she spun to engage their attackers, and she was immediately followed by the group spraying hundreds of rounds at the thrashing monstrosities.

The creatures looked to weigh 400 pounds easy, and for something so big, they were a blur of motion. There were dozens of them, and this must have been what the green girl had heard and was frightened off by in the jungle canopies.

The bullets smashed into the flailing horrors, and only Angel and Watt's heavy-caliber weapons seemed to deter them. The others came through the gunfire as if it didn't exist and were among the people in seconds.

Joe Edison yelled as he was grabbed by two of the creatures. Horrifyingly, they began to drag him toward the jungle line, and Maxine Archer went after him.

"*Get back in line,*" Loche roared.

Maxine Archer punched rounds into the creatures holding Edison who was dropped to the ground. He scurried back to the group on all fours while Archer gave him cover.

The veins in Loche's neck bulged as he yelled, "Archer, you get your ass..."

It was too late, as now alone and outside of their defensive ring, Maxine Archer was also grabbed. As the team tried to pick off her attackers, the things easily dragged her to the forest line and then lifted her into the trees. Just before she vanished, they saw two of the muscular creatures fighting over her in some sort of horrifying tug of war.

The woman screamed and then in a spray of blood and entrails, both monstrosities won as the top half of her body went one way and the lower half was taken another.

Loche had drawn the group into a circle, with the soldiers with the guns standing and Matt, Jane, Mike, and Janus kneeling at the center of the circle and firing out from waist level.

The amount of gunfire was holding the creatures at bay for now, but Jane knew that they were doing little damage, and if the attack continued, their ammunition would soon run out and they'd all be dead. She tried real hard not to think about the image of the female soldier being torn in half.

"On our six!" Croft yelled and spun his sniper rifle to point behind them.

More of the creatures erupted from the jungle at their rear and it was now clear that wherever these things were coming from, there were a lot more of them than the human beings.

"We need an exit!" Loche yelled over the gunfire. He turned about then selected a route. "We head to that fallen tree over..."

Even as he was talking, more of the tentacled things burst free from the spot he was indicating, their muscular arms coiling and unfurling as if in anticipation of getting hold of more of the soft-bodied human beings.

"*Ah, shit!*" he yelled and fired into the approaching abominations as he searched for more options.

Jane knew that their chances were diminishing while they were in the open. One thing she knew after being embedded with the last military team was if you were attacked, having to defend all four quadrants was a tough game; they needed cover or at least something at their backs.

Matt Kearns aimed and fired, hitting most of his targets, but even though the things coiled in on where they were struck, they weren't stopped or even slowed. He turned to Jane and grimaced. "This is crap."

Loche yelled orders over his shoulder. "Angel, Watts, go big!"

"About time." Angel loaded his grenade launcher.

"Fuck yeah." Watts did the same.

The two men fired, and Angel's grenade was first to strike, totally obliterating one of the land cephalopods. Watts did the same.

The creatures fled from the explosions, but their boiling frenzy was only switched to somewhere else.

Both men aimed and fired the stout grenade plugs again and again, each time hitting and blowing apart one of the creatures. But they soon began to exhaust their grenades.

"There's more coming in," Matt observed.

The trees surrounding them now waved and bristled with the tentacled things, and Jane knew that with one concentrated rush it'd be all over.

"Hold the line. Get ready to form a wedge!" Loche yelled with a gun in each hand.

Jesus, Jane thought. *We're going to try and make a rush to the jungle line, which might be no better.*

Jane reached out to grip Mike's hand and he squeezed it back. She guessed then that it might not be the cancers that was going to get them after all.

"Incoming!" Watts yelled and raised his gun to the sky.

Loche looked up. "Hold fire," he replied.

From out of the sky, dozens of the green flying people appeared with long spears, and from fifty feet from the ground threw them with unerring aim into the closest creatures. They skewered many of them, but though the creatures coiled in on the trauma areas, they soon managed to pull the lances free.

Jane saw then that attack wasn't meant as a deterrent, but more a distraction—as a ring of the flying women kept the land cephalopods at bay, more of the green women dropped down and grabbed each of the people in their team under the arms and then lifted off.

"Hey!" Watts exclaimed as they took the heavy gun from him and tossed it away. "I need that." He began to fight the woman.

"Let it happen!" Matt yelled.

"I've got it." Edison went after the man's gun.

The others lifted off like a squadron of mini helicopters, taking everyone else with them.

One hovered over Edison who held the gun tight to his chest. "I need this gun, honey," he said.

The flying woman grabbed him and tried to lift him off but couldn't quite get airborne. She let him go and hovered a dozen feet above him for a moment, as if in indecision.

Edison held the weapon and turned to see the ring of flying people that had been holding the tentacled creatures at bay also begin to lift off.

Then Edison's flying girl also began to rise into the air.

"Hey." Edison held the gun up. "I just needed…"

"Oh no." Jane watched as the green woman began to lift away while staring down at him. "We need to…"

"Come back!" Edison yelled. He tossed the gun to the side and began to run underneath them.

He was alone, and his movement was like a beacon to the monstrosities surrounding him. Unimpeded now, they slammed into him, and each fought for a morsal of the remaining human, tearing limbs, head, and even the torso into pieces. Jane couldn't watch anymore and shut her eyes.

When she opened them just moments later, they were already hundreds of feet above the tree canopy and being transported up toward the open mouth of one of the huge statues that now looked to be a massive tunnel.

She craned her neck to look up into the face of the being who held onto her. The green-tinged woman must have been enormously strong, as she was only around five feet tall, but the muscles in her chest and back were flexing powerfully as the wings on her back moved in a blur, like those of a bird or a dragonfly.

Jane could also see more clearly the extra ribs or bands of muscles at her sides and wondered at their use—*maybe an aid for balance or for flying*, she wondered.

"Hey!" Mike yelled.

She turned to see him wave just around fifty feet from her. She waved back.

She looked up again at the woman holding her. She knew from the last time she had been in the underworld that the kingdom in the crystal cave had been abandoned for around twelve thousand years, and that should not have been nearly long enough to evolve a significant and sophisticated physical characteristic like flight.

But that thinking was based on the normal order of things on the surface and down here, everything was washed by a constant bath of extreme radiation. *Could it have been enough time?* she wondered.

She turned back toward their destination—the colossal statue's mouth was open, and as they approached, she saw inside more of the green people waiting for them. Again, all were females, and she had to wonder, *where were the men?*

One after the other, the tiny squadron of flying women with their passengers entered the gaping cavern and softly lowered the people to the ground.

Loche called them into a group. "Everyone okay?" he asked.

"Except for Edison," Watts spat. "That bitch."

"Shut it, soldier. You're alive because of them," Loche replied.

It seemed all those lifted off were fine.

"Take me to your leader," Janus remarked as they looked at the growing number of green women surrounding them.

"Are they friendly?" Nina asked.

"They didn't disarm all of us, so that's a good sign," Loche replied.

"They may not have known what the weapons were," Matt replied. "I think they took Angels and Watts' heavy-caliber guns away only because of the weight."

"Well, this is why we're paying you the big bucks, Professor." Janus held out his arm toward the group. "Work your magic."

Matt turned back to the women. "Notice something?" he asked.

"Yeah, like they're all chicks," Croft replied.

"Sure, there's that, but that's not so unusual. We had the ancient Scythians, all women, on the steppes of Russia, which some said were the basis of the Amazons legend." Matt shook his head. "But not that." He turned back to Janus. "They're silent. Totally silent. None of them has uttered a word of joy, fear, greeting, or any sound at all since we've arrived."

The group turned back to the throng of green women. It was then that Jane observed that there was another feature about them. Though they were all attractive, they all seemed to be the same age, build, and height, with the same facial features but a few variations as to make one think they were all related.

Their clothing was a tunic dress that wrapped around their waist, but their breasts were bare. Jane squinted and saw another difference—they had normal, firm breasts, and there was an areola situated where it should be, but there didn't seem to be nipples.

"Valley of the clones," Janus remarked.

Matt spotted the original being they had met earlier and recognized the small slash of an old scar above one of her breasts. He stepped toward her and raised his hand.

"Hello, again." He touched his chest. "It's me, Matt Kearns. Do you remember me?"

The woman also walked forward with her wings now folded down behind her back, making it look like some sort of gossamer cape. She held up her hand and placed it against Matt's.

Once again, Matt could feel the odd coolness of her hand and wondered whether one of the adaptions to the heat down here was a lower body temperature.

She took hold of his hand and placed the palm against her cheek first, and then her chest. She turned to the assembled green throng, and all their heads swiveled toward her.

Jane could just make out a high-pitched whine and frowned as she concentrated. "Did you hear that?"

Matt nodded and turned to her. "They may be communicating with each other in a way that we can't process."

One after the other, the green women came and placed a hand on or just touched the exposed flesh of the humans.

"I think I'm in heaven." Watts smiled and nodded, loving the attention. "I forgive you," he said.

More and more of the clan wanted to experience the warm skin of the people, and after a few moments, another group of women appeared and took their hands to lead them further into the cave. It seemed that the colossal statue was riddled with tunnels, but it was by design as the walls weren't hewn rock but a mosaic of small interlocking stones.

They were led along a passageway with many offshoot caves or rooms that had strands of things like pearls over the doors, obscuring their contents. But then in a few moments, they were taken into a room of their own. It was large, and inside were the familiar blue crystals.

"This must be our room," Watts said and turned. "Can I order room service?" He grinned at the small woman, who just stared back at him with her large, black, doe-like eyes.

"Careful, Watts," Nina remarked. "You may end up married before you know it."

He chuckled. "Fine with me. But I can only stay for the honeymoon." He winked.

In another moment, a cohort of the winged women brought them a few dead insectoid-looking creatures, which they laid out on a bench.

Nina frowned at the bodies. "What's this supposed to mean?"

"I think…" Mike approached. "I think this is supposed to be food for us."

After a moment of being observed, the green woman with the scar on her chest turned to the other women in the doorway, and then moments later more of them appeared holding armfuls of different-shaped fruits and vegetables.

"I guess this might be more like it." Matt turned to the women. "Thank you." He picked up one of the fist-sized fruits and began to tear it open. Inside was a purple syrup and flesh that filled the cave with the smell of sugar. He licked a little off one of his fingers.

"Hmm, okay, not as good as it smells—a little like a cross between a banana and cabbage."

"Well, that sounds like shit," Croft scoffed. "Anything that tastes like steak and beer?"

"Don't insult our hosts." Loche smiled and turned to the women. "Thank you. And thank you for saving us. Most of us," he added.

Once again, they were met with silence, but a few of the small women looked at each other and then they all departed the room, dropping the pearl curtain in their wake. Except for one.

It was the green girl with the scar on her chest and she stared at Matt. He walked forward and raised his hand.

She did the same and placed it against his, her fingers small, but strong looking. He saw that the lines on her face were deep like they were scars—he knew of some primitive tribes that used scarification as a sign of adulthood or beauty.

"Matt," he tried again and tapped his chest. "Can you say that?"

Her mouth never moved, and she didn't even attempt the word. Instead, she touched where he had tapped his chest and then ran her hand down his stomach and then to his groin. She then took his hand and began to lead him away.

"Forget it," Loche said. "We stay together."

Matt nodded and pulled his hand free. "Maybe later." He smiled. "Call me, okay?"

The green girl stared for a moment more and then exited through the bead curtain, leaving them alone.

"Seemed friendly enough," Janus said.

"Overly friendly, if you ask me," Nina added.

Watts guffawed. "No such thing as an overly friendly woman."

"But where are the men?" Nina asked.

Janus shrugged. "Maybe they're asexual. We haven't seen what's under those tunics yet."

"By the way she took to Matt, I'm not sure they're asexual," Jane replied. "She looked clearly interested."

"A race of women, thousands of miles below the Earth... that are hungry for men." Watts chuckled. "Man, I'm livin' the dream. Pick me up on the way back, will you?"

"We're not here on holiday," Loche replied. "We rest, eat, and then if we can't work out how to convince our flying hosts to transport us to the end of the jungle valley, then we're going to have to find our own way out."

"That's a long way down," Mike added. "Got to be a thousand feet of sheer rock."

"I never said we had to scale down," Loche replied. "We're at the top, so we keep going up."

Nina nodded. "Sounds like a plan."

Loche took off his pack, grabbed a few pieces of fruit, and slumped down with his back to the wall. "Everyone eat, rest, and recharge."

Jane turned about, really examining their room for the first time. It reminded her of one of the red people's caverns in that there were alcoves and some stone furniture. But it looked to have remained unused for hundreds of years, or maybe more.

"Mike, Matt." She waved them over. "Might be some clue to the origin of this humanoid species."

Matt nodded. "I'm sure they communicate, but not in a way that allows our inclusion. I'm not confident it's possible for me to understand them."

"Could they be using a form of telepathy?" Jane asked.

Matt shrugged. "Anything is possible. But I can detect a faint whine passing between them, so I still think it's an audible form of communication." He looked about. "Unless we find some sort of Rosetta stone, I'm screwed."

They walked around the perimeter of the large room. The crystals were only placed toward the front, perhaps for their benefit, which meant the rear of the room was left in darkness.

Jane held up her flashlight into an alcove. "Mike, look, just like the red people's cavern."

Mike joined her. "Looks the same."

There was a mosaic of picture glyphs. Matt came forward and used his sleeve to wipe a heavy layer of dust from them.

"This is more like it." He put a finger into a few of the grooves. "Timeworn stone. Maybe ten, twelve, even fifteen thousand years old."

He stepped back. "Magnificent." He retrieved his flashlight and held it up. "Look, it shows an army, humanoid, and not winged. All marching into the jungle." He turned to Mike and Jane. "Maybe your red people?" Matt said softly.

"The time period is right," Jane replied.

The next images showed the construction of things like pyramids, and also of the carved monolithic statues in the valley wall.

"Seems they built these statues." His eyes narrowed. "But then they found trouble," he whispered.

The next glyph showed the warriors being attacked by long insectoid-type creatures.

"Not our green people, by the look of them. But they certainly found the local creatures to be a problem. Just like we did," he said.

"I just can't see there being enough evolutionary time for the red people to evolve wings and fly, even if they're constantly bombarded by radiation," Jane said.

They moved along to the next alcove. This one showed the insect monstrosities capturing many of the small warriors and flying off with them.

"It seems the wingless people were being tormented by these giant insects," Matt said and then pointed. "And this could have multiple meanings." The next image showed a feminine face, surrounded by what could have been hieroglyphics and all manner of markings.

Matt took a picture. "That face could be that of their ruler, their queen, but the writing tells the story. If I can decipher, we might be able to understand what happened here."

"We'll need to," Mike said. "Because from then, that's when the censors moved in."

"Damn," Matt whispered.

The wall was scraped clean from then on. Mike wiped down the rock. "Either removed or perhaps this was a blank slate still waiting for the story to finish."

"One thing is for sure." Jane turned about. "These grand rooms certainly aren't in use anymore. And haven't been for millennia."

"It's like a fallen kingdom," Matt observed. "Like a civilization that has declined back to its infancy."

"It's certainly got its secrets." Jane tugged on Mike's elbow. "Come on, we better get some rest while we can." She waited. "Matt?"

"No, no, I need to work on this. You go." Matt sat down on the cave floor, crossed his legs, and looked up at the writing. He never blinked.

CHAPTER 15

Matt Kearns' chin dropped to his chest. Everyone slept. Except their lone sentry.

While soft snores filled the air, the pearl curtain parted and one of the green women peered into the room. Watts was taking his first stint on watch and smiled and waved at her.

She stared at him, and he crossed to her, careful to step lightly over his sleeping friends.

"Hi there, pretty woman." He held out a hand.

She did the same and lifted her hand to let it trail over his face, pulling his lip down and looking inside his mouth. She then let her cool fingers run down his chest to his stomach all the while keeping her dark eyes on his.

"Yeah, I like that." Watts grabbed her hand and pushed it lower.

Her hand went to his groin and gripped him, squeezing his hardness. "Ooh, your hands are a little cold, baby." Watts grinned eagerly now. "Yeah, that's it." He briefly looked over his shoulder. "Just a quick one, okay? And we need to be quiet."

She took his hand. Behind her, the pearl curtain automatically moved aside and she gently led the man from the room.

***

"What do you mean you can't find him?" Rick Croft's neck jutted as he faced Chris Angel.

Angel shrugged. "He never woke me, and when I went to take over the shift, he wasn't here… or anywhere." His brows lifted. "Hey, maybe he's takin' a piss."

"For fifteen minutes?" Croft thumbed over his shoulder. "Fuck that, you tell the boss."

"Tell him what?" Loche loomed up behind the men who both came to attention.

Croft was closest and Loche glared at the man. Croft's lips pressed together for a moment until he gave up and spoke in a rush.

"Lieutenant Watts is missing, sir."

"Then we better find him. And he better have a good reason for being AWOL." Loche checked his watch. They'd rested for a good three hours, more than enough, so he clapped his hands together, making a sound like a gunshot.

"Okay, people, we need to be up and at 'em." He looked to Nina Masters and motioned her over.

"Sir?" she said.

"Watts has gone for a walk. He's a numbskull, but I don't know if he's that much of a numbskull," he said evenly.

She shrugged. "He's always had an eye for the ladies. But I doubt he'd abandon his post and leave it open. We'll find him."

"Damn straight. We all will. It's time we got on our way anyway." Loche turned. "Okay, people, let's go. We're moving out."

He waited while the team organized themselves a moment more for the civilians to fall into line. Loche then went to the door and peered through the pearlescent bead curtain to look along the corridor. On seeing nothing there, he put a flat hand through the curtain to move it aside, but then stopped. He frowned.

"What the hell is going on here?"

The pearls hanging down on their strings didn't move aside easily, and in fact were as tight and tough as piano wire.

"Is it to keep something out, or us in?" Janus asked.

"Doesn't matter. Somehow, Watts went through and so are we." Loche clicked his fingers to Angel.

"Loche," Matt called.

Loche turned. "What is it?"

"The stone writing." Matt pointed back at the wall. "From what I could decipher, I think it's a warning. From the original owners."

"Original owners?" Loche lifted his chin. "Aren't these people the owners?"

"No, I don't think so. Well, they are now, but they came later. After the red people. I just need to finish the last few sections, to find…"

"Then you do that—from your notes—because we're leaving." Loche turned away. " Angel, make me a hole."

"Yes, sir." Angel first pulled a long blade and tried severing the strands, but they refused to cut. Nina handed him some wire snips, and after grunting from the effort for several seconds, he managed to cut one of the strands that fell to the ground where it immediately melted.

"That shit is weird." Angel looked at the snips, shrugged, and then went back to work on the next strand.

In a few minutes, he had cut enough for them to all squeeze out into the corridor. Loche looked one way then the other—both were empty and looked largely disused, so no clues as to which direction Watts went. Time was against them, so he decided to split them and check both areas.

"Nina, you're on the east tunnel. Take Croft, Angel, and you get Janus. I'll take the civs. We meet back here in ten minutes."

"Yes, sir." She made some hand gestures in the air and headed out, with Janus staying right on her shoulder, followed by Angel and the large form of Rick Croft at the rear with his gun held tightly.

Loche turned back to the western tunnel. "And we get to go deeper. Everyone keep their eyes open."

They headed in and Matt Kearns pushed to the front. "Captain Loche, please, their language. Or rather the language of the people who were here first."

"You already said. So, these little green pixies are not the original owners? So what?" Loche asked.

"That's right," Matt replied. "The original owners were the ones that settled here thousands of years ago. After a while, they came under attack by swarms of these intelligent bugs. They suffered heavy losses, but soon worked out how to defend against them and began to push them back."

"If they won, where are they now?" Mike asked.

Matt turned. "According to the writing, the bugs changed their tactics, found another way to—"

The scream made the group cringe and spread to flatten themselves to the walls of the tunnel.

"Was that Watts?" Jane asked.

"I damn well hope not," Loche replied without turning. "Everyone be ready to move quick."

Loche double-timed down the corridor with flashlight in one hand and gun in the other. The group followed right behind him.

***

Nina Masters suddenly held a hand up as they came to a corner, causing Janus to bump into her. She turned to glare for a moment while Angel and Croft waited with guns ready.

She peered around and seeing nothing but more labyrinthine depths of the disused ancient tunnel system, she waved them on.

Soon they came to more side corridors and one of them had another of the bead curtains hanging at its front. She tilted her head closer; sure enough, she could hear something like a soft mewling coming from inside.

"Might be Watts." She stood back. "Croft, open it."

The man stepped forward, pushed his gun over his shoulder, and immediately set to using his wire snips to cut through the hanging strands of pearls.

Once again, they dropped to the ground and lost their shape like they were made of some sort of wax that had been left out in the sun. Croft completed his task and then stood aside.

Nina held up three fingers and lowered them one after the other. She then lifted her light and handgun and went in, followed by Croft, Janus, and then Angel, who took one last look around outside and followed.

Nina's eyes widened, and she put a forearm over her lower face from the stench.

There were what at first looked like a lot of pudgy children with a green tinge to them. But as she stared, she saw that they were older, stunted, or somehow deformed.

"I think they're adults... male," Nina breathed out.

"They've got cocks like men, anyway." Croft made a disgusted sound in his throat.

When they could drag their eyes away from the dangling genitals, they saw that the green male's eyes were compound eyes set in tiny gargoyle-like faces, and the wings on their backs were stunted.

"Ugly little bastards," Croft spat. "What's wrong with their eyes?"

The small creatures were all crowded in among each other and covered in some sort of greasy excretion. Running beside the group were troughs, empty now, but looked to have a dark brownish-red stain inside.

She also saw now that they were all silent and the noise she heard was actually their bodies rubbing up against each as they were so tightly packed in on one another.

Around the room were scattered bones and also mummified bodies—many of them insectoid-looking creatures, but there were also some small human-looking skulls.

Janus coughed and put a hand over his lower face. "So, now we know where all the men are," he said between his fingers.

Croft peered into a side chamber. "Fuck me. Get a load of this." He recoiled. "This is what they're feeding the little monsters."

Nina stuck her head in. There was another long trough and tied to the ceiling were three bodies, red, humanoid, and from their necks were pipes that allowed their blood to fill the trough.

Several of the stubby, green men had their faces buried in it.

"If they think they're gonna do this to us, they're in for a fucking shock," Nina spat. "Let's get the hell out of here." She began to back out.

As she did, the group of humanoid males began to get agitated and reached out toward them, as if begging them not to leave. They seemed to remain silent except Nina was sure she could hear the familiar soft whine filling the air.

"Fucking horror show," Croft said, his mouth turned down. "Say the word, and I'll drop a grenade in their dinner bowl."

"Stay cool, stay silent… for now." Nina waved them out.

As they exited the cave, Angel snapped his gun up. "*Contact.*"

Nina and Croft spun while Janus scurried in behind them. The corridor was now filled with the green females.

The women were silent, with large unblinking, dark eyes, but this time they had their spears with them.

"Here we go," Angel whispered. "Show time."

The green women spread out. And horrifyingly, so did their bodies—from beside them, those strange bunches of muscles at their ribs unfolded into another set of arms, which reached forward to also grip the spears.

A high-pitched whine filled the air as the green women began to move forward.

***

Loche went along the stone corridor, fast. The moan was the first human sound they had heard, and he was sure it had come from his missing man. If Watts was alive, he was in trouble.

They came to a side cave once again with one of the strange bead curtains barring their way.

"Cover me," Loche said and used the barrel of his gun and brute force to stretch the curtain strands aside. When nothing leaped out, he peered in for several seconds and then spoke over his shoulder. "Professor." He stepped back.

Matt walked forward and looked inside the alcove. He began to smile. "Hello."

Loche then used his knife to saw and slash the curtain out of the way, and he entered with Matt. Mike and Jane followed.

Inside were about two dozen red children of varying ages, clothed in little more than rags.

"The remnants of a defeated civilization," Matt whispered.

He held up his hand. He used the word for greeting but had no idea if he was pronouncing it correctly as he had seen it written but never actually heard it spoken.

The children just stared, frightened to the point of immobility. Jane eased closer to the children, but her large size caused them to back up.

"We're friends," she said in a soft voice and crouched to their level.

She smiled and slowly reached out a hand. They stared for a moment more, and then one of the tallest children came forward. He touched her hand, and she felt the warmth and in feeling the heat from Jane's hand, he seemed satisfied there was no threat. He turned, whispered, and nodded, and the others came forward to crowd around them.

The children surrounded each of them, touching their hands and clothing and looking up with grimy faces.

"Prisoners," Matt said. "They decimated the race and then took the remnants hostage."

"And for what purpose?" Mike asked. "Slaves?"

"Doesn't matter now. Come on," Loche said. "We'll come back for them. We need to find Watts and then link up with our team."

Jane looked about to protest but changed her mind and instead held a hand up. "You wait here, we'll be back. Promise." She backed out of the cave, with the moon-eyed children watching in silence.

The group continued on and at a junction of three intersecting tunnels, Loche slowed, not sure which way to go, wanting to move silently. *But it was time to take a chance*, he thought.

"Watts!" he yelled. "*Lieutenant Chuck Watts*." He waited but there was no return sound. He shook his head. "Any ideas, people?"

"Got to check them all, I guess," Mike replied.

Loche nodded. "Good a plan as any."

He went to the first tunnel and headed in a few dozen feet. Behind him was Mike, then Jane and Matt. After a while, he stopped.

"Smell that?" he asked.

"Yes, fresh air," Jane replied. "Might be a way out."

From back the way they came, there was a low moan.

"That's Watts," Loche said. "Come on." He headed back at a jog.

At the junction, he called again, and this time from the middle tunnel there was a weak call, definitely human.

"This way, fast." Loche sprinted now and kept his gun ready.

Mike, Jane, and Matt also held their handguns when they came to a side cave and skidded to a stop.

Loche peered inside and his eyes widened. "Mother of God."

It was Chuck Watts, spread-eagled on a table, and surrounded by a group of the green women.

Matt gasped. "Holy shit, that wasn't decoration."

The lines on the women's faces opened up, and the group saw they weren't decoration or scars and had instead been interlocking plates, creating a fake visage like a mask. Now there was exposed another face underneath—their true face.

One was bristling with insectoid hairs and quivering mouthparts. And from the now-open plates, a long proboscis elongated and pierced Watts' torso.

Watts looked visibly drained and shrunken, and as they sucked his fluids, the women's abdomens swelled red with his blood. If that ghastly image wasn't enough, they saw that the women had extended smaller arms from their sides that gripped the man to hold him in place.

"Oh shit. That's what the carved story meant—the insects that attacked the race here, the former race said their attackers adapted their attack… they adapted by mimicking the human beings."

The green women withdrew their hypodermic-like proboscis and turned, their large compound eyes shivering and twitching in their direction, and immediately the room filled with a high-pitched whine.

"They're giant fucking mosquitos," Loche said and lifted his gun.

"Now I know what these monsters are keeping the children for," Jane said, feeling ill. "We need to save them."

"Back up." Loche gritted his teeth and half turned. "Get ready to grab Watts."

The green women's wings extended and like they were jet-propelled, they shot from the ground. Though the stone room didn't have a high ceiling, the green women were extremely fast and navigated the small space easily.

Loche kept his gun on them, but they headed for the exit and vanished outside. Jane rushed to the man on the table.

"How is he?" Loche joined them.

Watts looked ash-grey, and his eyes had sunk into deep sockets and his cheek bones were sharp. It looked like he was being mummified, as there was very little moisture left in his body.

The puncture marks on his torso were still leaking a clear liquid. She pointed.

"Massive blood loss. That liquid dribbling out is more likely to be something they injected into him to stop coagulation. Might be like a sedative or anticoagulant." She looked up. "Just like mosquitos."

Mike pulled one of Watts' eyelids back, but the man's eyes were rolled up and unresponsive. "He's lost too much blood. He needs a transfusion."

"We need to get him out," Loche said. "We can rig a field transfusion, but not in here."

Jane looked at Mike, and they shared a glance—they both knew he'd never make it. But they weren't going to leave him behind.

Mike called to Matt who was looking at a large flat wall covered in writing. He turned to them. "This was a ceremonial chamber once. Like a chapel. The king's name, the last king, was *Usan The Great*." Matt shook his head. "Except for these kids, they've all gone now."

"Give me a hand," Mike said and lifted Watts.

Matt took his other arm. The man weighed next to nothing and felt more like a bag of twigs. He sagged between them, his feet dragging.

Loche looked back down the tunnel. "We find Nina and her team, and then head to that cave with the draft."

"After we rescue the children."

"We don't have…" Loche began.

"We make time," Jane insisted. "You want us to find the other red people, after we left some of their children behind? We bring the children, that's final."

"She's right," Mike urged. "We get them. They saved us once."

Loche exhaled. "Okay, fine, we get them. Then we find a way out, or we *make* a way out." Loche went to the exit and peered out. "Let's go."

He moved quickly but not fast enough to leave the rest behind.

"Hear that?" Matt called.

The whine filled the air, coming from behind them, ahead of them, and inside every alcove around them.

"Yeah, seems like the jungle drums are beating. We might have a lot of company real soon," Loche replied.

In minutes more, they came to the junction and Watts made a wheezing sound and sagged even more between the two men. Loche turned back, drew his blade, and made an 'X' next to the cave they had felt the earthy breeze emanating from.

He then quickly stepped in closer to Watts and lifted his head. He examined the man closely for a few seconds before his shoulders slumped. "Ah, damnit."

Jane also checked him. "We've lost him."

"He was already dead," Loche sighed. "Put him down," he said to Matt and Mike, who laid the desiccated body of the man on the cave floor.

Loche crouched in front of him. "Thank you, soldier." He reached into the man's collar, took his tags, and wrapped them around his fist. He saluted the body and then got to his feet and turned. "We need to find..."

From one of the tunnels came the staccato blasts of automatic gunfire.

"That's Nina. *Hurry.*" Loche sprinted into the tunnel ahead.

Mike ran with Jane, and Matt was close behind. Loche was already outpacing them, and just as he passed by the mouth of an open cave, something came out of it like a green torpedo to snatch him off his feet and keep going.

"*Loche!*" Jane yelled uselessly.

From up ahead in the darkness more gunfire and yells smashed out; they were closer now.

The trio looked indecisive for a split second until Jane started into the cave. "Loche first."

The trio headed in, both flashlights and guns held up. They moved cautiously, and in seconds more, they heard a grunt of effort and rounded a small bend to find Loche holding one of the green women by the throat. Its face plates were pulled back, the probing spike of a proboscis extended just inches from his face.

It used its two longest arms to try and draw him closer. They could now see that its small arms had sharp talons that raked and tore his clothing. Loche's gun and light were on the ground, and Mike lifted his own gun and aimed. But the pair moved too erratically for him to get a clean shot.

"Can't get a shot," he said, seething.

Matt charged in and grabbed one of the long wings of the thing, causing it to immediately crash to the ground.

Loche ignored the damage being done to his body, reached down to pull a blade, and then thrust it up into the side of the thing just between its first and second set of arms. The result was immediate and eerie as the green woman soundlessly folded in on herself. It released

Loche and spun toward Matt who still had hold of its wing. It darted straight at him.

"*Gaah*." Matt released the wing, threw his arms up, and fell back. The small green woman then sped from the cave.

Loche quickly looked down at his bleeding ribs covered in lacerations. "We've got to help the others, and then get the hell out of here."

"You might need stitches, you're losing blood," Jane said.

"And if we hang around here, we'll lose our lives. I'll deal with it. Let's go." He began to jog back out of the cave, only pausing momentarily at the corner before leaving to enter the main tunnel, and then began to run.

As Loche ran, he reached down into a side pouch on his pants and drew forth a plastic package. He used his teeth to rip it open and tugged out a patch with something reddish-brown on the pad side—iodine, Jane bet—and he lifted his shirt to slap it on the lacerations.

Air escaped his lips in a hiss for a second or two as he dealt with the pain and then once plastered on, Loche began to accelerate again.

Jane, Matt, and Mike worked to keep up with him. But they could all hear that the battle ahead was close now.

***

Nina, Croft, and Angel backed up, firing as they went.

Until they hit the wall.

The green insectoid creatures were fast, darting and changing direction faster than the soldiers could track and shoot. For every half dozen shots they expended, they hit one target, and as there seemed to be many dozens of the things crowding into the cave, they'd burn through their ammunition long before they took down enough of the creatures to be safe.

"Fucking monsters." Angel jacked a grenade into his launcher and lifted the weapon.

"Negative!" Nina yelled. "We could bring it all down on our heads."

At that moment, with Nina's head turned, one of the green women sped in and latched onto her with its four arms, and immediately the two smaller limbs with the dagger-like claws dug in. Being smaller than the two men, she was immediately dragged from their group.

Angel and Croft went to go after her but were swarmed and just as they began to get pushed back, saw Nina fighting hard, but then another landed on her back, gripping with its four arms, and spearing into the back of her neck with its proboscis.

"*No!*" Croft yelled and tried to charge forward, but more insect women dove into him, shredding his clothes and forcing him back.

Nina gurgled in pain, and whatever toxin it pumped into her acted quickly. Her arms dropped, and she slumped over.

"*Can't. Get. To her.*" Croft gritted his teeth as he battled the swarm, shooting, stabbing, and clubbing them with his fists. But he could only watch as his team leader was drained of fluid. Nina twitched as the life was sucked right from her body.

"Fuck you, you ugly sonsofbitches." Angel lifted his launcher and fired a grenade round into the center of the mass. "*Fire in the hole!*" he yelled and both men dove to the ground.

The pug only traveled a few dozen feet, and just as the insect beings began to land on the men, the brilliant red and orange thump of the blast filled the cave with blinding light and heat.

***

"*Whoa!*" Loche stopped and held his hands out to each side of the tunnel wall as the explosion shook the entire passageway. He waited a few seconds, and the group just stared at each other, waiting, as horrifyingly, there then came a sound like cracking ice from all around them.

"It's gonna collapse!" Mike yelled.

"We gotta get 'em." Loche charged on.

"This is insane—*wait.*" Jane made a guttural sound in her throat as she watched the man sprint away.

"No choice." Mike grabbed her arm and they continued to run, followed by Matt.

The professor cringed as dust rained down on him. "We've got about two minutes!" he yelled.

They burst from their tunnel into the chamber with a scene of carnage all around them.

"There." Loche sprinted to the body of Nina among all the shredded green people. He immediately turned her over but saw she had suffered the same fate as Watts.

"*Ah, shit, shit, shit.*" He pounded the floor.

"Here, Croft, he's alive," Mike said.

"And Angel too." Matt lifted the man who coughed and shook his head, trying to clear it.

"Nina," was all Watts said.

Matt turned to Loche, who shook his head. "We've got to get out, now!" he yelled.

As their hearing started to return to normal following the blast, they all heard the growing high-pitched whine coming from the tunnels.

"Here they come," Jane said.

"We're outta here." Loche lifted Croft and began to jog with the man stagger-running beside him on his shoulder.

Mike and Matt got Angel up between them and luckily for them, the big man was able to help by half staggering along with them. As they ran, the sound of their ragged breathing and the whine of the approaching insect women was drowned out by the cracking of stone.

"Here we go." Jane began to sprint and urged them even faster.

Loche spotted the knife marks on the rock beside one of the caves and pointed. "This one."

Jane skidded to a stop. "You go, I'll get the children."

"No," Loche ordered.

Croft jacked in another magazine. "I got this, boss."

The captain pointed at the man's chest. "You got two damn minutes, soldier."

Without anther word Jane sped off, with Mike right on her shoulder. The large form of Croft, still staggering, came up from behind.

As they careened down the tunnel, they heard the first thump of heavy stones coming down.

"In here!" Jane yelled and sped straight into the room. The red children were still there, and they all backed up when the huge people suddenly appeared.

Croft stayed at the door, looking up and down the corridor, and Jane went to the taller kid who had greeted her previously. She held his face in two hands and looked into his eyes. "I know you don't understand me, but you must come with me, all of you, *now*." She kissed his forehead, hard, and then took his hand and began to lead him to the door.

There she placed his hand in Mike's, and then went back to urge the other children to follow. She grabbed another child's hand and took the girl to link hands with the boy Mike held.

Each seemed comfortable doing this until she had all of them, all twenty-three.

"*Gotta go, gotta go, people!*" Croft yelled as the room began to fill with dust.

Jane nodded to Mike, and the procession headed out.

***

"Come on, come on, come on." Loche bared his teeth with impatience as he waited at the cross tunnel.

Behind him came a whoosh of air and a dust cloud surged past them, obviously as some of the tunnels further in were beginning to collapse.

Just when he felt they were lost, he saw the pinprick of Croft's barrel light come bouncing down the long tunnel.

"*Hurry up!*" he roared.

In seconds more, the long line of adults and children appeared, and Loche immediately pushed them into the marked tunnel. "*Go, go, go!*"

They sprinted for a few minutes until they all charged into a large, dead-end vault-like room that was crowded with skeleton fragments around the edge of a large pool of water. On its surface were revolting-looking bristling bulbs, five or six feet long, that shivered and jerked.

The children screamed and crowded in behind Mike and Jane.

As the group watched, one of the things at the surface started to spit down the back, and then rising up from within the casing came an abomination that was part green woman and part spindly insect.

"The birthing room," Jane said.

"Not today," Croft snarled. "For Nina." He fired a stream of rounds into the rising insect body.

It was like an electric shock had been run through the pool of stagnant water as all the bodies flicked and jumped and then vanished below the dark surface. The green woman-creature he struck flopped sideways into the water and lay still.

"There." Loche pointed.

In the ceiling above them, they could see a crack of red light, and water dripped down from it onto the water's surface.

"It's how the pond fills—maybe rainwater from outside," Mike said.

"If the water's getting in, then that's how we're getting out." Loche looked up.

Beneath their feet, the rock jerked to the left, then right. He threw his arms out like a tightrope walker, just as the rock jerked again.

"Time's up." Loche stepped out of the way. "Angel, make a hole for us."

Angel nodded. "Everyone take cover." He lifted his launcher and pumped one of the explosive plugs into the chamber and fired.

He then dove backward as the plug struck the ceiling and detonated.

Rock blew in all directions and when the cavern settled, they could see a shaft of brilliant red light in the curtain of dust.

The cavern jerked again, this time by Mother Nature. But above the thundering sound of the shifting stones, a high-pitched whine was building.

"Here comes the army," Croft said, as he raced to the tunnel they'd just exited from, and peered back down. "Time to go, boss."

"Up and out!" Loche yelled, and one after the other, the group scaled the tumbled rocks to the exit. They had to wait for the small children to climb as Angel and Croft guarded the exit, and as Loche got to near the top, he turned. "Angel, shut the door, and we're out."

Angel nodded and turned to his friend, Croft. "Go, I'm right behind you."

"Don't make me come back for you." He slapped Angel on the shoulder and turned to bound up the stones. At the top, he and Loche watched as Angel fired several rounds back down the shaft, and then turned and ran.

The explosive rounds detonated as he bounded up the rockslide. Loche pulled him up the last few feet as the rumbling continued after the blasts.

Then got louder.

"Oh shit." Loche backed up, and then turned.

The group found themselves on top of the massive statue's head and spread out before them far below was the jungle valley. But now cracks were running through the stone head that was the size of a football field.

The group began to cautiously back up as a sound like thunder reverberated right through the cliff wall. It finished with a fissure opening in front of them.

There was silence and they all waited, holding their breath.

Then it started again, massively shaking the entire cliff face.

"*Run!*" Loche yelled to the group.

In front of them, more cracks began to appear and open.

"She's gonna go!" Mike yelled and he, Jane, and Matt grabbed up two each of the smallest children in their arms, put their heads down, and sprinted.

More cracks opened, mostly behind but some in front of them. Mike leaped across one massive rent in the cliff top, followed by Jane, Matt, Janus, Loche, then Croft and lastly, Angel.

The last few dozen feet to a ridge of rocks they dove and then sprawled on the ground. They turned, just as the entire thousand-foot-high statue parted from the cliff. It hung there for several seconds before slowly tipping forward. Then the millions of tons of stone figure fell like the mightiest tree in the world.

Mike got to his feet. "Keep going."

They ran back further, looking over their shoulders, and when the titanic weight of rock struck the valley floor, everything jumped as if an earthquake ran through the inner world. More land fell off the cliff edge into the void.

Janus was on his belly hugging the ground, and the others stood but had their arms out wide to maintain balance until the earth stopped shaking.

For many seconds afterward, there were still the sounds of huge rocks striking the valley floor as the last loose boulders were shaken out to fall free. Eventually, it fell to silence, and the group felt confident enough to straighten.

"I guess toppling a thousand-foot-high statue and destroying it is leaving a small footprint in the greater scheme of things," Matt chuckled.

Croft snarled. "Yeah, and I'm just happy those green bitches got what they deserved."

Loche turned and walked a few paces up through the trees on top of the cliff wall. He put a hand over his eyes and exhaled. "The end of the valley."

The group joined him and stared out over the vista—the jungle valley ended in just a few miles, and like someone had drawn a line on the ground, there began the desert. He checked his GPS and turned to Jane.

"According to our positioning and your maps, we're nearly there." Loche half smiled. "We can still do this." He glanced back at the children. "But they aren't going to make it any easier."

Jane nodded. "I know, but we just pulled them from a fate literally worse than death."

Matt was kneeling before them, practicing his language skills, and a few had begun to respond. A few even smiled.

"I can't imagine how many generations were brought up to be

grown like cattle to then be fed upon as soon as they reached a certain age." Mike shivered. "They were monsters."

Matt turned. "No, they just had no humanity." He stood. "They saw them, and us, as food, nothing more."

"I'm glad they're all dead. They were a parasitic race," Jane growled and looked back out over the red desert that ran to the horizon. "We need to finish our job."

Loche nodded and hefted his weapon. "You heard the lady—let's get this done."

He waved them on and then led them down to the desert floor.

CHAPTER 16

Viktor Zhukov handed Ally his field glasses and she looked out at the shimmering red desert.

"Hot," he said redundantly.

"And it's gonna get hotter," she replied.

Ally scanned the distance. The sky was its usual boiling red, the ground was red, and the very air seemed to shimmer as red waves of dry heat hung like oil in the air. She lowered the glasses and turned to look over her shoulder.

The red landscape was punctured by gnarled trees that looked to have been dead for hundreds of years. And there was something else— cones—that reminded her of clay termite mounds. They'd been avoiding them when they could because she had no idea what sort of creature had made them—a lot of something small in a nest, or something big that used them to whip out and ambush its prey; either one was something they didn't want to tangle with.

Zhukov turned. "Valentina, you okay?"

The Russian woman's face was dry, and her eyelids drooped. But she nodded. "Yes, I can do it."

"Good. Drink a little more water." Ally reached into her pack and felt several of the fleshy bulb-leaves remaining. She pulled one out, cut the top off, and handed it to the Russian woman.

"I've got plenty, so make sure you drink from it. There's also sugar in there, which you'll need." She held it out as the thick liquid welled up.

Valentina took it slowly, her limbs seeming to move in slow motion.

Zhukov smiled and nodded. "Thank you."

One side of Ally's lips curved up into a smile as well. "No, thank you, both of you. For saving me." She sighed and turned back to the desert. "We still heading in the right direction?"

Zhukov checked the GPS and then pointed. "That way. Maybe just ten miles."

"Over the horizon." She blew air from puffed cheeks and wished there was a better way to cross it. Ten miles over that landscape, on foot, without shade, when they were already fatigued, was an eternity.

Ally sucked in a deep breath that singed her lungs. She'd survived her military training. She'd survived missions in Afghanistan and Syria. And she'd damn well survived being taken alive and kept in a hellish darkness for nearly a year by some sort of troglodyte monsters.

Ally knew she'd walk until she was nothing but leather stretched over bones if need be. She turned and looked at her companions. She thought the captain would make it. But would Valentina? She doubted it.

"We need to travel for a few miles and then rest. And no matter how tired we are, we must never stop being alert. There'll be things living out there that would love to chow down on us for our fluid alone."

"Agreed," Zhukov replied.

"Okay, I'll lead, Valentina next, and then you, Captain." Ally looked at Valentina who had her head down. "Valentina... *Valentina*..."

"Huh?" The woman looked up as though she had been nudged.

"Valentina, if you need to rest, say so. But you must try and stay with us, okay?" Ally tried to look into her face, but the woman's hair hung forward from under her makeshift head covering and obscured it. She nodded.

"Good. We'll be there soon. And there'll be food, water, and shade. You'll see." Ally turned away. "Let's go."

They headed out over the red desert and the miles of skillet-hot sand began to burn her feet through the soles of her boots. Ally tried to keep her wits about her, but the endless sameness was hypnotizing.

A dry breeze blew little ghosts of dust across their path, and its breath was the only thing breaking up the deathly silence and sterile dryness.

Or almost the only thing.

Ally lifted a hand and tilted her head. She could hear something. She had a rag tied over her mouth and nose to stop inhaling the chalk-dry dust and she tugged it down to sniff, long and slow.

"What is it?" Zhukov asked, tightening his grip on his gun.

"Like I said before, in the caves when without sight your other senses are amplified. One thing I used to be able to detect was fresh water—it has a sweet, subtle smell." Ally turned slowly. "And it's somewhere close."

Zhukov turned slowly. "Please find me an oasis like in the movies—with the palm trees, pool of clear, cool water, and maybe a nice fat bird or two."

"There's nothing," Valentina wearied. "I think the heat is cooking all our brains."

"Possibly," Ally said. She sighted on something. Her mind wondered at it. She pulled out her gun. "Time to take a risk."

She fired a round into one of the four-foot-high, clay-looking cones. The bullet struck it and the top two feet were blasted away.

She held the gun on it, waiting for some swarm to come bursting forth like a torrent of fire ants. Or maybe some long, whipping tongue to slither forth trying to grab anyone nearby.

But after many seconds, there was nothing.

She took a few steps closer. The half cone was now showing a larger hole in the top and darkness below.

"Cover me," she said over her shoulder as she crept forward.

Zhukov came with her and kept his gun trained on the cone. Valentina stayed back a few steps and kept watch on the surrounding landscape.

The first thing Ally did was pick up a stone the size of her fist and dart forward to drop it in the dark hole at the cone's top.

Nothing came launching out. But there was a surprising and most welcome noise—*a splash.*

She turned and grinned. "There's freaking water down there." She immediately pulled out her flashlight and shone it into the hole. She stared for a moment, the grin widening on her face. "It's moving water— – a river."

"Which direction?" Zhukov asked.

Ally stared for another moment, her eye and the flashlight sharing equal space over the six-inch hole.

She pointed. "That direction… *our* direction."

"Do you think…?" Zhukov's dusty brows were raised.

"It'd be too good to be true," Ally replied. She drew out her blade, and used the hilt to hack at the cone's base. Zhukov joined her and together they smashed out a ring at its base, and then the Russian pushed it over where it fell like a hollow tree trunk and broke apart. The trio then stood looking at the two-foot-wide hole in the ground.

Ally jammed her head in with her flashlight. After a moment, she scoffed. "It's a freaking river down there." She pulled back and turned with a half-smile. "Don't suppose either of you have an inflatable raft in those packs of yours?"

Zhukov grinned. "Ms. Ally Bennet, everything we need is right here." Zhukov grinned and pointed to one of the gnarled trees. "What do they teach you in the American military?"

"How to kill people," Ally chuckled. "Okay, I get it. We build a raft, of course."

Zhukov nodded. "We have knives, rope, wood, and much strength left." He put a hand over his brow and sighted into the distance. "Our only risk is if we are able to exit this underground river when we need to."

Ally grunted, knowing the Russian captain was right. She got down on her belly and leaned her head and arm with the light deep into the hole. She moved it around, examining what exactly was down there. She inhaled the blessed cool wetness that seemed like nirvana after the deathly dry desert they had been crossing. She pulled back and sat up.

"Fairly large river cave, easily ten feet across. And about the same distance to drop to the water. Can't tell how deep it is from here. And also, not sure how long it stays like that."

"You mean, our river might suddenly disappear into a hole below the ground," Zhukov said.

"Yeah, I do," she replied and leaned on her elbows. "So, here's the thing—the river is not moving all that fast. Backtracking is not impossible, but it will be damn hard."

Zhukov bobbed his head, and then looked at Valentina, who was like a shell of the woman who had started out with them.

"What I think is, if we try and cross much more desert, we will not make it. At least not all of us." He turned to Ally. "I vote we chance the river. Besides, if its fresh water, and therefore drinkable, it will replenish us."

"It smells like fresh water." Ally reached up to touch her dry, cracked lips. "Then there's one thing left to do…"

"Build a raft," Zhukov finished. He got to his feet, held out his hand to Ally, and hauled her up. He turned to the Russian doctor. "Valentina, I need you to keep watch for us, okay?" He handed her his near-empty water bottle. "Drink this, rest, and shout if you see or hear anything."

The woman nodded dreamily.

Ally turned about looking for the most suitable dead trees, and also ones as far away from the sand drifts as possible; she sighted three candidates. "There, there, and there. I'll take that one. We cut them down and drag them all back here to work on."

Zhukov grunted. "I think this will work." He pulled his long blade.

"So we begin."

***

Several hours later, Ally dragged her last logs to the stack near the hole in the ground. She let it drop and staggered a little, almost swooning from exhaustion.

Her throat was parched, and she had stopped perspiring now—a sign that dehydration was setting in. She closed her eyes and drew in a deep breath, filling her lungs, but had to quickly open them as her head began to spin.

She staggered to the side, and Zhukov was there to throw out an arm and grab her.

"Let's not go lying down now, yes?" He looked into her face.

"I'm sorry," she said and held a hand to her hot forehead.

"Why? You are the strongest woman I have ever met. Okay now, you sit and finish whatever water you have left. I'll prepare the raft, and then we can lower it down."

Ally nodded slowly, being too bombed out to resist. She knew Zhukov's preparation meant that he would lay out the materials as a physical blueprint because they couldn't assemble it above ground or it would never fit through the smallish hole. They'd just need to get an idea of how to put it together, lower it down, and then assemble it in the water cave—not ideal, but there was no other option.

It took the Russian only another three-quarters of an hour to have the main raft logs laid out, the cross beams, and also the rope. He stood to survey his work.

"It will do. Keeps us above water, and we have one paddle." He looked about. "First, we take sounding."

He grabbed up a stone and took his rope from his pack. He wound it around the rock and went to lay by the hole. He then dropped it down, letting the rope play out. The stone touched the water and sank down, only gently being pulled a little by the current.

In a few seconds, the rope went slack.

"Very good. Best news, only about three feet deep." He looked up. "We can stand to build our raft."

"Not a good idea being in the water," Ally replied.

"I know," he replied. "But the only other option is to assemble the raft suspended in the air, and that would require a lot more rope, and a lot more strong arms—neither we have right now, Ally Bennet." He smiled.

"Ally… just call me Ally." She returned the smile. "No one has called me that in nearly a year."

He shrugged. "My friends call me Viktor. So not many people call me Viktor." He laughed for a moment before getting serious. "But you can."

Ally got to her feet to go and pat his shoulder. "Viktor." She then walked around the raft framework. "Good work. It will do."

"It will have to." He then knelt and set to bundling all the wood into three piles and lashing them together. "This one first. Then this, then lastly this," he said.

He looked up at her. "And I get to go first." He got to his feet.

Ally stared into his face. "Do you know, when we first came here, my mission profile was to hunt you Russian guys down and stop you by any and all means?"

He nodded, knowing exactly what that *any-and-all-means* meant.

"You're a good person, and I think we are the same." She gave him a crooked smile.

Zhukov shrugged. "We are sometimes hostage to the politics of war." He reached up to grasp her hand. "And now, wish me luck."

She squeezed his hand and released him. The captain dragged the first bundle to the hole's edge and the rest he laid out, awaiting their turn to be lowered down to him. He then set about tying a loop around his waist and securing it to the closest boulder.

He tested it, went to the hole, took a last look down, and then turned around and began to wriggle backward into the hole. Holding the edge, he paused.

"Wish me luck."

"Good luck." Ally got down on her belly and looked into his face. "I'll cover you."

He nodded, his face a little pale, and then dropped backward. Ally slid forward and shone her light down, watching him drop the ten feet or so to the water.

Zhukov waited a few seconds, holding the rope and spinning slowly. He held out an arm with his flashlight and panned it around.

"It's cool in here. Can't see anything unfriendly above the water." So, he let himself lower down to the water.

He sunk into his waist. "It's solid underfoot, rocky." He took one last look around and then back up. "Lower the first batch of wood." He went to untie himself.

"No, keep yourself lashed up. We've got extra rope, and if you need to get out quickly…"

"*Hmm*, yes, yes, good idea." He left the rope at his waist and raised his arms as Ally slid the wood forward and lowered it.

Zhukov untied it and quickly began to lash the base together while doing a great job of stopping any stray bits from floating away.

Ally slid in the next batch, and the Russian captain then anchored the support beams to the structure. The last tranche of wood was a strengthening layer for the top and his large paddling stick. Zhukov tested it and nodded his approval.

"Won't win any races, but good enough." He looked up. "Lower the packs and come down. Valentina first."

Ally tied Valentina to the rope and helped ease her down. Zhukov grabbed her legs and guided her onto the deck of the raft, where she sat cross-legged. He handed her the packs and the paddle.

Up top, Ally untied all the rope, including Zhukov's tether, took one last look around, and then wriggled backward into the hole. She lowered herself down to her fingertips, hung for a second or two, and then allowed herself to drop.

Zhukov caught her. He held onto her. "You're a very capable woman."

She grinned. "That's the nicest thing anyone has ever said to me." She softly punched him in the chest and quickly panned her light around. She looked up into his face. "So, how's the water?"

"I don't know." He cupped some in his hand and lifted it to his lips to sip. He swallowed and then began to slowly nod. "Clean, is okay."

That was enough for Valentina, who leaned over the side of the raft to gulp down water. Ally brought some to her face to sip first, and then swallow great drafts. Finally, she used more to rub the grime and dust from her face.

"Oh God, that's good." She splashed some through her hair.

After a few more minutes, they had their water bottles refilled and already felt better.

"We needed that," she said.

Zhukov checked his GPS. "Time to leave. All aboard." He held the raft as Ally clambered on.

He did the same, and the raft sank to the waterline but stayed afloat. There was little room left and only enough for the Russian man to sit with his feet over the edge. The raft was barely above water and Ally knew that if they encountered anything aggressive, they'd be screwed. But she guessed that if they tried to trek one more mile above ground, they would have been doubly screwed.

Zhukov picked up the paddle and used it to keep them facing forward, as the current was already starting to move them along just a little under walking pace.

As they continued, every hundred feet or so, they encountered a shaft of red light that in the darkness was as bright as a laser beam.

"Probably more of those cones," a much revived Valentina remarked.

"I wonder what made them?" Ally asked.

"Could it be a natural thing?" Zhukov asked. "Maybe this place floods now and then and the water pushed upward."

"Down here, the rules of biology and geology are different. So that could well be true. Or it might be something else again." Ally shone her light at the walls and for the first time noticed that there were green mosses covering some areas.

She wasn't a biologist, but she remembered from her past trip that this simple organism was usually the basis of a food chain. Where there was moss, there were tiny things that fed on it. And where there were tiny things, there were bigger things to feed on them. She just hoped that there wasn't anything large enough down here to feed on them.

They were all still armed, but down in the dark, she knew that the night-hunters always had the advantage.

***

Two hours in and Zhukov had to do little more than keep them from touching the walls as they drifted in the current. All Ally needed to do was strain her above-average hearing to listen to the sounds of the river cave. But so far, she heard nothing unusual.

Even the walls and ceiling had been mostly smoothed by the millennia of soft rubbing of the languid stream. And where it wasn't smooth, it was coated in a layer of cushioning moss.

She shone her light at the ceiling, and rather than dagger-sharp stalactites hanging there, she saw round lumps the size of miners' helmets that she could only guess at how they were formed. *Rock blisters*, she thought.

Valentina tried to pull her knees up and keep as far from the dark water as she could manage. Ally didn't blame her one bit. Everything down here seemed dangerous.

"How much further?" the Russian doctor asked.

"I'll check." Zhukov handed Ally the paddle and he looked at his

GPS. He bobbed his head from side to side for a moment. "Probably another five miles. At this speed, maybe three hours."

"Three hours," Valentina repeated wearily.

Ally inhaled. "This air down here is so pure. Something, maybe the lichens, must be producing oxygen."

She exhaled with a whoosh and pulled out her flashlight. She had been preserving her light's batteries but switched it on now and scanned the mats of lichen on the walls. There were a few more varieties in the crevices that hung with bulbs like glistening grapes, and she had the horrible impression they pulsated as if breathing.

Ally shone the light around one last time. There was little to see other than impenetrably dark water, the cave walls, dripping with mosses and lichen, and a ceiling hanging with the rounded nodules.

She didn't mind if it was boring because boring was safe, boring meant life. She sighed and handed Zhukov back his paddle.

Three hours, she thought. She could almost grab some sleep.

***

Ally's exhalations combined with the breath of Valentina and Zhukov soon filled the tunnel with a wave of carbon monoxide, as well as the smell of warm animal. It changed the environment, even if it was only temporarily.

The scent of the humans was dragged along with them in a wave just behind the raft, and as the gases passed over the walls and ceilings, changes occurred. The main ones were the rounded things on the cave ceiling lifted and a swathe of small eyes on tentacles appeared first. Then came strong, sharp legs that extended along with powerful, grasping claws.

Like a wave of army crabs, the many-legged things began to move along the ceiling, following the delicious scent of the warm human beings.

***

Zhukov poked the wall again with his paddle-stick to ease them a little further out into the center of the stream as they moved near silently down its length.

Ally turned to Valentina and examined the woman closely. She seemed to have physically improved with better hydration, but she still looked haunted with dark rings under sunken eyes. She guessed the woman had been in her late thirties, but now with her blonde hair matted, grimy face, and disheveled appearance, she looked at least a decade older.

She wanted to try and lift the woman's spirits. "Val?"

The woman looked up.

"Do they call you that, *Val*? Val for short?" Ally smiled. "My full name is Allison, Ally, for short."

Valentina shook her head. "No, nobody calls me Val. It is always Valentina." She looked back down at her hands.

"Can I call you Val?" Ally persisted.

Valentina shrugged. "Okay, sure, I don't mind."

"Thank you, Val. So, what's the first thing you'll do when you get home?" Ally tried again.

The woman lifted her sunken gaze again. "Have a chemical bath…" She shared a fragile smile, "… and take a big dose of iodine."

Ally tilted her head. "For the radiation, huh?"

"Yes. It is debilitating and deadly." She pointed. "Look at your arms."

Ally didn't need to. She knew the lesions were there. Plus, she had felt their soft crustiness on her neck and back. She remembered the old Russian woman named Katya; it wasn't a great path ahead for her.

"That was from my time before. I've been down here or in some sort of mid-world, for around a year. You'll be fine." Ally was determined to get the woman's thinking on something positive, so she tried one last time. "Do you have children, a husband, or a lover maybe?" she asked.

Valentina tilted her head back and her eyes took on a faraway look. "Sergei, at the base. Sometimes my lover, sometimes my boss, and sometimes a pain in the ass." She looked to Ally, and for the first time, really smiled.

"I'm not married," Ally replied. "But I'm always on the lookout for the next Mr. Right." She chuckled. "Or the next Mr. Right Now will usually do."

Valentina's smile widened. "We wouldn't talk to them if they didn't have penis, yes?"

"Yeah." Ally snorted loudly.

Zhukov looked back over his shoulder. "You know I have ears, yes? As well as a penis."

Both women shared a look and then laughed out loud, their voices carrying up and down the dark water-filled cave.

"Quiet," Zhukov hissed. He checked his GPS. "Not long now." He paused for a moment. "But the gentle river current has meant we have been moving downhill for the last few hours. We may be several dozen feet deep now, and I've seen none of the cone-pipes in the ceiling for a long time."

"I know," Ally sighed. "We'll need to plan our exit soon. Do you still have some grenades?" she asked.

"Yes, but last resort only." He turned away.

As they continued, Ally noticed that the smooth walls were now more riven with cracks and rents, and then a few hundred yards further on, they came to their first side cave; that might have been the good news for a possible way up, but the bad news was their little river was beginning to increase in its flow speed.

It was still silent, as there wasn't the hint of a ripple or wave yet, but for the first time Ally thought she could hear some sort of background noise.

She turned then pulled her flashlight and shone it back at the cave they had just traveled from.

Zhukov also looked over his shoulder. "What is it?"

She continued to stare, lifting her light. Ally shut her eyes for a moment and concentrated on listening. There it was: a hard, clicking sound, a little like distant chopsticks. She opened her eyes.

"Something is coming. It's just out of reach of our lights."

"Oh no," Valentina whispered.

"Then, we speed up." Zhukov began to paddle for the first time.

He dug the makeshift oar in deep and dragged it back along the raft on one side, and then the other. The oar wasn't very flat, and the raft wasn't built for speed, but it did manage to give them a lift above the current's languid pace.

"Still there?" Zhukov asked.

Ally listened hard and held up a finger as she concentrated. After another few moments, the sound didn't seem to be gaining on them. But the odd thing was the Russian captain's voice echoed, even more than usual.

The stream they were paddling on finally came to its end and it poured them into a vast underground lake. They were pushed out about forty to fifty feet, but shining their lights around, the walls seemed distant and the ceiling now around a hundred feet over their heads.

There were a few red pinholes in the ceiling, indicating there might be more of the cone-pipes way up there.

"So, that is how far we are now underground," Zhukov said and dug his oar and arm down but couldn't find the bottom. "It's deep in here."

"Take us to the side," Ally said softly. "If it's deep, I don't want us out in the middle. Because that'll be where the big things live."

Zhukov paddled them back to the wall close to where they exited from the river cave. He placed the tip of the oar onto the rocks to anchor them. "What now?" he asked.

"We can't see the end of the lake so we have no idea how large it is. If there's an exit, we may spend days looking for it… if there even is one."

Zhukov nodded. "It must drain away somewhere as the stream is filling it. But for all we know, it drains below the surface."

"Yeah," Ally replied softly.

Zhukov checked his GPS. "Less than a mile short of where we want to be. Now is the time to leave."

"Let's do that." Valentina's voice was trembly.

Ally looked up, and then slowly lowered her light beam down along the wall. "It'd be a tough climb. Probably some of it free-climbing. If we had more equipment, it might be possible." She glanced at Valentina. "But we're tired, short of rope, and just about everything." She sighed. "We might need another option."

"Then we need to find another stream to continue our journey. We skirt the outside of the lake." Zhukov shrugged. "There must be other openings."

"And what if the other openings are not in the direction we want to go?" Valentina asked. "Or they keep going lower?"

"Yeah, personally, I'll be happy if any river exit is uphill. It'll be hard to paddle against a current, but we need to get closer to the surface, so if we need to climb, we can do it." Ally shone her light around. "There are more side caves here." She smiled. "I'm feeling confident."

Zhukov winked at her. "I'm always confident." He looked both ways. "Left or right?"

"I think…" Ally held up a hand. "Wait…." She narrowed her eyes. "Can you hear…?"

"Is that a breeze blowing up?" Valentina asked.

"No." Zhukov's head snapped around to the cave they had just exited from.

Just then, the cave mouth vomited a boiling mass of scuttling creatures. They immediately spread to the left, right, and up the wall, as they poured from the dark interior.

Ally's eyes widened. "This is what I heard following us."

"Get away from the wall, get away from the wall." Valentina tried to paddle with her hands.

Zhukov rammed the oar into the rocky cave edge and pushed hard. They only scudded out about six feet but it wasn't enough, as some of the closest creatures began to leap at them.

The dinner-plate-sized arthropods spread ten sharp legs wide. The first arrival, Ally batted aside with her flashlight, but others landed on and among them.

Zhukov yelled as one of the things struck his shoulder and clung there. It immediately set to digging in its legs and using its powerful, sharp pincer claws to try and pull pieces of his flesh away.

More thudded like falling meteorites onto the raft. Ally turned and began to drag, kick, and smash them, but their armor plating was far too thick, and their blows were ineffectual.

The raft was still within landing distance and fighting the crab things meant less movement.

"Just fucking paddle!" Ally yelled.

She resorted to trying to knock them off the raft where they momentarily sank but then bobbed back to the surface. For every one she managed to dislodge, another two took their place.

Zhukov ignored one of the things clinging to his back and began to strike with his oar. Valentina shrieked as one of them landed heavily on her head and used its sharp pincers to snip off the tip of her ear and jam the tiny pink piece of cartilage and flesh into its buzzsaw-like mouthparts.

Ally did her best to try and keep them free, and she herself was covered in cuts and abrasions. Whatever the things were, they were aggressive, strong, and hungry—*just like every damn thing down here*, she thought furiously.

"Shit." The walls were now a moving tableau of waving pincers, pointed legs, and armored bodies as more and more poured from the cave mouth.

And then the bigger ones started to arrive. The crab creatures had started out the size of miners' helmets, but the bigger ones were now as big around as manhole covers, with clawed pincers a foot long. Ally knew that if the small ones could cause as much damage to them, the big ones would easily take off a limb.

In minutes more, they were fifty feet out into the center of the lake.

"Fuck off." Ally kicked the last invader from their raft, and then looked up.

"Oh no." Valentino pointed. "They can swim."

"What?" Ally swung to where the Russian female doctor was pointing her light. Sure enough, the bigger crab things had taken to the water. They used their legs like oars, and the smooth round backs and waving eyes on tentacle stalks were all that was above the water line. And they were coming fast.

There were dozens, and worse, there was one now exiting the cave mouth that was easily as big as their raft.

"*Paddle, paddle.*" Ally dropped to her knees and began to use both hands to shovel water backward. Valentina did the same from the other side.

But even with all three of them frantically rowing, the crustaceans were more adept at swimming and were gaining, fast.

Ally glanced over her shoulder, and then just kept her head down, counting her strokes to take her mind off the approaching horde. And then she saw the shadow pass underneath them. Then another. And they were big.

She sat bolt upright. "Hands out of the water. *Now!*" she shouted.

"What?" Zhukov did as asked and then spun to her. "Why?"

"Something in the water," Ally grimaced. "We need... to get out."

"What is it?" Valentina shrieked while holding a hand over her bloody ear.

The first of the big spider-crabs only had a half dozen feet to get to the raft, when suddenly it vanished below the surface in a swirl of water. Then another, and another.

Zhukov stared. "What's happening?"

Suddenly, a huge greyish body lifted from the surface among the swimming arthropod creatures. It went over the top of them and when it submerged again, about a dozen of the swimming things, large and small, were gone.

"They're eating them." Valentina began to laugh a little madly.

The crab thing's small eyes on the end of their twitching stalks were becoming more agitated, and then like a retreating armada they began to turn and swim back to the rocky shoreline, perhaps now thinking that the meal on the raft wasn't going to be as easy to catch as first thought.

"Now's our chance. We need to get out of here." Ally saw that the spider-crabs were retreating into the cave. "Head to the shallows at the cave wall. I don't know what the hell these big things under the water are, but I don't want them suddenly wanting to see if we're edible or not."

Zhukov paddled them back to the wall as the smooth, grey lumps of large backs rose and fell among the retreating spider-crabs.

"Maybe they're like whales," Valentina offered. "They can be friendly."

"Down here? Not a chance." Ally helped Zhukov paddle.

As if to put to bed the Russian woman's suggestion, there was one of the biggest spider-crabs up on the wall. The thing must have been four feet across, and its muscular pincers looked powerful enough to cut them in half if it got hold of them.

It edged along the wall, and when it was just a dozen feet from the cave entrance, something rose before it, higher, and higher still, until it was a long length of muscle and glistening grey flesh in the light of their flashlights.

Along the length of the water creature, small arms or legs opened wide, one set on each of the segments.

"Not a whale, more like some sort of giant caterpillar," Ally said.

The massive thing's end opened in a giant maw and it slammed forward to totally cover the fleeing spider-crab.

With a crackle and crunch, the arthropod was ground up as the whale caterpillar pulled back into the water.

Ally looked to Zhukov and his eyes told her exactly what she already knew—the things were big enough to eat them as well.

While the feeding frenzy was finishing, the trio worked to move their raft around the perimeter of the underground lake.

They passed several rock platforms at the water's edge, and on some, laying out like basking seals, were the grotesque pipe-like creatures, but thankfully much smaller.

"Seems they only stay in the water when they're bigger," Ally whispered.

"Or older," Valentina replied. "Maybe the juvenile stage is less aquatic."

As they eased past, trying to be as silent as possible, one of the creatures must have got spooked and began to inch upward. The three-foot-long caterpillar glistened in their flashlight beams, and its tiny grasping arms at the front pulled the long, grey bag-like body up the cliff wall.

"Look," Ally urged.

It headed up toward a dot of red light in the ceiling, which was one of the cones they had encountered to enter the river cave. The thing climbed and slithered vertically and didn't stop when it got to the hole, it kept going until it vanished outside.

"So, they really are only semi-aquatic," Ally scoffed. "And now we know who made the cones."

"Maybe they start out as something different altogether," Valentina mused. "Maybe another species of the sandworms we encountered."

Ally and Zhukov were at the front of the raft, with Ally sitting and the Russian captain kneeling and using the paddle. Ally shone her light up and around the walls.

"The cliff walls are getting more broken up with more hand and toe-holds. We might be able to climb soon. At the top, we can open one of those cone entrances and climb out," she said.

"Do you think the worms will bother us?" he asked.

"They might. But they're not so big, and there's not a lot of them," she replied, sniffed, but then frowned. "You smell something?"

***

At the rear of the raft, Valentina listened to her two companions as they worked on a way out. She felt nothing was in her control anymore, and she was just a hostage to strange events now. She never signed up to come here to this center of the Earth hell. She still felt she was living in some sort of nightmare and any second expected to wake up and find she had been sleeping on the chopper ride to the Kola Borehole.

For some reason, that made her smile.

She was lost in her reverie and didn't hear the slight tinkle of water or smell the overpowering stink of something from the depths of the Hadean-dark, slime-filled lake. But she did feel the drops of cold water as they began to tinkle down on her.

There was no shadow, of course, but a sixth sense screamed at her to turn around. She did. And wished she hadn't.

Looming over her was something that froze her blood. One of the lake worms, as wide around as a pine tree and rising twenty feet in the air, hung over their raft.

The small gripping legs along the side of its head flared wide and even though there were no discernible eyes, the Russian woman knew it saw her.

The great stinking hole of a mouth opened wide, displaying a perfect ring of comb-like teeth.

Valentina was like a small rabbit in the hunter's spotlight and could do nothing but sit frozen with her eyes wide as the mouth came down... and over her.

***

The raft rocked hard, and Ally and Zhukov glanced at each other then spun.

Valentina wasn't there anymore.

"*No.*" Ally half got to her feet, ready to dive into the water, but Zhukov lunged for her and grabbed the back of her pants, dragging her backward.

"Don't..." he pointed, "...*look.*"

About two dozen feet from the rear of their raft, a broad, glistening body lumped the water surface and then went under again. But it wasn't the only one. There were others now. They were the big ones that had obviously finished dining on the spider crabs and, drawn to the area by the abundant food, were still hunting. The humans on the raft would be easy pickings.

"Oh no." She eased back down.

One of them glided closer, making a V-shaped wave in the inky water.

"We need to, we need to..." she began but knew there was no way they'd out-paddle the huge thing.

"Off the raft!" Zhukov yelled.

He grabbed up his pack and made a lunge for Valentina's pack as well. Then with them looped over one arm, he used the pole-paddle to drag them close to the ledge where the young worms basked. He tossed the bags.

Ally leaped onto the ledge, followed by Zhukov. The pair ran to the wall and as far back from the water as they could, and watched as their raft was smashed from below and then pulled under.

Zhukov went to one knee and pointed his gun back at the dark lake. One of the creatures rose, towering above them, dripping water. The pair stayed still as stone and watched the thing for several moments.

They couldn't see any eyes on it, and maybe it was sensing for movement, or heat, or scent, or something else. After another moment, it slid back below the water.

Zhukov lowered his weapon. "Poor Valentina," he said softly, and then lowered his head. "My team, all of them, now gone."

"This place." Ally sighed and rested a hand lightly on his shoulder.

"Yes, this place," Zhukov replied and crossed himself while whispering his lost friend's names. He slowly got to his feet.

"Fuck off." Ally kicked one of the small worms that had started to investigate her boot. Thankfully, the others ignored them.

The pair looked out over the lake and watched as the huge bodies patrolled the dark water, some of the backs that breached easily the size of whales. They stayed as far back from the edge of the rock shelf as they could manage. But it was still a risk, as given the small ones were equally at home on land and water, then maybe the big ones had no problem coming up onto the shelf when they wanted to.

"So, we're committed now." Zhukov turned away from the dark lake, and the pair both looked up to the dot of red light a hundred feet, straight up, above their heads.

"Yup." Ally exhaled loudly through her nose. "I get the feeling that sooner or later one of those big bastards is coming up here, and I don't want to be here when it does."

"Agreed," Zhukov said while running his light over the crags and crevices of the rock wall. "I think it can be done. Maybe."

"*Hmm.*" She turned to him with a half-smile. "You ever free-climbed?"

"I have done a lot of cave and cliff climbing. But not free-climb," the Russian replied warily. "Is the same but without ropes, yes?"

She grinned. "Is the same, but ten times more deadly."

He nodded. "Good, I was getting bored." Zhukov then moved his light up a broken seam in the cave wall. "We can climb easily along there." He lifted his light. "And then this shelf of stone will get us close." He sighed. "But then there is just cave roof for twenty feet out over the water. Maybe hand holds, but that's all."

Ally nodded. "Well, if you slip, it won't be the fall that kills you." She looked back to the dark water still being patrolled by the leviathans.

Just as they turned away, something splashed close behind them, sending a surge wave up over their rocky platform. Both whipped around, but nothing was climbing behind them.

"Well, I'll take that as a little incentive to get moving." She took her pack off her shoulders. "Throw out everything we don't need and keep Valentina's pack, as we don't know how much harder the trek will be if, *ah,* when, we emerge."

Zhukov set to work rummaging in his pack. Their water bottles had remained full, and they had little to throw away, but they held onto the last scraps of food, their weapons, last ammunition, and their remaining fleshy bulbs of the cactus-like plants. They pulled their packs back on, and Ally shook her head.

"Too heavy." She looked up. "We need to ditch some of the weapons."

Zhukov's brows went up. "That will be suicide."

She remained looking up. "It'll be suicide if we don't."

The Russian stood firm. "No, we climb with the packs until we need to free-climb the ceiling. We remove them and wedge them in the rocks and tie a rope from us to them. If we make it to the hole, and can climb it, then we can recover the packs."

Ally looked back up, working the angles. They could get to within twenty feet of the hole, and they had a good fifty feet of rope. She nodded. "Okay, Viktor, doable." She slapped Zhukov on the shoulder. "So, let's do it."

Ally led the way, skirting the pipes of living flesh that lay on the rock shelf and even jammed in the cracks of the wall. The pair followed a natural rift upward for about fifty feet before they had to ease across to another crack. It took them another thirty minutes to get to the shelf of stone that they slithered along, and then reached its end.

Ally looked down; they were about eighty feet up, and with little light on the lake, it was nothing but darkness below them. That was good, as the last thing she wanted to see was the beasts circling in the dark water like a school of monstrous sharks.

They both slid their packs off, and Ally withdrew her length of rope. She drew Zhukov's pack closer to hers, and she tied one end of the rope around both pack's shoulder straps. Lastly, she checked the long blade she had strapped to her hip to make sure the hilt band was keeping it in place.

"I go first," she said.

He shook his head. "No, I think I am strongest and should—"

"Thanks, Sir Galahad, but you don't need to. I'm lighter and an experienced free-climber." She looked toward the shaft of red light that seemed to be coming from a hole no bigger than her fist.

"Okay, here's the plan. I'm going to climb across, and hopefully will be able to break through the clay cone. Then I'll climb out and tie the rope off." She snapped the rope between her fists. "This stuff is elasticized rope and extremely strong—it'll hold a small elephant. That means it'll hold the packs *and* you. You can climb it out."

"Good." He laughed softly. "Because I'm sure I was going to fall."

"I won't let you fall. Ever." She held his eyes for a moment before turning away.

Ally mentally mapped out her route, noting the handholds, toe placement positions, and risk spots. Thankfully, it looked dry and maybe that was due to it being so close to the vent and the red, bone-dry atmosphere outside.

She then drew in a deep breath, also sucking in all the courage she could muster. "Here goes nothing."

She reached out a hand and grabbed a small knob of rock, tested it, and then stretched out a leg to a toe hold. It held. And then she was off.

Ally scaled slowly. Her arms and legs were still not as strong as she would have liked, but the lower muscle mass from being underweight meant she had less bulk to pull upward.

In a few moments, she was halfway and refused to look back or down, instead staying focused on the red dot of light ahead of her.

She clung for a moment like a human spider and tried to work out her next handhold. There was a tiny crevice she thought she could jam a couple of her now abraded fingers into and stretched toward it.

As she wormed her fingers into it, she felt something soft that wriggled.

"*Fuck.*"

She jerked her hand back as a luminous blob of jelly with a dozen legs scuttled out, looked at her once with too many unreadable button eyes, and kept on going along the rock face.

"You creepy little bastard." Ally calmed her breathing and reached for the crevice again. This time, nothing was disturbed, and she hung for a moment to compose herself.

After another few seconds, she looked toward her destination—only another few feet until it started up into the beginning of the cone.

She started off again but purposely slowed herself. She remembered that overeagerness can cause mistakes, so even though her fingers, wrists, biceps, and shoulders screamed at her, and she just wanted it over, she forced herself to be patient as she scaled up into the base of the cone.

The red heat was like a laser beam as it fell on her skin after the many hours in the total darkness of the cool river cave. And as she wedged herself in, she rested her head for a moment and closed her eyes.

"I'm in," she yelled.

"Very good," the faint voice of Zhukov yelled back. "Can you see anything?"

"Not yet." She reached down to carefully pull out her long blade and began to dig it into the base of the clay cone. After several minutes, she had punched a hole roughly the size of a baseball through the clay matrix, and she put her eye up to it.

The heat and light stung her but when her vision cleared, she saw there was nothing but red, dry earth.

She groaned. "Desert. More damn desert."

She had hoped for some sort of forest, or at least for some sort of cover. She hoped it was worth it, losing Valentina, and she began to smash more of the cone out.

Ally paused for a moment. *What about things being outside waiting for me?* she wondered. She rejected the idea as they had no choice; they were marooned with their backs literally to the wall.

She doubled her efforts, smashing and hacking until a foot-wide piece of clay fell outward.

"Ow." A blast of red heat bathed her face and she squinted from the full assault on her eyes.

"Okay?" Zhukov yelled.

"Yeah, yeah, it's just red, hot, and dry," she replied

There was still nothing moving about outside or any risk she could see so she continued her hacking, working her way around the pipe until the entire cone shifted. She then reached up and pushed it, toppling the cone to the side where it fell onto the dry, cracked earth and shattered like a clay pot.

"We're out," she yelled back down.

Ally then turned to look behind her for the first time, and a huge grin split her face.

"A goddamn forest!" she yelled.

She heard Zhukov's muffled reply and briefly looked down. But now after being in the red light, anything below her in the darkness was impossible to see. She quickly hauled herself out and pulled along some of the rope tied to her waist with her.

In a few more seconds, she found a stout rock that was perfect for tying the rope around. She tested it, and then went back to the hole in the ground, and leaned in.

"Rope is secured, come on up."

She continued to lay down, looking back into the darkness, and felt the rope being slowly pulled back down for a moment until it was tight.

Then it strained as weight was added to it.

The rope swung from one side of the hole to the other as the man must have been swinging free now. She made sure it never got hung up on one side of the hole lest it become abraded and cut. She then hung her arm down with the flashlight and saw the Russian captain, no more than ten feet down, slowly pulling himself up.

"Nearly there," she said with her lips curled up in a smile.

In seconds more, his head breached the hole, and he blinked a few times and looked around. Ally grabbed his shirt and dragged him up and out, where he rolled to lay on his back for a moment.

He turned his face to her. "Thank you."

She leaned over him and kissed his forehead. "We made it."

"This far, you mean." And he sat up. "But yes, we survived the cave." He turned back and gave a small salute. "Thank you for your service, assistance, and friendship, Doctor Valentina Adrina Sechin."

"Adrina. I never knew her full name." Ally also saluted. "I won't forget it."

Zhukov got to his feet and held out his hand. Ally took it and he hauled her up.

"I hate this place, but I hated down there even more," she said.

Zhukov looked at her, and then looked harder.

"What?" She frowned.

"Your skin…" He lifted her hair back off her face.

"God, is it worse?" She held fingers to her cheek.

"No, looks, better. Much better." He pushed her hair back behind her ear.

Ally trailed her fingers over where she knew the lesions had started. They seemed to have shrunk. And some weren't there at all anymore.

"Maybe you hated the caves, but maybe they were good for you," he said with a half smile.

"And maybe it's just all the dirt washed off." She placed a hand over her eyes and turned about. "A few more hours out in this and I'll be right back to how I was." She sighed and began to rummage in her kit. "And I'm starving." All she saw was a few of the fleshy cactus-like bulb-leaves. "And I'm definitely sick of sucking on these things. Last resort only."

Zhukov chuckled. "Well then. Let's see where we are, and how much more we have to travel." He checked his GPS and turned slowly. In a moment, he stopped and looked up toward the forest. "We're close," and then he suddenly craned forward, frowning at the device.

"What?" she asked. "Problem?"

He began to laugh and looked up, his eyes beaming. "You want some more good news? Another signal blip appeared on the GPS—it must be the other team."

Ally closed her eyes and rocked her head back on her neck. "Thank you, thank you, thank you." She then grabbed the man and pretended to waltz with him for a few seconds.

"Home," she said and let him go. "*Home*! I'm going home!" she yelled to the boiling red sky.

CHAPTER 17

"Hey." Joshua Loche had stopped them on the cliff top and frowned down at his GPS.

"What is it?" Jane asked.

"Croft, Angel, what do you make of this?" Loche asked.

The two men slung their rifles and came to look at the small device. The others also crowded around.

"That's weird. Says there's another team down here. Who could that be?" Croft asked.

"Malfunction?" Angel asked, then snapped his fingers. "Hey, could it be the Russian woman you left behind? Or maybe an old device from the last mission?"

"Katya didn't have any GPS or other devices," Mike said. "And I'd be surprised if any device would keep working nearly a year in these harsh conditions."

"Maybe you're right. But the signature is moving." Loche looked up. "And it's converging on our position, from the north. So, we're gonna find out real soon."

"Wait a minute." Janus blew air from between his lips and held a hand to his forehead. "This is mind blowing." He continued to hold his forehead. "There was another mission we sent that entered in Russia via the Kola Superdeep Borehole."

"Russians?" Mike asked.

"Yes." Janus paced for a moment. "They were never meant to come to the center of the Earth, only travel as far down as necessary to rescue Ally Bennet." He turned and held up a finger. "But what if something went wrong? What if they were forced to come all the way?"

"Did they know about our mission?" Loche asked.

"Yes, I'm sure they did," Janus replied.

"No way they could survive without help," Matt said.

"Then that's what they're looking for. If it was me, I'd try and improve my odds of survival by linking up with another team." Loche pulled his small field glasses from his pack and scanned the forest edge ahead, and then the line of red desert. After a moment, he lowered them.

"Do we link up, or do we proceed?" Jane asked.

"We proceed," Janus shot back. "We have a mission."

"If they managed to rescue Ally, I vote we link up," Mike shot back.

"Why?" Janus' brows were up. "They're going to come to us anyway. I'm betting they're tracking us as well. We continue on, they'll catch up—two birds, one stone, right?"

Jane turned to Joshua Loche. "What do you think?"

Loche's face was devoid of expression. "Mr. Anderson is right. The mission is the priority. We proceed on course."

"Good man." Janus nodded.

"But." He lifted his gaze to Jane. "We move slowly, and maybe allow our mystery party to catch up to us. Besides…" He nodded to the children. "Little legs can't move that fast anyway, right?"

Jane smiled and nodded.

The group set off again and spent the next few hours winding their way down from the cliff top at the end of the jungle valley and toward the plain. There was still plenty of forest left to navigate, but then they expected to be out on the desert within a few more hours.

Croft led them through a wall of large-leafed ferns, and they came out onto a pleasant-looking meadow with a stream running through it. The large trees overhead had grown to create a canopy roof, just allowing filtered red twilight to shine through.

There was a soft ground cover like a fleshy clover on the broad, flat riverbanks, and twenty feet back there were types of wildflowers—some had iridescent bells that looked like stained glass, others had upward-facing white cups with blood-red stamens, and some even had an occasional crimson bulb that was like a tulip but with a closed end and a soft glow inside like it was lit within.

Loche checked his GPS. "Okay, people, this is the last green area before we hit the desert. We take a break, recharge, and then we head out." He looked about. "Croft, Angel, take first watch. Jane, can you check that water is drinkable? If it is, I want everyone to fill their canteens before we set out."

Jane nodded and quickly searched for her water-testing kit.

Matt settled the children in the shade, and Loche shucked off his heavy pack. "Everyone else, take a break… but leave one eye open. And no one rest underneath any goddamn red apples." He dropped his pack, sat in a pool of shade, and briefly glanced upward.

After Jane had given the stream water her seal of approval, Mike and Jane sat together, and he lay down with his head on his pack. She did the same and turned to him.

"Wish I never found that stupid manuscript, or met with Katya, or brought you down here." He sighed. "I'm sorry." His voice trailed away.

She saw his eyes glistened. "It's funny," she began. "Sometimes, I think we never left. That we stayed and we only dreamed we went back to the surface. That in reality we've been here the whole time."

"That'd be a nightmare," he replied.

"I don't know, is it? You said that we'd do something that no one else has ever done before. That we'd see wondrous things. And you were right." She sat up and hugged her knees. "There are terrible dangers and unbelievable wonders." She held out an arm and pulled up her sleeve, exposing the red, crusted lesions. "But there is a price to pay for the knowledge and adventure."

"A terrible price," Mike sighed.

She lay back down. "I have one request."

He propped himself up on an elbow. "Anything. What is it?"

"Next time, ask someone else to come with you." She laughed softly.

Mike reached out and took her hand. "We'll make it out, don't worry. And I don't know if this is hell or paradise, but I do know I'm glad I'm sharing it with you."

She smiled broadly and brought her face a little closer to his. "I can tell you one thing—it isn't paradise." She lay back and looked around. "But this place looks familiar."

"Yeah, I thought so too," he said and eased up on one elbow. "I think this was the oasis before we set out onto the desert." He drew in a deep breath. "It was the calm before the storm."

"But then we had the *Y'ha-nthlei* on our asses." She looked around. "But where are they now? I don't think we wiped them out."

"Neither do I. But really, if we never see them again, that's a good thing." He turned at the sound of splashing from the stream and saw Loche step into the shallow water, quickly bend forward, and grab hold of something then throw it up on the grassy bank.

The silver torpedo thrashed and flipped. "Fish," Loche said.

Sure enough, it looked like a small mackerel, with a strong body and yellow fins. There were a few catfish-like feelers around its nose, but other than that, it looked normal.

"There's more." He turned to Matt Kearns. "Matt, get in here and help me grab a few more. We've got a lot of mouths to feed now." He paused before going back to his task. "Croft, start a fire."

In ten more minutes, the two men had caught a dozen good-sized, fat fish, which Loche expertly cleaned with his knife, finding no scales, just a leathery skin which he stripped and then threaded onto sticks to hold over the fire.

The smell was intoxicating after living on food bars and dried fruit, which was rapidly dwindling anyway. The children looked interested, and Matt pulled off several cooked fish pieces and loaded a broad leaf up with the hot white flesh and then handed it to them.

"Try this." He lay it down before the group of children who simply stared at the strange meat.

Matt picked a small piece up to put in his mouth. He spoke softly in their language and their eyes went to the food again. He smiled and mimed rubbing his stomach. "Yummy," he said.

Jane watched as one of the older boys reached for a small piece and sniffed it before popping it into his mouth. He chewed thoughtfully, and then spoke softly to the other children.

That seemed good enough as the other children's hands darted out, grabbing handfuls and stuffing it into their mouths.

Matt turned. "They approve." He stood to go and get another fish for them.

Each adult then took a portion on a broad green leaf and ate with their fingers. Jane smiled as she ate, the oil coating her lips.

"Okay, maybe here there are some aspects that might be paradise." She pushed another fingerful of flaky white meat into her mouth and looked over her shoulder. "But I still have the feeling we're being watched."

In ten more minutes, Loche called the end of rest time, and they packed up, heading hopefully on the last leg of their mission.

While he had Janus and Matt bury the remnants of the fire and the meal, he showed the GPS positioning tracker to Jane.

"Our second party is coming right at us. And about two miles out. We might even intersect with them on route." Loche straightened, took one last look around, and then threw his pack over his shoulder. "Mr. Angel, take us out, please."

They set off along the stream's shoreline until it eventually pooled at a pile of boulders and then was sucked below the ground. Then another quarter-mile and they came to the last vestiges of the forest. The group stood on the border between the jungle and the desert.

"I remember it wasn't far from here—half a mile, maybe a little more," Mike said. He put a hand over his eyes and squinted out onto the shimmering, red, hard-packed earth. "The last time we set out across the desert, the red clan were watching. I wonder if they know we're coming."

"If you're there, Katya, tell them we're friends, okay?" Jane whispered.

Loche lowered his field glasses. "Nothing significant I can see at surface level. But you said everything was below ground, right?" He turned to Mike.

"That's right. We basically walked right over them—they had fortified doors set into the ground. Hopefully, they're still out there," he replied.

"So do I, because that's why we're here." Loche nodded to his men. "Croft, left flank, Angel, right. Eyes out, gentlemen. Everyone else stay close and keep up. Matt, you're king of the kids—keep them bunched in nice and tight behind us."

Matt saluted and practiced more of his language skills with them, this time eliciting some smiles and giggles.

Jane watched as the two military men gripped their firearms a little tighter and set foot out into the hard-packed and brutally hot desert. Loche headed up the middle, followed by Janus, Mike, and herself, and then Matt and his gaggle of tiny red children that reminded her of a lot of little ducklings following an adult bird.

Jane turned briefly back to the forest and concentrated for a moment. There was no sound of war drums or the scuttling of thousands of sharp arthropod feet.

She turned away and moved quickly to catch up with the group. It only took about ten minutes before she felt the scalding heat singeing wherever it touched her bare skin. On her forehead, her hat was sticking to one of the lesions that was now weeping a clear fluid.

Jane looked at her hand, spotting another of the crusty sores—they're getting worse, she knew, and wondered whether she'd even make it home. She looked across to Mike, who smiled back at her. She had seen his own ulceration. The pair of them were literally rotting before each other's eyes. And if there was no cure, did it matter if they died here, fast, or made it home, to die slowly?

Think positive, she demanded of herself. Making it home with a cure is first prize, so work with that goal in mind.

"Something up ahead," Loche said with the glasses to his eyes again.

In a few more minutes, they began to pass across stained soil and bodies, or rather skeletons, and hundreds of them.

They were strewn everywhere, some with shattered bones and missing limbs, or some were totally torn to pieces. Loche stopped and looked around.

"Your red people?" he asked.

"Yes," Jane replied. She could see a few of the remains wore the adornments she had seen some of the warriors wearing in the labyrinths below ground.

"A last stand," Matt added softly.

"Who were they fighting? Your shell people?" Loche frowned. "So where are *their* bodies?"

"They tended to remove their own dead," Mike said. "But it's strange. They used to take away *all* the dead, usually for food. We were just meat to them."

Loche bent to pick up a dagger, its blade about a foot long and seeming to be carved from crystal. He held it up to the red light to look into its clear depths. He tested its sharpness on his gloved hand.

"It's beautiful," Matt said. "A lot of work went into that."

"And effective." Loche noted the cut on his glove from the blade edge.

"You can't see it in this red light, but underground, it'll probably glow blue," Jane added.

Loche tucked it into his belt. "Not that we're on a scavenger hunt."

Mike turned back to the red earth plain. "The entrance was close by here. But it's well camouflaged, so everyone keep a look out for a heavy door set into the earth."

Loche turned and lifted his glasses to scan back the way they'd come. "No sign of pursuit so we can spread out, move in a line, a dozen paces between us. We need to find that entrance."

They did as asked and formed a skirmish line nearly a hundred feet wide. They moved forward for several minutes, covering the ground slowly.

Jane saw more evidence of a great battle—stained earth, a shattered jawbone, broken spears. But still no sign of any fallen *Y'ha-nthlei*.

The other thing that gave her a sinking feeling in the stomach was if the red people had prevailed, or even survived, would they not have returned for the bodies of their fallen kin?

If there was enough left of them. She sighed. *Not looking promising*, she thought.

"Here!" Matt Kearns yelled.

The group joined him at the edge of a slight depression. Below were the remains of a stout door. But it had been shattered.

"Looks like it was hacked to pieces by fire axes," Croft remarked.

"No, by claws," Jane replied.

"Well..." Loche pulled his gun from over his shoulder and attached the flashlight under the barrel. "This is why we came. Croft, lead us in. Professor, you on his shoulder with me. Then Janus, Mike, and Jane in tight behind us—they will be our guides and Matt will be our spokesman. Everyone else stay in tight. And Angel, guard our six and mind the children."

"Aw..." Angel pointed at the moon-eyed children.

Loche glared. "I said look after them, mister. Not play games with them. Just keep 'em quiet." He turned away.

"Tell them a story," Croft chuckled.

"Battle of Midway?" Angel lifted his brows.

Loche gave Croft a nudge. "Go."

Croft nodded, walked down into the depression, and pulled the shattered door aside. He headed on down and found the ladder still intact.

At the bottom, he and Matt paused for a moment, and Jane and Mike moved their lights around the space. There was nothing but the sound of their own breathing.

There were more bodies, but these were obliterated, just in pieces. Even the skulls were broken into shards.

"They were overwhelmed," Croft said. "Hey, there's light up ahead."

"Proceed," Loche ordered.

Croft moved in, gun up.

They passed along the rubble-strewn corridor until they came to an alcove that had a single blue crystal giving off a soft blue glow.

"Your crystals," Loche said.

"And yours." Jane pointed to his waist.

Loche pulled out the crystal dagger that glowed like there was a light inside it.

"Amazing," he whispered as it illuminated his features.

"Got something here, boss," Croft said as he peered around a corner. "There's a large antechamber with a new wall—fortified, I think."

Loche spoke over his shoulder. "Keep the children here. Everyone else, let's take a look."

They followed him and came to a barrier. There were the remains of ancient, dried blood everywhere, but no bodies. But there was a wall, strong, heavily fortified, and still in place.

"This was where they held them, the warriors. Maybe giving their lives so the people inside had time to build that." He nodded to the wall.

"And then get their people behind it," Jane said.

"So, they're in there?" Janus asked.

"Let's see." Loche stepped forward. He used the butt of his handgun to rap hard on a wooden beam—three times first, then twice, then once.

"No way they're going to know we're friendlies," Janus said.

"I know," Loche replied. "But if there is a Russian woman in there, she'll know it's humans and not the crab freaks out here."

He waited, and then rapped again, same pattern. After the echo died down, he leaned his ear up against it.

"Anything?" Janus whispered.

"Nothing." Loche stepped back and let his eyes run over the structure. He stopped moving and spoke without moving his head. "Jane, Mike, come up here."

"What is it?" she asked as she and Mike joined him.

He turned his back on the barrier wall. "Top left corner, about eleven o'clock, there's someone watching us." He winked down at her. "If they're anyone you know, now is the time to announce yourselves."

Jane frowned. "I don't know their language."

"But we know the name of their leader, *Ulmina*... and Katya," Mike said.

"You're right." Jane cleared her throat and stepped up closer to the wall without letting on she knew they were being watched.

"We come to see the great Ulmina. And we are friends of Katya." Jane waited a few moments and then repeated herself.

Again, she waited, but there was still nothing. She turned to Loche. "Give me the dagger."

He did as asked, and she turned to hold it up. "We are friends of the *Grunda Omada* people."

She waited and again there was nothing.

"Got any dynamite?" Janus asked.

"Yeah, that'll win them over," Matt snorted.

Janus cursed as he turned. "Listen, Professor, for all we know, the person behind there might be deranged and the last one of his or her kind." He stepped back. "We came a long way and spent several hundred million bucks to get here. And lost a lot of good people, just to get some answers... and those answers are behind that wall."

Loche's mouth turned down for a moment. "Yep." He put his hands on his hips. "He's right. We came this far. Come hell or high water, we need to see what's beyond that wall."

"Damn," Matt said. "If we do, and there's an indigenous race behind there, they'll never talk to us."

Janus bared his teeth. "*Jeezus*, if only we thought to bring someone who is a language expert."

Matt pointed a finger at the smaller man. "Hey, listen..."

"No, *you* listen." Janus knocked his hand away. "Just fucking make these sawn-off red people understand what's at stake, *Professor*."

Matt pushed him back a step. "Piss off."

Matt felt he had been suckered. He already had a basic understanding of the language, probably faster than anyone else could have achieved on the planet. But as he had only ever heard the kids speaking scraps of it, and their language might have been altered over the many generations they had been slaves, he felt he had little chance of ever pronouncing the words correctly.

He began to pace and surreptitiously looked up to the top left corner of the wall, but the eye had pulled back. Perhaps they had lost interest in watching the strange people squabble among each other.

The others were silently watching him, maybe hoping he could conjure some linguistic magic trick. But he had nothing.

He stopped. Or did he?

Matt turned. "We have something far more valuable than daggers or fluent language."

Matt called the children over to him. Then he turned back to the wall and walked right up close to it.

"Let's try something else first." Matt took a deep breath and cupped his mouth. "*Katya Babikova, my proshli dolgiy put', chtoby uvidet' vas.*"

"Russian." Jane grinned. "Of course, why not?"

Matt listened for a moment more and then raised his voice even more, once again in fluent Russian. "*Katya Babikov, your friends are here from the surface. They need help. And you can see, we rescued some of the red people's children.*"

"Who is it?" came the reply in Russian.

Jane drew in a breath. "That's Katya, I think," she whispered. "But sounds a little different."

Matt nodded and turned back to the wall. "My name is Professor Matt—"

"Not you, who are the people you say are friends?" the voice asked again.

"Mike Monroe, Jane Baxter—they came to find you," Matt replied.

"Who else is there?" the voice asked.

Matt turned to look at his companions for a moment. "Some soldiers to protect them."

"Russian?" the voice asked.

"American," Matt replied. "You are Katya Babikov, are you not?" he asked.

The eye returned and fixed on the children. "Where are the young ones from?"

"The jungle valley," Matt replied.

There was silence for nearly a minute, and Matt turned to shrug. And then.

"Back up," the voice said.

Matt looked along the wall of tumbled boulders, fallen crossbeams, and metal plates, and wondered how the hell it was going to open.

"If they're going to pull it down, it'll take a while," Loche said.

In response to this, a slab of formerly invisible and slightly recessed rock to their side slid back into a recess, leaving a dark passage beyond. As they watched, now with guns pointed at the entrance, a blue glow began to emanate from deep inside as someone or something came closer.

In another moment, a woman emerged and straightened. She wasn't red. The woman looked along the group until her eyes found Jane and Mike.

"An explorer comes here once. A fool comes twice..." One side of her mouth quirked up. "... but what is someone who comes for a third time?" she asked.

"Insane, I guess," Mike replied.

"Katya," Jane said. "But. You look...*how?*"

The woman that stood before her had long silver hair, but she was in no way the decrepit, bent-over skeleton they had left behind. Her back was straight, and her skin, though lined by time, was clear of the nasty canker-type sores that plagued her, and Mike knew had also been working their way into her body—just like with he and Jane now.

"The salve," Mike said softly. "It works."

"Yes, it does," Katya replied.

She stepped forward and Jane noticed she still wore the small gold disk around her neck that had once belonged to her sister.

"The Grunda Omada people gave me most of their remaining stores to apply to my skin and make into a brew to drink for the internal cancers eating away at me. They healed me, but unfortunately, it is running out. And when it does, the cancers will return. It is a temporary shield, not a cure."

"Doesn't matter," Janus inserted. "Just let us know where it comes from, and we'll do the rest—we'll make you gallons."

Katya ignored him and crouched before the children. She looked into many of their eyes and cupped their faces and smiled. Then she stood and turned to Mike and Jane. "You look exhausted. You are welcome inside. But the remaining people of the cave are now fearful after the last attack."

"The attack... what happened here?" Loche asked.

Katya looked at the tall American, and then her eyes slid to his gun. "Put your weapons away. The red people have poison darts they use for hunting. They can kill you all before you'll even see them."

Loche nodded and waved his men to lower their weapons. "Sorry, we've been through a lot."

She half smiled. "I can tell."

"What happened?" Jane pressed.

Katya sighed. "Come inside and rest." She pointed at Matt. "And you stay close, Mr. Russian speaker. I have not used English in a long time, and it is a struggle for me. I may switch to Russian when I tire."

Katya turned and led them into the small side cave, and the group followed in single file. Once inside the blue-tinged cavern, the door was slid shut, fitting neatly into the wall and becoming invisible once again.

Katya led them onward and for the first time, they encountered the small red people, with the dark, screwed-down hair and coal-black eyes. The men and women had weapons now, and they watched the surface people go past with a mix of fear and awe.

Jane wondered about their leader. "Katya, is Ulmina still here?"

"No, she died in the great battle." Katya half turned. "Down here, the leaders lead, even in battle. More than seventy percent of our people died in the attack." Her eyes grew dark. "The last push meant those outside had one job: to slow down the advance so the wall could be completed. They knew they were going to die when they were left on the outside. Ulmina was one of them and just her being there stiffened their spines. Such bravery."

"Shit," Mike said softly.

Katya stopped. "Yes, it was, *shit.*" She turned away. "Follow."

Katya led them into a large room that they recognized with the alcoves and blue crystal rods around the walls illuminating the space. The enormous table and the picture frescos with the stories of their history were still there.

"Wow," Matt said.

"So far, we have preserved much behind the wall. But they often return, and we fear the next attack will wipe us out," Katya said.

Mike found the crude drawings he had carved into the tabletop. He turned to Loche and Janus. "My explanation of the outer and inner world. Seems like years ago now." He looked up. "Katya, with Ulmina gone, who is the ruler here now?"

Katya turned. "I am."

"You?" Jane said.

Katya smiled and spoke in a lyrical language to the small warriors who seemed to be guarding her. They bowed and vanished.

"They'll bring you food and water. But remember, it will be sparse, as Dagon's minions are always watching and waiting. They do not forgive our, *your*, attack."

Jane remembered her injuring the great beast. "I'm sorry."

"Don't be." Katya smiled. "I'd like to see them all destroyed. They are a scourge on the entire inner world. They are like locusts that swarm and consume and feed their great god all they can capture."

Her lips pressed flat for a moment. "And sometimes they intrude on the surface world. Same as Dagon. And then he returns with his own feasts." Her level gaze was on Loche. "Your ships."

"We came via the gravity well in the sea, beside the *Y'ha-nthlei* village. But it was empty—they were gone," Mike said. "Maybe they moved somewhere else."

Katya laughed wearily. "No, they are there. Their cities reach deep below the red ocean." She looked up. "You see, the great beast wanted you here. It will have seen inside your dreams and it will never let you leave now. All here belong to it."

"We'll see about that," Loche replied. "Our vessels pack quite a bit of punch."

"You've also got to get to those vessels, Captain." Katya turned to Jane and raised her eyebrows. "He's never seen Dagon, has he?"

Jane shook her head.

"Question?" Matt held up a hand. "How did you learn their language so quickly? You're not a linguist."

"Ulmina was her teacher," Jane said. "You were working on a guide together."

Katya nodded. "She was a good teacher. Far better than me. Through great patience and skill, she taught me their language. But I could never teach her mine. I just wasn't smart enough."

"You have a Rosetta stone? A manuscript?" Matt grinned. "Can I see it?"

Katya paused as some of the red men and women returned bearing plates of food. They turned and bowed to Katya who thanked them. Many were stunned into immobility by the sight of the children, who stared back with a similar rapt interest.

Katya spoke again and then a few moments after a group of red women came and hugged the children. Many of the women had tears on their cheeks.

"Who are they?" Jane asked.

"Mothers who lost their own children. To the war, to famine, to disease... to Dagon." Katya sighed. "The children will be very welcome." She looked up at Matt, and then the others. "Thank you for rescuing and caring for them."

"You're welcome. But it was a team effort." Matt beamed. "They've been teaching me a lot. They came from the jungle valley. Their city was wiped out by a race of things that looked like people but weren't."

Katya nodded soberly. "We had heard the ancient legends, but we never had the power to rescue them. It is terrible. Such is the brutal life down here."

The other red people were about to depart but before they left, Katya said something else, which caused one of them to come closer and examine Mike and Jane's faces. He nodded and then also vanished.

Katya smiled. "I guess the people here believed that because Ulmina spent so much time with me that I became imbued with her strength and wisdom." She went to a shelf that had a curtain in front of it. She pushed it aside, brought out a leather-bound book, and turned to hold it out to Matt.

"They are a good people. And I do not want them harmed in any way." Katya faced Loche. "That's why you are going to destroy Dagon for us."

"That's the plan," Janus shot back.

Matt held the book open and grinned broadly. "You even added how to pronounce the words and phrases. Very cool."

More of the small red people returned with a small, lidded bowl of glistening white salve, which they handed to Katya. She looked down into it and sighed.

"Not much left." She stepped toward Mike and Jane and began to first daub and rub it on Jane's lesions. "Like that," she said and handed the bowl to Jane. "Do it all over." She tilted her head. "But you really need to have ingested some as well, to ensure the minerals work their way right throughout your system. It will be a temporary reprieve, I'm afraid. Because this is the last of it."

"What? That's it?" Janus shrilled. "But where does it come from? Where did they get it from originally? Did they make or harvest it?"

Katya watched the man for a moment before responding. "It comes from a rare plant like an agave called the *Youta*. It is extracted and eaten raw. But it is most potent when it is boiled to condense into a paste for application to the skin and mixed with warm water as a drink." She smiled. "But the plants are all gone from our area now and are too far away for us to travel to. I won't let the people here put an expedition together to travel to farther lands—even if it is for me." She shrugged. "All things must end."

Katya walked to one of the frescos, and Jane saw it was the one depicting the old people rising up in the gravity well to what they believed was their ancestors in some sort of heaven.

"One day soon, I'll need to make the walk into the darkness. And if the mother of the caves allows it…"

"Mother of the caves?" Matt asked.

Katya nodded and turned to him. "Legend has it that there's something in the caves, that sorts the believers from the non-believers…"

"Oh yeah, we've met," Mike said and turned to Jane. "The spider-woman in the caves."

She nodded. "With all the hatchlings."

Katya turned back to the frescos. "If I pass her judgment, I will ascend, and perhaps meet my ancestors." She smiled benignly. "And maybe my beautiful little sister, Nina, will be waiting for me."

"No." Jane shook her head and lowered her voice. "There's no ancestors, Katya," Jane sighed. "There is just a race of monsters, that might once have been human beings, that live in the caves. The people who arrive, thinking they're meeting their ancestors, well, they may well be ancestors, but they've devolved into monstrosities that feed off flesh."

"They'll be waiting for you," Mike said softly.

Katya smiled at him. "That talk is blasphemy down here."

"It's worse than that," Mike said. "It's a horrible truth."

Some more of the red people returned and chattered briefly with Katya. She nodded and her brows came together.

Matt listened in and then tilted his head. "Seems we have more visitors."

Katya nodded. "You learn fast, Professor Kearns."

He held up the manuscript. "I do because you write well."

Loche held up his GPS to Janus. "Our mystery guests have arrived. I'd say they have been tracking us like we have them."

"Well, let's go meet them," Janus replied.

Katya shot him a distrusting look, but Loche motioned for Croft to accompany them. "Jane, you come as well. Everyone else, stay put."

Mike watched them go and then turned back to Katya. "When we leave, will you come with us?"

The striking old woman scoffed. "Return to a world that rejected me? Disbelieved me? Locked me up? I think that is a world I want to be no part of."

Mike shook his head. "There'll be no disbelieving or rejecting anyone anymore. Besides, how can you stay down here now when you're a prisoner off the *Y'ha-nthlei*? Sooner or later, they'll break in and massacre or capture everyone down here."

"No." She smiled knowingly. "We have other options. They are high risk, but we can escape if we want to."

"By ascending?" Mike shook his head. "You would ascend to darkness and madness, and a certain brutal death. There is no heaven or meeting up with friendly spirits that are your ancestors."

Mike pulled his collar across, exposing a circular mark the size of his fist. "This is a bite from one of them on my last trip. Not my imagination."

Katya reached up to pat Mike's other shoulder. "Thank you for caring about me, Mike Monroe. There are a few good people left on the surface, so I have great hope for all of you."

***

Jane watched as Loche positioned Croft at the mouth of the tunnel entrance and then motioned for Jane to wait just inside. He then checked his GPS. "They're here." He stepped up the ladder and stood at the top, cradling his gun. She saw him scan the horizon, and then fix on a position to the north.

In another moment, he raised his arm in a salute. "Lieutenant Ally Bennet, I presume." He smiled broadly and quickly let his gun drop to hang on the trap from his shoulder. A woman launched into his arms.

Croft turned to Jane with a grin. "I guess they're friendlies."

Jane ran up the steps to see two people—one, a Russian soldier that looked like he had been dragged through a briar patch, and the other, a thin, but healthy-looking Ally, dressed in an oversized Russian uniform.

Upon seeing Jane, Ally burst into tears. "I'm sorry, I'm so sorry for leaving you..."

Jane rushed to her, shaking her head. "No, we didn't know. We thought at first you had made it out. Then we thought you were dead." Jane couldn't help her own tears flowing. "I'm so happy you made it."

The Russian soldier came and saluted Loche. "Kapitan Viktor Zhukov, last member of Special Forces rescue mission, *Glubokaya Zemlya*, to rescue American woman." He nodded toward Ally. "Mission *almost* accomplished."

Loche returned the salute, introduced himself, and held out his hand. He gripped the Russian's hand, and then his wrist with the other hand. "Thank you for rescuing our soldier. And thank you for surviving." He let his hand go. "But we have more work to do just yet."

"If it involves getting home, then I stand ready," Zhukov replied.

Croft had appeared beside them and was scanning the distance. He held up his tracker and pointed at the far line of trees that marked the start of the forest to the east.

"Strange, I thought it was our two stragglers coming home. But there's something else moving out there," he said.

"*She-it.*" Loche looked along the horizon but saw nothing. "Then why don't we go back down and not advertise there's people back in here."

Jane grabbed Ally's hand and led her down into the dark tunnel. Inside, they went quickly to the side alcove with the hidden door.

"What happened here?" Ally asked.

"War," Jane replied. "After we left, the *Y'ha-nthlei* came and massacred most of the clan."

"Oh, that's sad," Ally said.

Jane rubbed her arm and half smiled. "It is. But come and meet their new leader."

They walked down along the tunnel until they came to the large room again and entering, Jane waved. "Look who we found."

Mike clapped and rushed to her. "We hoped it was you." He hugged the woman.

Ally kissed him, stepped back, and held an arm out toward Zhukov. "My hero." She grabbed him and pulled him forward. "This is Captain Viktor Zhukov. He risked everything for me and has been my guardian angel the entire way. He kept me alive and my spirits high even when I wanted to surrender."

Zhukov blushed a little as he shrugged. "It is a soldier's job."

Ally spotted the silver-haired woman. "Katya? Katya Babikov?"

Katya held her arms wide. "Life is long and strange, is it not?"

Ally went to hold the woman. "What happened to you? I mean, you look like a different woman."

Katya shrugged. "I gave up smoking." She began to laugh but then scrutinized Ally's face. She pushed her hair back. "You don't look so bad for someone who has spent so much time down here either."

Ally's mouth drooped. "I wasn't down here for most of the time, but in a twilight world of hell. And I'd still be there, if not for this man." Her eyes welled up. "He lost his entire team rescuing me, and then getting me here through river caves and across deserts."

Jane saw the Russian man beaming back at her and guessed they had grown close in their time at the center of the Earth.

"How did you survive?" Matt asked.

"Determination," Zhukov replied. "And a lot of luck." He grinned.

"And those weird leaves like aloe vera that were filled with something like syrup." Ally pulled a face. "*Yeesh*, I never want to see one again."

She reached into her bag, pulled out the two remaining fleshy bulbs, and tossed them onto the table.

Katya began to laugh and picked one up. "The *Youta* plant." She looked up. "And the source of the salve. This is why you are not that afflicted by the radiation's poison. This has been your shield."

Janus snatched one up. "This is it?"

Zhukov emptied Valentina's bag that still contained half a dozen of the fleshy leaves. "They were everywhere."

"They were once everywhere here as well. But we took them without cultivating them." Katya held up the fat pod-like leaf. "We know more about that now, and this will be our second chance." She smiled at Jane. "And yours too."

"How do you, ah, prepare the salve?" Janus asked.

"Simple." Katya held up and squeezed the bulb leaf. A drop of pearlescent liquid appeared on the end where it had been pulled from its plant stem. "You crush the leaf, extracting the syrup. Then you heat it until the moisture is reduced to make a paste. It concentrates the medicinal properties."

Janus began to put the leaves back in Valentina's pack. "Ladies and gentlemen, our work here is done."

"Hey, leave some for Katya," Jane demanded.

"I only need two," Katya said. "They grow easily, and we now know we can grow them underground near a heat source."

"And by the way, our job is not done here until we're all safely on our way home," Loche said. "And we need to work out how we're going to do that." He turned to Katya. "Are you sure that the crab people will try and stop us?"

"They are there," Katya said. "Now and then, a scout creeps in here. But so far, they believe there is no life. Unfortunately, you being here will change that."

"So, they will come for you now?" Jane asked.

"Yes, with more warriors, and they will try and break in. They're mindless and relentless automatons when it comes to carrying out the orders of the great beast," Katya replied.

"So, we just wait here and try and repel them?" Janus scoffed. "That's not a great long-term strategy." He pouted. "We don't have many weapons, and a first wave is liable to exhaust our ammunition."

"Fight where we are strongest," Loche said.

"Sun Tzu?" Zhukov smiled.

Loche nodded. "Our best offensive strategy is to take these things and their master on with all the armaments we packed into the submersibles. We just need to get to them."

"Oh, is that all," Janus laughed derisively.

"There is a way," Katya said softly.

Silence reigned for several seconds before Janus lifted his chin.

"Yeah, okay, we're listening." He folded his arms.

"The labyrinths in the deep caves." Katya smiled. "There is a way."

"Hold on, Katya, we've been in those labyrinths, and I gotta tell you, there's some pretty unpleasant wildlife back there," Mike said.

"But we have the screechers now," Jane said. "That'll ward off anything that hunts by sound."

"We have them too," Zhukov added. "A gift from you Americans before we embarked. We've tested them, they work. But…" He looked at Jane from under his brows. "We found that there are things in the caves that do not need sound."

"Good news on the screechers. And I guess we deal with each threat as it comes," Mike replied. "Our chances just improved."

"Where do they come out?" Loche asked.

"In the jungle, but close to the shoreline… and the *Y'ha-nthlei* village," Katya replied.

"The abandoned village," Janus included.

"Don't be fooled," Katya said. "They are there, waiting."

"Will you come with us?" Jane asked again.

Katya shook her head. "My place is with my people. I will stay until the beasts are knocking down our wall, and I will pray that you are successful. If you are, then both our problems will be solved. If you are not, it will undoubtedly mean you have been killed, and my world will end also."

She tilted her head back. "I am home here. They cured me, and I have a love for them as much as they love me." She smiled softly. "On the surface, no one had loved me for fifty years."

"We love you." Janus' attempt at a warm smile didn't reach his eyes. "Hey, don't suppose you have a map?"

"There are maps." Katya turned to one of the red guards standing, watching them silently. She said a few words, and Jane could tell Matt followed along, fascinated.

The man left the room, and then appeared back with some rolls of parchment that he placed on the table. Katya unrolled several before choosing one.

She pointed to a place on the map. "We are here."

Like veins and arteries running through a body, Jane saw the diagram illustrated a vast network of the kingdom's underground tunnel system. Katya traced a finger to a line across one of the larger tunnels.

"This is where you begin to leave our domain. The caves run deep." She looked up. "And unfortunately, very hot." She traced the line again. "They are ancient caves, not used for many centuries. We keep them sealed off, because as you said, there are some denizens down there that we'd prefer to keep out of the city."

"Just great," Janus breathed out.

"If you have your sonic devices, you should be safe." She paused. "However, there is light down there." She paused, looking from Jane to Mike, and then Ally.

Ally nodded. "I understand. That means things will also hunt with sight."

"They might. No one living here has been down there. Maybe they don't even survive anymore, or maybe they never did. Just stories to scare the children into never going exploring there."

"Let's hope," Matt said, following the map from over her shoulder.

"But the heat is real. There are hot mud pools there. They will be dangerous, and you must stay on the path and not wander." Katya showed them where the danger areas were and then continued her explanation. "When the cave starts to lift and slant upward, you will know you are heading out. Where you finally exit, you will be only a few hundred yards from the shoreline, and close to the city."

"This is great news," Loche said.

"The exit is concealed." Katya straightened. "When you leave, you must seal the exit again and hide it as best you can. We don't want the *Y'ha-nthle* discovering the exit and coming at us from behind as well as the front."

"We will. And thank you. Thank you for everything." Jane took Katya's hands.

Katya smiled and pulled Jane close. Then she held her at arm's length and looked into her face. "I remember, years ago, a fresh-faced American girl coming to see me with a tall, handsome man named Mike Monroe. The questions you asked led you here." Her smile fell away. "Maybe I should never have answered your questions."

"It was meant to be," Jane replied.

"I blame Arkady Saknussov." Mike half smiled. "If only that brilliant fool had never indulged his wild theory, then maybe no one would have ever learned of this place."

Katya and Jane broke their embrace and Katya called two warriors to accompany them.

"We will just take you to the entrance to the labyrinths. The rest must be up to you," she said sternly.

"When do we leave?" Matt asked.

"Now," Janus ordered.

"We have all we need." Loche organized his people.

"Where do you want me?" Viktor Zhukov asked.

"You and Ally are two very needed soldiers. Ally can assist covering the civilians, with Croft at point. You can work with Angel at our rear."

The group began to file out with the two small red warriors leading them. Jane and Mike turned at the door and Katya held up a hand.

"Kill Dagon. Free us all," Katya ordered.

"Can you kill a god?" Matt asked.

"You will find out. If you do not, then even the surface world will not be safe. He sees you in your dreams, and his vengeance knows no bounds."

"Is it, *Dagon*, the only one?" Matt asked, his questions rushing now.

"I believe it is the last one of its kind," Katya replied wearily. "Legend has it, Dagon has been alive forever. But no one has ever tried to hurt him before, or even could. Until you came."

"We'll finish it this time," Jane replied.

Loche saluted. "We'll do our best, ma'am. Thanks for everything." He nodded to his soldiers and followed them out.

Mike and Jane waved and rushed after the group.

EPISODE 14

"When I returned to partial life my face was wet with tears – Never was solitude equal to this, never had any living being been so utterly forsaken" — Jules Verne, Journey to the Center of the Earth

CHAPTER 18

Matt followed the small red warriors as they moved quickly along the well-lit tunnels. He had been in the remnants of fallen civilizations before, and he saw all the signs—cracked and crumbling edifices, moss-covered monuments, and large areas that looked unused, perhaps for centuries, perhaps for millennia.

He tried to quickly interpret and read everything he saw as they passed by ancient writing, picture frescos, and glyphic symbols. He learned more about the three great rulers and how they had been attacked by Dagon and his minions and had broken into several groups. The three kings then organized their quests to find a new home, each taking some of the crystal cave's inhabitants with them.

However, one smaller group were determined to stay behind to climb into the higher caves, and this is the one that seemed to have become the hideous creatures inhabiting the mid-world. He remembered Mike's report that had sampled DNA evidence of what they believed these "ancestors" were—the malformed remnants of that colony that over thousands of years had devolved back into raw, animal savagery.

Of the three great clans that did depart, there was one that voyaged by sea, another entered the great desert—this one—and then the last one traveled into the deep jungle. He bet they were wiped out by the green insect people within the great idols in the valley wall they had encountered. It was sad, as they looked to have grown and flourished for centuries before being infiltrated by the parasitic mimics, the green women. And what became of the clan that took to the seas? Perhaps they would never know.

The group took a turn into a side tunnel from the main thoroughfare, and they noticed that the blue crystals became sparser. Down in the center Earth world, their glow would be eternal, but it seemed they weren't wasted on a place no one was going to go.

Matt practiced his language skills on the men, and though he knew they understood each other, he got the impression they were scared shitless and just wanted to get their task done so they could retreat to their own clan.

The small red men stopped and waited for the surface people to catch up to them. When they did, the small men pointed. Matt turned to where they indicated and saw the huge door.

One of the men held out a crystal four-pronged key to Matt. "May your journey be everything you hope for." His face was grim as he bowed.

Matt took the key and returned the bow. He responded in their tongue, "Thank you, and may you…"

The two men turned and vanished back along the tunnel without another word.

Matt watched them go for a moment and turned back to the door. The first thing he noticed was there was writing set into the heavily corroded iron. He held his luminous crystal closer and rubbed a millennium of dust from the words.

"*Beware all who enter here.*" He scoffed. "How about that? It seems even the underworld has an underworld."

"What else does it say?" Janus asked.

He shook his head slowly. "It presents as more an image than sentence text. Something about being burned and consumed." He turned. "By demons."

"Well then, we came to the right place," Loche said. "Open it."

"On it." Matt tried to turn the key. He then gripped it with both hands and ground his teeth as the key finally turned. There was a sliding sound of bolts being slid back, and then the door swung inward with a shower of rust flakes.

"*Ach.*" Mat held up a hand in front of his face as a wave of heat billowed out at them.

Janus had his eyes as slits. "Jesus, is anything easy down here?"

"The easy stuff ain't worth doin', right?" Croft finished with a grin. "Orders, boss?"

"Take us in, Croft. Everyone else, same formation as before. We all stay alert. And we all stay alive." Loche nodded to Croft, who turned and headed in through the large door.

***

Matt did as asked and pulled the door shut behind them. On closing, he used the key again to lock it and watched as two horizontal stone cross beams slid into the wall.

He turned back to see the group waiting for him at the top of a downward-sloping tunnel. Or rather, partial cave, as the walls looked to have been hacked out by hand but didn't have the finish that the bricked and sculpted tunnels did behind them.

Some huge boulders were as nature had carved them and intruded on their path, perhaps of some mineral composition that resisted the primitive instruments used to widen and enlarge their avenue.

Matt moved past Zhukov and Angel at the rear to take his position at the center of the group. With him was Janus, Mike, Jane, and then Ally. Up front were once again the large forms of Croft and Captain Loche.

From somewhere down in the darkness, a hot and fetid breeze blew into their faces. It must have been a hundred ten degrees and smelled of sulfur and something else that gave the place an eggy, corrupted odor.

"Smells volcanic. But that's impossible down here," Jane said. "Got to be some sort of natural heat source."

"For all we know, the gravity and magnetism of the core is still generating geological friction," Mike added. "Maybe rubbing some deep crustal plates together. We think it's solid iron, but we have no idea what's really below us now."

Loche led them downward, and they moved slowly as there were no blue crystals, just lights from their flashlights or the crystals they brought with them. They dropped down quickly, and as they did, the heat and humidity started to rise. In no time, perspiration ran freely from their faces and soaked their shirts.

"How much further down?" Janus asked.

Loche half turned. "The map gives direction, not depth. But we're not even a third of the way yet, so let's all just keep moving forward and get through it quickly."

Matt noticed that all sign of intelligent habitation had disappeared. There were no carvings, no embedded crystal rods, and even the caves had stopped looking like the stone had been worked and were now just raw and dripping rock.

As they traveled, they came out onto a ledge that dropped into darkness. From below, they smelled molten magma, and steam rose, filling the cavern with a stinking fog.

"Don't want to fall here," Janus remarked. "Boiled alive."

"Thanks, I'll keep that in mind," Mike replied.

They entered another cave, and after another half hour, Loche told them they had traveled exactly half the way.

"Not so bad," Matt said.

They then passed through a narrowing section under a shelf of stone and then came out into the next cave before Loche finally stopped them. This time, there was a raised path, a bridge, that traveled across a lake of mud that boiled and popped, belching sulfuric smelling gases and was continually churning like a giant pot on a stove.

In among the boiling mud was the occasional rock showing like a small island. No one could guess at its depths, but everyone knew that the heat would have been skin stripping.

Loche exhaled as he stared. "This is gonna hurt."

Even though the bridge across the mud lake was raised about three feet, they could see that there were splashes of mud on its top, some of which still steamed. The first problem was the bridge was only about two feet wide.

The soldier turned. "Okay, people, we need to get across this as fast as possible. Stay focused and steel yourselves. If you get splashed, it'll burn and hurt like a bitch. But suck it up and ignore it. Try not to overbalance, as the result could be... unpleasant."

"Yeah, I'll bet." Janus grimaced as he stared at the popping, bubbling mud.

"Everyone hold up while Croft and I see what the lie of the land is like," Loche said.

The captain tightened his pack and then he and Croft started across. The bridge or raised pathway went for a couple of hundred feet and at about fifty feet, he stopped and turned slowly, surveying the lake of boiling mud on either side of him.

After another moment, he turned back to the waiting group. "Okay, come on over, it's solid and easy. Just try and ignore the mud."

The group started after him and he waited, watching them cross toward him. Jane couldn't help glancing at the scalding mud and several times a larger than normal bubble popped, splashing her legs with the thick, hot sludge. Even through her pants, she felt the sting of its heat as it stuck and continued to burn. But it wasn't unbearable, and little more than when you are frying bacon and the fat pops and splashes you—it burned like hell but eventually cooled.

When they were about halfway, just shy of a hundred feet, Jane glanced again at the mud—just in time to see something surface. And then submerge.

"Hey." She pointed. "There was something there..."

Everyone stopped and turned to where she indicated.

"What?" Janus asked.

"Something came up." Jane frowned down at the mud, focusing on the spot she was sure she had seen movement.

"Maybe it was just a bubble or some sort of surge," Mike said. "Or maybe a coagulated lump. The mud is viscous and constantly moving from the heat."

"Could have been," she said, now doubting her own eyes.

As Jane watched, she saw the bubbles rise and pop, some of them no bigger than golf balls and some the size of basketballs. Most burst, sprayed their splatter, and then fell back to the red-brown volcanic-looking mixture.

But others didn't. Now and then, larger bubbles rose, and then stayed as lumps on the surface. Jane thought that the air remained trapped, probably because of the thickness of the mixture.

"Let's keep moving people." Loche waved them on.

They still had a hundred feet to travel, and they tried to balance moving as fast as they could manage while also as carefully as was humanly possible. It was a curious human trait, that a pathway at ground level presented no problem, but that same pathway, with same width, when raised high, suddenly became like a tightrope when asked to keep balance and walk a straight line.

From time to time, one or other of them had been sucking in their breath or groaning as a splatter of hot mud found an exposed piece of flesh, but then Janus screamed, loud and high-pitched, and it jerked everyone to a stop.

Jane and Mike turned to see the man standing with eyes wide. Janus stood in a crouch, pointing, and holding up Ally, Angel, and Zhukov behind him.

"What the hell is going on back there?" Loche yelled.

Janus continued pointing, and they followed where he indicated but saw nothing but the roiling mud, with its large and small bubbles like a witch's cauldron but on the scale of a dark lake.

Not unusually, the bigger bubbles sometimes remained, and that was where it got weird. Jane craned forward.

"He-*eeey*." Her eyes narrowed.

The bubbles weren't just remaining now, but they seemed to be moving. Not as if being buffeted by the liquid in furious movement from the heat, but more all moving together, in unison. And toward them.

"What's going on here?" Croft shouted from the front.

"That's what *I* saw!" Jane exclaimed.

"This is not good." Zhukov pulled his weapon.

"*Beware all who enter here,*" Matt uttered. "*For you will be cooked and consumed. By demons.*" He looked up. "The warning on the door."

"Thanks, Matt." Mike pulled his own sidearm. "Can we get moving? Like now."

Angel put his gun to his shoulder and fired a round into one of the large domes that was moving toward them. He hit it, and rather than popping, it simply submerged.

"Got it!" he yelled.

And then the shit went sideways. From where he struck the bubble, out of the boiling mud a long strand reached out to wrap around Angel's wrist and thigh. In a flash, it pulled him onto his side.

"Get it off, get it off!" Angel yelled as he began to be dragged to the path's edge.

Ally was closest and she reached up to grip the mud-dripping tentacle but immediately recoiled and held her hands up, screaming.

"It fucking burns!" she wailed.

Croft and Loche piled rounds into the mud where the long lash had emanated from. But there were now other domes that were crowding in, and the tips of more tendrils started to appear up out of the scalding mud.

"Get back!" Loche yelled to the group.

Unfortunately, that meant the group split—some going toward Loche, Ally, and Zhukov, and the rest backing up the way they'd come.

For now, Angel was still being held just at the side of the land bridge. But the creatures started to mass in the mud at the bottom of the rise. And then they began to lift themselves up the sides.

"Jellyfish," Matt whispered. "They're like jellyfish."

Jane's face screwed up in horror as that's exactly what they looked like— – gigantic jellyfish with bulbous bell-like heads that dangled long tentacles or tendrils from under the bell. As the mud slid from them, deep inside their nearly transparent bodies came a red glow, like the heart of fire. *Or the devil*, she thought, remembering the warning about demons.

"Take 'em out," Loche said.

"On it." Croft pumped a grenade into his launcher. "Fire in the hole!" he yelled and fired it into the mud at the center of the monstrous swarm that seemed to have hold of his friend.

The projectile entered the mud as everyone cringed back and then it detonated. Scalding mud flew in gouts, covering and burning most of the group.

The creatures sank. Angel had been held at the edge of the path, but as the things retreated, they didn't release him, instead taking the man over the edge.

Angel's screams made their blood freeze as he was drawn down into the scalding mess. As he shuddered from pain on the surface of the boiling lake, the creatures closed in now that he was in their domain.

In seconds, the boiling mud began to flush red, and the smell of cooking meat overrode the odor of sulfur and methane.

Jane guessed then that the grenade had startled the creatures, but only temporarily. And now they were massing to return.

"Run!" Janus screamed.

Mike stayed put and pointed to Ally and Zhukov, now a long way back. "Hurry!" he yelled.

The two started to move as fast as they could manage along the bridge that was now spattered and slippery with the slimy mud, but perhaps the taste of human flesh had excited the creatures to greater pursuit of the rest of the people.

Ally had her gun and held it in a tight, two-handed grip as she fired round after round into the blobbish bodies with their waving tendrils that began to climb the sides of the land bridge.

Zhukov did the same, trying to stay close to Ally, and fired at anything that tried to get too close to her.

Jane could see his face, and it was torn by fear—not for himself, but for Ally. The man had been charged as her rescuer, and perhaps saw himself as her guardian angel. Or maybe even something more now.

Close to where the lead group huddled, a huge mound rose, easily five feet across, and trunk-thick tentacles rose beside it.

Croft and Loche filled the bell-shaped head or body with several rounds, but the bullets passed straight through the boneless form of the creature.

Matt reached into his pack and pulled out his water bottle, spun the top from it, and then splashed a long gout of water onto the approaching tentacles.

The effect was immediate and astounding—the tentacles he managed to splash steamed and cracked open, with several chunks of the thing's flesh flaking free.

It seemed a life lived in the Hades-like flames couldn't stand the sudden change in temperature.

The monstrosity withdrew straight back into the hot mud. Matt spun to Ally and Zhukov. "Use your water."

As he did, one of the things surged up the side and its long lash-like tendril circled Ally's waist. She immediately threw her head back from the searing pain. More of the tendrils grabbed at her legs and around one of her wrists.

Zhukov charged toward her, pulling his water bottle and yelling in Russian as the woman was lifted from the path and began to be drawn down into the mud.

Ally screamed and shuddered as if being electrocuted. It was too much for the Russian soldier, who without a split second's hesitation leaped from the bridge to land on a small rock island to grab Ally's dangling leg with one hand and splashed half his remaining water at the thing with the other. It immediately released her, and she dropped onto him, but the searing pain had stunned her, and she hung limp in his arms.

The others raced to the edge of the path in front of them, but Loche stopped any of them following Zhukov out. They could only call advice as the man held on, and they splashed their water out to try and keep more of the creatures from getting to them.

They were successful, only partially, because from behind him one wrist-thick tendril encircled his leg. They saw the steam rise from the thing as its hundreds of degrees limb clamped down.

Zhukov's teeth snapped together, and they heard him moan in pain. He held the unconscious Ally and looked toward the group. Jane could tell he was calculating the odds of trying to throw her, as he could never leap while holding her.

But this too looked impossible, as he was just too far, and as more tentacles wrapped around the man, Jane saw his face change and become more resolute.

"*No, no, no...* don't you dare!" she screamed.

Captain Viktor Zhukov leaned his face toward Ally's and kissed her cheek. He then used one arm to splash his remaining water behind him over the creatures.

Captain Zhukov looked back to the waiting group, now about six feet from him, separated by that much boiling mud.

Zhukov seemed to steel himself.

And then stepped forward. Into the mud.

He sunk to his knees and his eyes went wide. But he kept his teeth clamped tight to stop from screaming his pain.

He took another step, this time sinking to thigh depth.

Tears ran down his face as around his legs, blood began to seep into the mud. More of the tentacles sought him out now that he was in their world.

The Russian captain kept going, and as he did, he lifted Ally high above his head and out of reach of the hellish beasts. His face streamed with tears as with his last ounces of strength, he lurched back and then threw the woman forward. Ally sailed the remaining three feet and was caught by Mike and Loche, who dragged her backward.

Through tear-blurred eyes, Jane held her hands out to the man, but he was totally covered in the tendrils now and he simply smiled, happy perhaps that he had saved Ally, the woman he had set out to rescue. And fallen in love with.

Viktor Zhukov was dragged down into the angry, boiling mud. And in seconds more, he was gone.

The group stared, and Loche straightened, his own face pale with shock. The man then turned to the group, his roar so loud it overrode their fear. "He gave us a chance. So now move it." He pushed Croft to lead them out and slapped their backs, urging them to speed. "Do not look down, do not look back, just keep going."

Mike hoisted Ally onto his shoulder and ran. Loche took one last look around, saluted, and then followed.

***

The caves remained raw stone, but within thirty minutes they began to incline slightly. When the group began to falter through sheer exhaustion, Loche let them slow.

Jane had treated Ally as best she could with the remaining med-packs each of them had but she was ringed with lines of blisters that were raw and painful looking. She'd need water soon as while her body wept clear fluid to try and protect itself from the burns, it drew liquid from her system—just when they had used most of their water to keep the mud creatures at bay.

In a broadening of the caves, Loche called a brief stop so they could catch their breath.

"What were those fucking things?" Janus demanded.

"Some type of extremophile," Jane replied between rasping breaths as she continued to tend to Ally. "There are some species, called thermophiles, that thrive in high temperatures. Some live near deep-sea vents where it can get to over 600 degrees."

"They looked like jellyfish." Matt had his hands on his knees as he sucked in air. "I've never seen or heard of anything like them."

"No one has." Jane stood. "It's a new species, at least to us. It might be as ancient as time down here." Jane saw Ally begin to come around. "But jellyfish do become more active the warmer the temperature is. These things must be a variant on the ones we know."

"Demons from the heat of Hell," Matt said. "I'm paraphrasing the red people's ancestor's words. They tried to warn us."

"Unlike the military to walk us into danger." Janus gently touched at some burns on his face.

Loche slowly turned. "We just lost two military people who were dedicated to keeping your ass alive... and died doing it." The man's eyes blazed, and he took a step forward.

Janus threw his hands up. "Hey, no offense."

"The red people tried to warn us, but we had no way of knowing what to expect." Matt stepped between Loche and Janus. "Even the current red people probably had no idea what it meant."

Mike put both hands in the small of his back and straightened. "Yeah, well, vague warnings are no warning at all."

Loche grunted and turned away. "We're past it now." He checked his GPS. "We're not far from the shoreline, so we must be coming to the exit soon." He kneeled in front of Ally and looked into her face. He reached out and pulled one of her eyelids up but she gently batted his hand away.

"I'm fine," she whispered.

"She needs more rest," Jane said.

Loche continued to stare at the young woman. "We all do. And the best and safest rest will be aboard the submersibles."

"I'll be okay," Ally slurred. "Help me up. I'll walk it off."

"That's the spirit." Loche gripped Ally's hands and hauled her to her feet. "Well done, soldier. You're as tough as nails."

"I don't feel it." Ally winced and then blinked a few times, and then lifted her shirt and checked the line of raw blisters that wrapped all the way around her. She exhaled with a whoosh. "I'll be fine." She dropped her shirt and looked around. "Did Viktor...?"

"Dead," Loche said flatly.

"*Jesus*, Loche, way to break bad news," Mike responded.

Loche turned back to Ally. "I'm sorry. He was the one who saved you. A very brave man."

Ally's mouth turned down and she shut her eyes, nodding after a moment. "I thought it was just a bad dream."

"This whole place is a bad fucking dream," Janus said, seething.

"I'm sorry, Ally," Mike said.

"They're all gone." She shook her head. "Every one of the Russian team who came down to save me. And they *did* save me. And then guess what? I'm still here and they're not. This place punished them for it." She covered her face.

"Cut that crap," Loche barked.

The harsh words made everyone stop and stare.

"They did their duty. And thank heavens you did survive, or their sacrifice would have been for nothing." Loche lowered his brow. "Now, you can return the favor by making sure you keep your chin up and stay alive and help me get the civilians home." He eased back. "Then light a candle for Captain Viktor Zhukov and his team later."

Ally wiped her eyes and then tried to stand a little straighter. "Yes." She nodded. "That's what I'll do."

"Protect and defend." Loche placed a hand on her shoulder.

Ally nodded. "Protect and defend."

Loche stepped back and turned to the group. "Are we ready?" He glared at each of them. "Because we aren't home yet. And I sure as hell don't want to say goodbye to any more of you."

There were nods and confirmation.

"Then let's do the last nine yards." He circled a finger in the air to Croft who turned to lead them on.

***

In another fifteen minutes, the cave had sloped upward significantly so they had to climb in some places. It was only when they neared the top did there start to appear some sort of glyphic writing, and the raw cave became worked stone.

"Professor?" Loche waved Matt over. "Please tell me this isn't another warning."

Matt looked at the writing and he half smiled. "The first part *is* the same warning about fiery demons consuming all who enter." He frowned and stepped forward. "And then there's a message for us—or anyone about to leave this place."

He put his finger on the first glyph and traced it across the whorls, dashes, and images as he spoke.

"Something like, *the great dreamer is now awake. Beyond this barrier, all belong to him.*" Matt turned. "Not exactly uplifting."

"Fuck it, we have no choice," Janus said, sneering. "Because I'll

222

tell you something for nothing, we ain't going back the way we just came."

"He's right," Loche said. "We go forward now. GPS says we're close to our submersibles. We go fast and quiet. Outside this cave, we should be able to contact the subs."

"And Dagon and his minions?" Jane asked.

"We get to the submersibles. That's our only plan for escape. If need be, we fight and keep fighting until we have nothing left." Loche smiled ruefully. "After what we've been through, this looks like it's the last leg. We can do it."

"We can and will." Mike gripped Jane's arms. "We'll make it."

She kissed him and then stood back a step to investigate his features. Her brows came together, and she quickly pushed up his hair from his sweat and grime-streaked forehead. A grin spread across her face.

"It works." She grabbed his chin to turn his face and then looked at his temple. "The lesions are smaller."

He cupped her face and did the same to her. "Yours too."

Janus came between Mike and Jane and gripped both their shoulders. "A cure for skin cancer—we'll be richer than King Midas."

Jane looked up into Mike's face. "We already are."

Matt held the long iron key and lifted it to the locking mechanism. "Are we ready?"

Croft and Loche went to each side of the door, and the captain looked along each of their faces.

"Let's do this slowly, Professor. Let's not surprise anything on the other side of the door."

Matt nodded and turned back. "Count of 3-2-1 and…" He turned the key.

Once again, there came the sound of ancient bolts sliding, and Loche motioned for Matt to step back. He gripped the old door's edge and eased it open while leading with his gun muzzle.

As the door opened, the dark cave was flooded with red light. Then the sounds of life, followed by the scent of plants, flowers, and gloriously, seawater.

The group stayed in the darkness of the cave for a moment, scanning the world outside. They saw that they seemed to be under an overhang of stone with vines growing down over its front in a fringe that hid them from the wildlife outside.

Loche nodded and he and Croft moved out. Loche went to the

right, and Croft to the left. The others followed, spreading out between the soldiers. Loche motioned them down into a crouch.

"Let's just watch a while," he said softly.

There was jungle, large trees, some with the familiar fake candy apples hanging in their branches that proved deadly when they arrived. There were soft grasses and things the size of small birds zumming in and out of the greenery on stiff, membranous wings.

"I don't see anything dangerous. Anyone else?" Janus asked.

Loche used his field glasses, and Croft used the scope on his rifle to slowly pan across the under-foliage. He then lifted his gun to do the same in the tree canopies. "I can't see anything above those bird things flitting about." He lowered the glasses.

Jane turned to him. "That's not necessarily a good thing. I'd prefer to see something larger, predator or otherwise. The only places devoid of large beasts were overrun by the *Y'ha-nthlei*."

"Yep, I remember," Loche replied. "We don't have far to go." He pointed. "The river and our submersibles are just a few hundred yards through that stretch of forest. We need to get to them." He packed his glasses away. "So, we go low and fast, and stay tight. Got it?"

Everyone agreed and began to tighten pack straps and suck in breaths. Loche held up a hand.

"One more thing—everyone say a prayer—here goes." He put the mic to his ear. "Abyss-1 and Abyss-2, this is Captain Joshua Loche, come back?" He waited. "Submersible pilots Albie Miles and Joni Baker, come back."

He waited with his head down, listening.

The seconds dragged.

The comm unit finally pinged, and Loche's head came up.

"Boss, welcome back, and good to damn well hear your voice," Albie Miles replied.

"Same right here, Captain," Joni Baker chimed in. "Where are you? I still can't see you on the grid."

"You will when we step out of the cave system. We're only a few hundred yards from you. Is the situation clear?" Loche asked.

"We had a few nosey visitors, large and small, but we saw them off. Right now, land, sea, and air—above and below is all clear, boss. How's the team?" Miles asked.

Loche's lips pressed together momentarily. "We lost Angel, Masters, Edison, Williams, and Archer."

"Ah, damnit," Miles replied, and he heard Joni Baker also curse softly.

"But we are bringing in Ally Bennet," Loche said.

"Say again? The missing American woman?" Miles asked.

"That's the one. Long story," Loche said. "Put a drone up and give us eyes in the air. We're coming in fast. Prep the submersibles, as we are leaving as soon as the hatch closes."

"*Yes, sir*," Miles said with Baker also acknowledging the command.

Loche turned. "Are we ready?"

"Are we ever?" Mike replied.

Jane saw the nods and the mental preparation on their faces—even though there were seven of them, hearing all the names of the fallen brought it home how many had been killed. And then there was the entire Russian squad that had been lost.

She drew in a breath and let it out, feeling the knot of sorrow and regret in her gut. This place ate people, literally. It was never meant for them.

"Let's go home," she said.

Mike bumped up against her and looked up. Above them, they saw the dot of the drone appear and this time the soft, almost insect-like whine was comforting.

Matt turned to close the door behind them as instructed.

"That's our cue," Loche said. "Croft and I will lead us out—stay tight, people." He nodded to Croft and the pair began to jog.

They came out from under the overhang and moved fast.

"I see you," Miles said into Loche's ear. "Keep moving east. You're going to enter the tree line for just two hundred yards and then you'll come out just to the north of where we are berthed."

"Got it," Loche said as he led them into the first line of trees.

Inside the jungle, it became dark and humid, but thankfully, there was nothing that jumped out at them, or for that matter anything at all. If Jane didn't know better, she might have thought it was more a sanctuary than a place of tooth and claw.

In just a few minutes more, they came to the end of the strip of jungle and Loche held up a hand. As Albie Miles had said, looking south, he saw the towers of the two submersibles waiting right where they left them, still moored in the mouth of the broad estuary. And beyond, the red ocean sparkled. For now, it looked calm and only small waves lapped against the bank.

Jane remembered that further down the coast the city of the *Y'ha-*

nthlei would still be there. *Had the creatures returned to it?* she wondered. Katya seemed confident they had. But then, where were they?

Above them, the drone dropped to just about fifty feet above their heads and dipped its propellor wings in greeting.

Loche touched his ear mic. "Miles, we're coming in. Take the drone down the coast to the city and see if there's any signs of life." He turned to nod to the group. "We'll be with you in a minute or two."

Miles confirmed the order and Loche signed off.

"Last lap," he said, his eyes fixed on the subs. "We've got to balance the submersibles. Croft, Ally, and I will go in Abyss-2. I want you civilians in…"

"Hey, no way, I'm sticking with the guys with the guns." Janus turned to Mike, Jane, and Matt, and shrugged. "No offense."

Loche exhaled. "Fine, you come with us. Ally, you're the military guy that gets to accompany the civilians. Any objections?"

There were none.

"Okay, then…"

"Boss." Miles' voice was tight.

Loche held up a finger. "Go, Miles."

"City is empty, but I'm getting some weird readings coming in from the sonar," the pilot replied. "You seeing this, Baker?" he asked the second pilot.

"Sure am," Joni replied. "So, it's not a malfunction if we've both got it."

"Describe what you're seeing," Loche ordered.

"Well, if I was at sea, I'd say we were approaching a landmass. But as I'm moored, then it looks like the landmass is coming to us," Miles replied.

Loche lifted his head to relay the information to the group. "Sonar said there's something big, the size of a landmass, bearing down on us."

"It's Dagon," Jane replied stiffly.

Loche nodded. "Pilot one and two, we are coming in. Prepare for immediate evac." He signed off, took one last look around, and then waved them on. "Move it." He began to sprint.

***

The single group burst from the jungle and then split as they crossed the last hundred yards to the submersibles.

The water looked calm and red, but Jane knew what it was bearing down on them from the sea. And she had seen the size of the beast before and knew if it caught them, it would crush the heavily armored mini submarines like tin cans.

Loche got to submersible Abyss-2 first and turned to cover Croft and Janus as they climbed the side and dropped down into the open hatch.

Ally did the same, urging Jane, Mike, and Matt up and over the side. Mike came last and after dropping down inside, pulled the hatch shut.

Ally went directly to the front and sat down. "2nd Lieutenant Ally Bennet. And you must be 1st Lieutenant Albie Miles."

Miles grinned and saluted. "Yes, ma'am, and welcome aboard. And glad to see you made it."

"We haven't made it yet, soldier." Ally became all business. "We need to get out and away from the behemoth bearing down on us and get to the gravity well, ASAP."

She half turned. "Everyone else sit down and strap in." She faced Miles. "What armaments do you have?"

Miles quickly ran through the list of weapons they had, and when he got to the last, the standard and nuclear-tipped torpedos, she stopped him.

"Get them prepped, all of them."

Miles had already begun pulling away from the shore and pressed a few more switches, which elicited a mechanical sound beneath their feet as the torpedos were armed and loaded on their rails in line for the torpedo tubes.

"Half kiloton load. Just one is enough to sink a battleship," Miles said proudly.

"Won't be enough. Just hope between both submersibles we can do enough damage to kill or at least dissuade it from following us." She exhaled. "And not just piss it off."

Miles whistled and then checked the sonar. "Big bogey is half a klick and closing fast." He half turned. "Water drone?"

"Good idea. Launch it," Ally replied.

Miles pressed a few buttons and reset some dials. Another screen opened beside the aerial drone's panel and the small craft launched, its camera immediately transmitting underwater images back to them.

Now they had two screens of data—the aerial drone delivered images from several hundred feet above the water's surface, where the outline of both submersibles could just be made out, and then the next screen showed them below the surface, that was eerily devoid of sea life… exactly as you'd expect if a monstrous predator was in the vicinity.

"Abyss-1, do you read?" It was Loche's voice in the other submersible.

Ally opened the mic to the entire craft so Matt, Jane, and Mike could hear. "We read you. We've launched a seaborne drone, images up now."

"Got 'em," Loche said. "We're going to try and get behind this big bastard to give us more room to move. I suggest we go in opposite directions so we're not a combined target."

"Roger that, sir," Ally replied. "We've loaded up nuke-tipped fish… just in case."

"Yeah, so have we. If we get a shot, we take it," Loche replied. "Opening it up to full ahead. Good luck and Godspeed to all. Over."

Ally nodded and sighed. "And same to you. All of you," she added.

Miles pushed their craft to top speed, and on their sonar, they saw their sister submersible heading west at the same rate. And right in between them was something so huge that it defied physical description and was even proving difficult for their instruments to capture.

The splitting of their submersibles had the desired effect as the mass paused.

"It doesn't know which one of us to chase," Ally smiled. "Confused, huh? Ya, big dumb brute." She turned to Miles. "Wait 'til we both have some space and then turn so we can put a nuke up its ass."

"Roger that," Miles said. "Getting images now."

The first small screen displayed the feed from the airborne drone and showed a shadow in the water now just a quarter-mile from them. It looked like a massive reef, but they knew it wasn't.

"Here it comes," Jane whispered.

The seaborne drone sped toward the mass, and they watched while holding their collective breath.

"Something weird is happening," Miles said.

It looked at first like the mass was fraying at its edges, but then they saw that it was in fact smaller objects breaking away from the center mass.

Dagon then seemed to have made a decision and began to move toward Abyss-2, while the hundreds of specks moved in a swarm toward Ally and her team in Abyss-1.

"It's got to be the *Y'ha-nthlei*," Jane said. "Dagon has released its minions."

"Can't fire a torpedo into multiple moving targets of that size," Miles said.

"Try and stay ahead of them. Dagon is still the main game." Ally leaned forward, read the new data from the screen, and then cursed. "Abyss- 2, Dagon is closing in on your position."

"We see it," Loche replied. "Just get yourself clear."

"There," Miles said as he glanced at the underwater drone's screen.

On the image, something began to fill the screen, larger and larger until that was all there was. The last image was of a tentacled mass, and then an eye that must have been fifty feet across. It burned as red as Hades and carried an eons-old intelligence. And a hate. Hotter than the sun. Then the drone's image vanished from the screen.

"*Argh*, s*hit*." Matt winced and placed a hand to his temple. "It's trying to get in our heads." He groaned. "It remembers us, remembers *you*, Jane."

"I hurt it last time. It wants revenge," Jane replied, now also feeling the pressure of an intrusion into her own mind.

"Those things are faster than we are," Miles said. "Can't outrun them for long."

"What else have we got in the arsenal?" Ally asked.

"We can set up a shock pulse—burn anything that touches us or set up a shockwave that might stun them from a range of around fifty feet but that means they gotta be real close." He turned. "One more thing, we can't fire a torpedo while we are pulsing or we're liable to detonate the torpedo as it exits the tube."

"Yeah, let's not detonate a nuke on our skin." Ally thought for a moment. "Only pulse if we need to. I want us to retain the ability to fire a nuke when we can."

Miles shook his head. "Can't do it while Abyss-2 is in range of the thing. Though we have toughened hulls, the blast shockwave might rupture them."

Ally threw her head back to look heavenward for a moment. "Come on, give us a break, will you?"

The aerial drone image showed the image of their submersible's sleek body below the surface like a dark fish. But then just a hundred feet behind it, there were hundreds of objects closing in. By scale, they looked roughly twice human-sized.

"Can they break in?" Mike asked.

"Unlikely," Miles replied. "But they don't have to. They could damage some of the external sensors, or worse, they could simply crowd us and clog our propulsion units…render us dead in the water. Or take us to the bottom… and keep us there."

"And then we're dead, full stop," Jane added.

Ally momentarily bared her teeth. "That ain't gonna happen." She sat forward. "Prepare for a pulse—full power."

The female soldier stared hard at the screen, obviously counting down either the seconds or the distance as the first wave of Dagon's minions bore down on them.

"Swing us past the approaching wave," she ordered.

Miles did as requested, and as the sleek submersible powered by the front of the approaching horde, Ally pounded a fist down. "Now."

"Pulsing," Miles said and pressed a button.

There was the sensation of vibrating beneath their feet and their instrumentation whited out for a second. Then the overhead drone image returned to show the first line of things that had been following them had stopped to hang in the water.

"Got 'em." Ally made a fist.

But then the next wave who were outside of the pulse radius began to catch up.

"Damnit, we've only bought ourselves some time," she said, tiredly.

Miles shook his head. "That big bastard is going to overtake Abyss-2. It's too close to nuke."

Ally nodded for a moment. "Okay, we've got to slow that thing down. Load up an impact torpedo."

"On it," Miles said.

Ally got on the mic. "Going to put a standard fish into that thing's back—hold your breath," she said.

"Ready," Miles said with his finger on the launch button.

Ally didn't hesitate. "*Fire*."

Miles pressed the launch button. "Fish away."

***

"Evasive action!" Loche yelled.

Joni Baker engaged full thrusters and spun the U-shaped wheel, turning the tail rudder hard to maneuver the small craft away from the approaching leviathan.

The impact from the torpedo into the thing was felt as a shudder through the miniature submarine, but the massive beast didn't even flinch or acknowledge the strike in any way. But what the attack did was draw away all the minions from Abyss-1 to defend their master, so now they had Dagon and his hellish horde all to themselves.

"*Come on, come on, come on.*" Janus was on his feet. "Get us the fuck out of here, Loche." He reached over Joni Baker's chair and grabbed her shoulder.

Loche spun, grabbed his wrist, and jerked his hand off. "*Shut up, sit down, and strap in.*"

Joni's teeth were bared from the strain on her arms. "It's goddamn everywhere. Can't get around, under, or over it. Need some options, sir."

Dagon was nearly on them, and now the approaching horde was ringing them in. They were trapped. Loche calculated his options and their odds—none of them worked. It came down to a simple strategy: save some or save none.

"We have just one." Loche reached for the mic. "Abyss-1…" He drew in a deep breath. "You need to withdraw to safe distance. We're going for the big burn on this thing."

Ally came straight back. "We can stay in the fight, hit it from behind again," she pleaded.

"No, you are to proceed at speed to the gravity well. Get those civilians topside. That's an order." Loche felt the endgame coming on. He turned to the large form of Croft sprawling in the chair behind him.

"Oh yeah." The big man grinned. "Burn that motherfucker down."

Loche turned back to Joni.

She nodded immediately. "Can't let this big bastard topside to go on sinking our ships, sir."

"No, we cannot," Loche replied evenly.

"Hey, I'm a fucking civilian too!" Janus screamed from behind him. He unbuckled his seat belt. "Don't you dare fucking do anything stupid. You all work for me, remember?" He grabbed Joni again. "Get us out of here."

Baker shrugged his hand off. "No can do, mister. It's already on us."

"Prepare to launch nukes—both tubes," Loche said.

Joni Baker smiled. "Can't miss."

***

Ally was conflicted and knew her options were limited and shrinking. She could stay and fight, and probably be destroyed. Or she could use the precious minutes Loche was giving her to get to the gravity well and escape with her crew. And maybe live to fight another day.

She turned and looked at the faces of Matt, Mike, and Jane. None showed fear. But all were wide-eyed with apprehension.

"Orders, ma'am?" Miles requested.

If she was alone in this craft, her choice would be simple.

But she wasn't.

Ally turned away from the small group. "Head to the mouth of the gravity well at full speed. Then wait," she ordered.

"Yes, ma'am." Miles turned the stick hard and the small submersible veered in the water, speeding to the huge column leading up to and then through the boiling red ceiling.

In just a few minutes more, Miles slowed the craft at the base of the huge monolithic column rising from the sea and vanishing into the red ceiling above them. He brought them around.

"Drone is still in the sky." He craned forward. "Oh my God... *look*, it's coming up."

***

Loche felt a sense of calm come over him. "Full speed ahead."

"Sir, yes sir." He saw Joni Baker's jaw clench and her eyes glistened.

Loche faced front and his eyes were like gun barrels. "Prepare to launch." He drew in a deep breath, filling his lungs, and then let it out. "Ladies and gentlemen, it has been a pleasure to serve with you."

"And with you, sir," Croft and Joni responded.

"*Fuck this bullshit. Fuck it.*" Janus' voice was like a siren it was so high. The man's eyes were wide and rolling in his head.

He went to launch himself at Joni Baker, but Croft was out of his seat in a flash, grabbing the man by the collar and slamming him into a chair. He looked deep into the man's face. "Why don't we sit here a while, Mr. Anderson. See what happens." He grinned into the sweating man's face. "You can pray if you like."

"You bastards. I'll... *sue!*" Janus struggled against the big man's grip.

Loche half turned in his seat. "You wanted to ride with the soldiers. So, you get to do what soldiers do." He turned back to the front and watched as the pilot brought the submersible around. "Amplify," he said.

Baker enlarged and used the computer program to clean up the screen.

"Jesus Christ," he whispered.

There it came—the behemoth—the living god of the underworld. The monstrous being filled the sea. It was as big as a mountain, and probably much more of it not able to be seen due to the limited range of the camera. Its head was a mass of titanic coiling tentacles below a set of burning red eyes that had fixed on the tiny vessel.

Loche couldn't help slumping back in his seat as he beheld a creature bigger than anything that did, had, or ever would exist on the planet. Its grotesque body was lumped with crusted growths and a few bristling hairs as thick as pine trees. Swarming over its body was a horde of the smaller crab people, its minions they knew as the *Y'ha-nthlei*, perhaps now living on it like lice instead of in their twisted and nightmarish city.

An icy calm came over Joshua Loche as he stared back into that hellish gaze. "Fire one. Fire two."

"Firing one. Firing two." Baker pressed the launch button and both nuclear-tipped torpedos sped away.

The man gripped his arm rests but knew being in this proximity to the blast meant they would be obliterated.

But as the torpedos sped away from the submersible, they felt themselves stop dead in the water. Immediately, the hull groaned from enormous pressure. And then they felt themselves lifted. Higher, and higher, and then they broke free of the water.

"It's got us," Croft said.

***

"Oh my God," Jane breathed out.

As they watched the screen, they saw the leviathan rise from the red water. It was so colossal in size it scrambled their thinking just trying to process what they were seeing.

"It's got Abyss-2," Miles whispered.

As they watched, it held the tiny, fragile submarine in its huge hand, making the craft seem like a toy. Its massive tentacled mouth bloomed open but before it could swallow Abyss-2, there was a blinding light followed by a massive double-thump, and their instrument panel went blank.

"EMP," Miles said. "The nukes just detonated."

"Good," Ally said softly.

Seconds later, when their screens flickered back to life, they saw that the blast had struck the creature below the water line, causing it to fall back. A bloody, dark ichor filled the sea around it.

But horrifyingly, it regained its footing and rose again, towering ever higher.

"It didn't kill it?" Matt's jaw dropped. "A nuke can't kill it?"

"It's too big," Mike said. "And being bathed in the constant radiation of the core means the nuclear radiation won't worry it either."

Once again, Dagon lifted the submarine up to its glaring red eyes and stared with a malevolence that was like a physical force. Below its eyes, the tentacled mass flared open, revealing a pitiless, dark hole lined with inward-curving tusks. The monstrosity held the submarine closer.

"No, no, no..." Ally shook her head. "Please, no."

The trunk-like fingers of the hand closed, crushing the submarine as it was held over the thing's mouth, and its super-reinforced hull broke in half. Jane was sure she saw several tiny bodies tumble out and fall into the dark maw.

The entire submarine went next, and Jane knew this wasn't done for food or sustenance, but because it wanted to totally obliterate all trace of the humans. And maybe send a message to them as well.

"*Fire, fucking fire!*" Ally yelled.

"Wait a..." Jane said.

"Fish away." Miles launched the nuclear-tipped torpedo.

The mini-nuke sped toward its target, and it crossed the half-mile distance in several seconds, striking the lower body of the nightmarish creature. The blast once again whited out their instruments.

They waited and waited, and then their screens flickered back on.

"Oh no," Jane said. There was a mountainous surge wave coming toward them. "It's coming for us."

"Fuck you!" Ally screamed. "Prepare to fire agai—"

"*No!*" Mike yelled. "Get us the hell out of here."

Miles looked up at her. "Orders?"

"Ally!" Jane yelled. "Remember Loche's final orders."

The woman blinked, wasting several more valuable seconds.

"Okay, okay. Live to fight another day." She eased back into her seat. "Set course to the gravity well and enter immediately. Full speed."

"On it." Miles swung the submersible away from the approaching behemoth and the shelf-like wall of water that preceded it. He sped the submersible toward the half-mile-thick column breaching the ceiling.

They were already close and in seconds, they passed into the hollow interior. Behind them, the wave struck. It had little effect on the column other than to give them a speed boost and in seconds, they were in the well's gravity pull and flew upward.

"Will it follow?" Matt asked.

"The well is wide enough." Ally turned to Miles. "Do you have a reading on it?"

Miles slowly shook his head after scanning the massive column that drew them upward. "Nothing yet. Pipe is empty in both directions."

The submersible began to accelerate in the pull of the underwater gravity well, and the five remaining people sat in silence, waiting, and watching the instrument panel.

After a few more minutes, they heard the sound they were dreading.

Ping.

"Hold everything," Miles said.

Ping.

"Not good." He shook his head.

Ping, ping...

"Confirmed, big bogey has entered the pipe." He leaned forward and cursed again. "Gaining fast."

"How far back is it?" Matt asked.

"Nearly a full klick," Miles said. "But won't be like that for long."

"Can we accelerate? Outpace it?" Mike asked.

Miles nodded. "Let's see." He pushed the stick forward. "Maximum thrust."

In the gravity well, there was no sensation of any more speed, but after a moment, Miles shook his head.

"Bogey has also increased rate of gain." He turned to Ally, a question clear on his face.

"We're drawing it up with us," Mike said.

"Exactly what we didn't want," Jane added. "It's furious... it'll destroy everything."

Ally sat back. "Then we fight it or we die fighting it."

"Yes and no," Matt said. "The torpedos don't affect the thing. But what happens if we puncture the gravity well's wall?"

"It could kill us all," Mike replied.

"Or it might not. If we target properly," Matt said.

Ally stared for a moment. "I like your thinking, Professor Kearns—detonation behind us, and before Dagon. It might create some sort of exhaust vent in front of the monster," she mused and then seemed to think on it for a moment more. Then...

"Spin us in the water," she growled. "Let's show this big bastard our teeth."

Miles did as asked, swinging the submersible a full 180 degrees, allowing them to be carried backward up the well.

"Target between us and that big asshole bearing down on our position." She leaned forward, staring through the dark glass of the front screen.

"Target acquired," Miles replied.

"Fire," Ally said without hesitation.

Miles carried out the order and they watched as the torpedo sped away in the blackness.

"Impact in 3, 2, 1... *brace*," Miles relayed.

There was a blinding flash away in the distance. Then there was nothing but dark inside and out for a few moments until their instruments cleared.

"Wait for it," Ally whispered.

A massive surge wave hit them, and it was like they had been thrown into a washing machine. With the wave came speed, an enormous amount of speed.

"Jesus Christ," Miles said. "I think the entire gravity well structure has been opened. It's venting."

"Could we drop?" Jane asked.

"Forget that, is that damn thing still following us?" Mike yelled.

Miles bobbed his head. "A lot of debris coming up, but I think we got it in front of Dagon, so he might have been caught and sealed off... or vented." He checked his instruments. "For now, the gravity pull above us is stronger than the gravity drag below. Seems it's sucking the remaining water to the surface."

They waited another 30 minutes, but nothing enormous appeared on their sonar.

"I think we lost it," Miles said. He checked his instruments again. "Gone."

"Okay, turn us around." Ally exhaled, rubbed her face, and then pushed her wild hair back. "Let's go home." She slumped in her seat and closed her eyes.

CHAPTER 19

A cloudless sky, and warm, cerulean blue water—Jane had her bikini on, and she ran along the shore in the shallows with Mike chasing her. She laughed like a teenager and looked back over her shoulder to see Mike in his swim trunks gaining on her, his body smooth, tanned to honey, and well-muscled. He flashed a white grin as he caught her, grabbed her by the waist, and spun her around once before gathering her in close to his chest.

He crushed her full and firm breasts up against himself and she looked up hungrily.

"Hey," he whispered.

He then prodded her arm.

"Hey," he said again and shook her this time.

The beach vanished.

"Huh?" She opened her eyes.

Jane looked around, feeling a claustrophobic depression settle over her. They were still in a tin can under the water.

Mike held her arm in the next seat. She blinked to clear her head and noticed that the light streaming in the porthole windows wasn't red, or night-black, but a twilight blue.

"Where are we?" she asked.

"Coming up, and near the surface. The maintenance ship is on the way to our area." He smiled. "We made it."

"We made it? We got away?" She began to laugh, but then choked up as her memories crowded in on her.

Mike squeezed her hand. "Yeah, we're out."

She sighed and leaned back. "Was it worth it?" she asked. "Croft, Loche, Nina, all of them?"

Ally turned in her seat. "Damned right it was. If you hadn't come, I'd still be there. Or be dead." She reached out to grip Albie Miles' shoulder. "Well done, mister."

Miles nodded and grinned. "All part of the service, ma'am."

Ally spun in her seat and reached down for her pack. She stood and crouch-walked back to the pair and then placed it in Jane's lap.

Jane looked up at her and then opened the pack. Inside were the bulbous leaves of the plant, about six of them from her and Valentina's stash.

"The cure." Jane held one in her hand and looked up. "You kept them."

"I figure we're all going to need it." She took the bulb from Jane's hand and held it up. "Mike here is going to work out how to cultivate it and grow it. And then we're going to cure skin cancer." She smiled. "And maybe make us a few billion dollars each."

"I'm going to buy a house somewhere high, in the mountains," Jane said. "And never ever think about going into a cave again."

"But who owns the rights?" Mike asked.

"We do." Ally tossed the bulb to Mike. "I kinda figure this place owes me something for all I was put through. And you pair of saps have been there three times. Anyone might start to think you like it down there."

Jane turned to Matt Kearns. "And what about you, Matt? What will you do?"

"Me?" Matt sat forward. "I want sunshine, blue sky, birds—I mean real birds, in the trees. And I want to go surfing."

"Yeah, me too," Ally said softly.

Matt dug into his pocket and then pulled something out, which he held up between thumb and forefinger. It was the gold coin that Mike had sent him months ago.

He looked up at it. "I went to the middle of the Earth. And there I fought a god." He turned to them and smiled. "How was your day?"

EPILOGUE

South of the Aleutian Islands, Bering Sea, far North Pacific Ocean – 6 months later

Oof. Klaus was temporarily winded when he dropped to the deck as the 184-foot-long factory longline vessel, the *Kodiak Leader*, dropped into another trough among the huge swells.

The ship's engineer widened his stance. They had the bottom-fill nets out and were in the north Bering Sea, skirting the Aleutian Trench. The helmsman was earning his pay this day as he tried to keep them over the fishing grounds and not be dragged over the deeper water.

Klaus gave up trying to smoke and flicked away his sodden cigarette with disgust. Their ship was the newest in the fleet and designed for longline fishing, targeting Alaskan cod and other ground fish species. But to get a good catch, they needed to fish in two hundred feet of water, and not the more than twenty-six thousand feet of the trench.

So far, their catch had been near non-existent, which was odd for this time of year. And a ship with a capacity of 1.7 million pounds of freezer space, its own processing plant, and a crew of thirty members, was expensive and needed to bring in big hauls to pay for itself.

Another huge swell side-swiped them with the boom of a titan's drum, and Klaus gripped the gunwale railing with both hands. He cursed; that was the problem with these north Pacific storms—they came at you from every angle at once.

The sodden man squinted into the beating rain and sea spray—they might as well pull in the nets as he bet his last buck they were now well out over the trench.

He scoffed at the memory: *never go over the trench*, the old fishermen used to mumble over their flat beers in the well-traveled bars that stank of ale, fish, and ancient pipe smoke.

Klaus gripped the gunwale and peered over the side. The water over the Aleutian Trench was iron-grey, freezing, and whipped up with flicking horse tails; there was nothing down there worth catching, not that he would know.

Klaus carefully made his way back to the external metal door when he heard the net winches start to be hauled in—*about time*, he thought.

Then with a massive tug, the man was thrown to the sea-slippery deck.

What the hell? he thought as he scrambled to his hands and knees. Klaus looked one way then the other. The net winch screamed with a sound he had never heard before, and frighteningly, the huge ship suddenly went stern down.

For several seconds, he was bewildered as to what was happening. And then it hit him; the *Kodiak Leader* had been stopped dead in the water. *No, not just stopped*—dragged backward.

Water exploded over the stern gunwale, as every rivet, steel plate, or thing not tied down, was being thrown about or shaken to pieces.

Maybe they netted a Russian sub, he wondered. They were close to the Komandor Islands, so it wasn't without precedence to see Russian fishing or even military vessels in the area.

Finally, with a sound like monstrous guitar strings snapping, the net cables broke and lashed back at the ship like bullwhips. The ship bounced back to its position and even the wind and storm seemed to have calmed for several moments as if it was holding its breath.

The silence was broken by a sound like a base-deep moan that seemed to come from Hades itself, and Klaus climbed to his feet and looked over the side.

He wished he hadn't.

Eyes, huge eyes, each the size of a Mack truck, were staring up at them. And worse, they were coming up.

Never go over the trench, the old fishermen used to whisper.

Now he knew why.

END

Made in United States
Troutdale, OR
04/19/2024